GETTING Real

New York Times Bestselling Author

EMMA CHASE

Getting Real
Copyright © 2022 by Emma Chase
Originally published as an Audible Original on Audible in 2021

Cover design: By Hang Le
Photography: Wander Aguiar Photography
Interior Book Design: Champagne Book Design

ISBN: 9798534537222

GETTING Real

For everyone who struggled in 2020 and anyone who is still struggling today. This story was my happy place, my hug, my sweet joyful escape. I hope it is for you too.

CHAPTER
One

Connor

I NEVER THOUGHT I'D BE *THAT GUY*.

You know the type I mean. One of those guys who makes it through the first few trial and error, fixer-upper decades of adulthood, finally gets life figured out—and then has to start all over again.

I thought, by now, life would be smooth sailing—as glassy as the lake on a still summer morning. In a lot of ways, it is.

I'm in better shape in my early forties than I was in my twenties. I'm blessed with one of those faces that just keeps getting better with age. I've got a great career, money in the bank, three most-of-the-time awesome kids, a fantastic dog, basically the whole world by the balls . . . except for the crash and burn of my marriage. And the big *D* of a divorce.

Some men don't mind starting over—getting a tattoo, buying a motorcycle, trading in the starter wife for a blonder, perkier girlfriend named Candy.

But I liked being married. Being half of a team. Having a partner.

I was good at it.

I was serious about the whole, "till death do us part" thing. But I guess everybody kind of is. It's not like you stand at the altar and think *I'm going to divorce the shit out of you one day.*

And yet . . . here we are.

"She took me to Nordstrom's."

My youngest son, Spencer, tosses his Minecraft green drawstring bag on the table and stands in the kitchen with shoulders that are more hunched than any ten-year-old's should ever be.

"To shop for a bathing suit for her trip to Miami," he tells me, after getting back from a clearly un-fun Saturday afternoon visit with his mom.

"We were there for *hours.*"

Once the divorce was finalized, Stacey hung up her stay-at-home-mom shoes and moved up north for a new job in Manhattan and a new apartment in Hoboken. I bought a four-bedroom house with a finished basement, built-in pool, and fenced-in yard that's literally a five-minute drive from the house we used to live in. And now the boys and Rosie, our eight-year-old German Shepherd who doesn't act a day over two, live with me.

Because we always said we'd raise them in Lakeside—the same small, Jersey town I grew up in. Because the boys are happy here—their schools, their friends, their sports teams, our family—all here. Because so much had already changed for them, I didn't want that to change too.

So now I'm also *that* guy. A single dad.

And Stacey? Well, she's . . . *something else.*

"Then she got her nails done at the salon and made me sit next to her," Spencer says. "I had to use my inhaler three times."

I don't hate my ex-wife. Really. Most of the time I don't feel anything for her, except a discomforting confusion over how the woman she was when we got married could be so insanely different from the person she is today.

But at times like this—when my sweet, soft-hearted kid

looks up at me with big brown kicked-puppy-dog eyes—hatred is really fucking tempting.

So is taking Stacey's prized possessions—her Christian Louboutin shoes and that stupid Birkin bag and her butt-ugly Chanel dress—and setting them on fire in the backyard. We could roast marshmallows—throw in a couple beers, it'd be just like college.

It would also be . . . unhelpful. Counterproductive.

See, I'm a doctor—an emergency department attending at Lakeside Memorial. I believe in science, medicine. I believe mental and emotional health is every bit as important as physical. I've seen sick kids—kids who will never, ever have the chance to get better—and there's nothing on earth more important to me than my sons' well-being.

Which means pyromania will only be happening in my dreams.

And while I'll definitely be calling my ex-wife later to tell her what she should already goddamn know—not to take Spencer somewhere that's going to aggravate his asthma—right now I crouch down in front of him and do what good divorced parents do.

Suck it up. Make this okay for him. Make him understand how this works, in the gentlest way possible.

My oldest son has other ideas.

"I don't know why you still see her on her weekends. Brayden and I barely go anymore. Mom's a bitch, Spencer."

"Aaron," my voice snaps, firm and disapproving.

Because a seventeen-year-old's brain isn't so different from a dog's—it's not the words you say, but how you say them.

"You're right; that sounded kind of messed up," he concedes. Then he puts his hand on his brother's shoulder. "Mom's an asshole, Spence."

I give him an irritated look and say the magic words that are guaranteed to remove him from the discussion.

"Isn't there an electronic device calling your name somewhere?"

He salutes me with his glass of milk. "Touché."

After Aaron walks out the kitchen door, I turn back to Spencer.

"Mom loves you, buddy."

"Then why is she acting like this?" he asks in that whispery, wounded tone that isn't anything like whining.

"She's going through something right now. A phase."

His little brows draw together.

"You mean like how Brayden is in the bathroom all the time and uses up all the tissues? A phase like that?"

Brayden's thirteen. It's a weird age.

"Yeah. Sort of, kind of. A little bit like that."

"But Brayden's a kid, Dad. Adults aren't supposed to go through phases."

Childhood is the only time you get to think your parents are perfect. There's a security and innocence that comes from believing your mom and dad control everything, can protect you from anything. It sucks that Spencer never got to have that.

I cup the side of his dark-haired head before bringing him in for a hug.

"I know . . . but sometimes they do."

My old man was not a knocker-on-doors type of guy when we were growing up. He ascribed to the belief that since he paid for the house, premiums like privacy were his to giveth and his to taketh away.

Mostly taketh.

He also strongly suspected that if any of his sons wanted to do something behind a closed door, it most likely involved drinking or "smoking the weed" or begetting him an early grandchild.

And—okay—he was totally right about that.

But one of the perks of having your own kids is you get to actively *not* do all the annoying shit your parents did. Feels a little bit like vengeance.

So, when I get to Aaron's closed bedroom door, I knock.

"Come in," is his immediate answer.

He's reclining on his bed, his light-brown hair that needs a trim pushed back by neon-red headphones, in a room smelling of sweaty socks and shrouded in tomb-like darkness thanks to perpetually sealed sunlight-blocking drapes.

"Can I talk to you a minute?"

"Do I have a choice?" he asks. Because my firstborn is both smart and a smart-ass—so that's always fun.

I shake my head. "Not even a little."

"That's what I figured."

He slips his headphones down around his neck as I sit on the end of his bed, bracing my elbows on my knees.

"I need you to lay off your mom in front of Spencer."

I pause to let that sink in and to give him the chance to object. When he doesn't, I go on.

"I know you're pissed at her and I'm not saying you don't—"

"I'm not pissed at her."

Aaron's face is expressionless, his jaw relaxed, his mouth passive, his dark eyes trained steady and dispassionately on mine.

It's his lying face.

Every kid has one, and while he may get an A-plus in smart-assery, he's always been crap at lying.

"It kind of seems like you are, Aaron. Like you have been for a while now."

"Nope," he pops the *p* at the end, stubbornly. "She decided to stop being a mom; I decided to stop being her son. Everybody wins."

"Right." I nod, choosing my battles. "But, Spencer's young—he idolizes you and still adores your mom. And when you badmouth her, it makes him feel like he has to pick between defending her and going along with you—and that doesn't feel good for him. Can you understand that?"

Aaron takes a breath. "Yeah, I get it. I'll lay off the cursing and the name-calling. But . . . I mean, she basically abandoned us, Dad. Dumped us on you and hasn't looked back. Don't you think it's better for Spencer to know that that happened because there's something wrong with *her*—and not because there's something wrong with him?"

Teenagers argue a lot, but they rarely make actual sense. The times when they do are always accompanied by an odd mix of pride and unease—the feeling that the baby bird is getting ready to fly the nest, that the student is becoming the master . . . that you're one step closer to possibly getting your ass stuck in a retirement home.

Still, I give the kid his due.

"Touché."

Growing up, my mother did her best to raise her four sons to be gentlemen. It was important to her that the Daniels boys were chivalrous, respectable, and mannerly.

Not an easy feat, considering we settled our differences by punching and shoving, and pinning each other to the floor and farting on each other's heads until somebody gave in . . . but she tried.

Which is why, when my ex-mother-in-law called to ask if I could move some furniture out to her curb that got ruined when her basement flooded last week, I didn't hesitate to say yes. I make the half-hour drive over to Hammitsburg, pulling my truck up in front of the two-story, beige stucco hacienda-style house that Stacey's mom redecorated with the life insurance money after her dad passed away when she was ten.

And I'm not alone. My brothers, Ryan, Garrett, and Timmy, came along to help. Because not only do they owe me a lifetime of favors for the various shit I helped bail them out of when we were teenagers, but also because we're close. The four of us actually like each other.

Most of the time.

"Hiiii, boys!"

Joyce Skillman, Stacey's mom, stands on the stoop with her right hand raised and waving vigorously, wearing high-cut black velour lounge shorts and a low-cut matching top that's at least fifty percent cleavage.

Joyce is a piece of work. She's not like my mom or any other mom I know—she never was.

Joyce is . . . youth-oriented. Blond and bouncy even at sixty. She's into yoga, clean food, and air purifiers, Botox and breast implants and just enough nipping and tucking to keep things fresh.

My boys call her by her first name, per her request.

"I made martinis!" She shakes a half-filled martini glass in her other hand, because she's also the kind of mom who loves martinis and isn't shy about sharing her passion.

She offered one to Aaron when he was eleven.

"Hey, Joyce," I greet her as the four of us approach the stoop.

She reaches up on her toes, clutching me in a full-body-pressing hug.

"Connor—it's been too long!"

It hasn't been that long. She was with Stacey a couple months ago during the weekend kid trade-off, when all three boys were still spending time with their mother.

"You look good." She gives my bicep a squeeze and strokes a hand across my T-shirt- covered chest.

And then lower, slowly . . . down over my abs.

"Have you been working out?"

A robot voice squawks in my head.

Danger, Will Robinson! Danger!

Joyce has always been affectionate, but she's never been ass-grabby. At least not with me.

"Uh . . . thanks." I take a step back, out of the grope zone. "Not working out any more than usual."

I glance at my brothers—gauging their reactions—wondering if I'm reading too much into it.

Timmy's grinning like a pervy idiot. If WTF had an expression, it would be Garrett's face at this very moment. And Ryan . . . Ryan's staring at the '67 Camaro in the neighbor's driveway, most likely not listening to a word that's being said.

"Well, bachelorhood suits you." Joyce says, picking up a clear-liquid-filled glass from the table and holding it toward me with a sly smile. "Martini?"

"I'm okay, thanks."

Never one to turn down a free drink, Timmy volunteers.

"I'll take it."

Joyce giggles as he drains the glass in one gulp. Then her eyes are back on me as she lifts a toothpick to her mouth and slowly slides the speared olive off with her lips.

And it's like I'm in the Twilight Zone—the dysfunctional family Twilight Zone.

"We should probably get started on the furniture." I hook my thumb back over my shoulder. "Aaron's keeping an eye on Brayden and Spencer, but Bray's been giving him a hard time lately so I don't want to leave them alone for too long."

I've been come-on to by the wrong woman before. Patients, the wives of a few hospital administrators—it happens. I know how to let a woman down gently. I'm hoping that mentioning the boys will steer Joyce away from the danger zone.

But she doesn't take the bait.

Instead, she bats her eyelashes in my direction and says, "Aren't I lucky—four big strong boys here just for me."

For the next hour, we drag two antique couches, a red chaise lounge, a dining table, and a dozen wooden folding chairs up the basement steps and out to the curb.

It's old furniture, heavy as shit, consisting of actual solid wood. And the narrow stairway makes maneuvering hard and tempers hot.

This isn't a problem for me and Ryan.

"You okay on your side?" I ask him from the opposite end of the table before I move.

"All good."

Ryan's only two years younger than I am, so he's always been less of a brother I had to watch out for and more like a partner in crime. He's matter-of-fact, direct, and to the point, and slow to piss off.

"Jesus Christ, Timmy—I didn't plan on getting my fingers crushed today. Can you turn it to the right and stop screwing around?"

Garrett's four years younger than me and definitely more like a little brother. He's perceptive, smart, caring—he can read people.

"But I'm so good at screwing around. It's my duty to show the rest of you how it's done."

Then there's Timmy.

My parents' final swing and miss for a girl. I've always felt extra protective of him. Being fourth in a line of three hard acts to follow couldn't have been easy. Plus, there's a seven-year age gap between him and Garrett, which in kid years is huge.

This one time, when Garrett was fifteen, my parents went

9

out to dinner and me and Ryan were somewhere and Garrett was supposed stay at home to babysit Tim all night. But Garrett's high-school-girlfriend-now-wife, Callie, came over to watch a movie and afterward Garrett wanted to walk her home. He told Timmy to lock the door behind him and stay in the house until he got back.

Timmy—being the annoying eight-year-old baby brother he was—threatened to tell Mom and Dad, and whined about how much trouble Garrett was gonna be in if he got kidnapped.

Garrett told Tim that if he let himself get kidnapped, he was going to beat the shit out of him when we eventually got him back. Timmy flipped Garrett the bird with both hands and slammed the door in his face.

And that pretty much set the tone of their relationship for the rest of their lives.

"You're such a dick sometimes," Garrett grumbles.

Timmy is unrepentant.

"That's why you love me, bro."

Once the final piece of furniture has been moved, Joyce pours each of us a glass of ice water with lemon in the living room.

"Since you boys weren't interested in the martinis, I've brought some alternate refreshments."

I feel her eyes on my throat when I take a drink from the glass. And I feel her gaze intensify when I wipe my forehead with the bottom of my T-shirt, because I'm sweating. We're all sweating. Except Joyce.

She walks to the thermostat and says in a breathy voice, "Oh, silly me! I had the heat on instead of the air."

Then she weaves through my brothers and stands in front of me—close to me—and leans forward to get even closer.

"Thank you for your help today, Connor. I don't know what I would've done without you."

I lean back.

"It was no trouble."

Joyce stares at me a moment, licking at her full bottom lip.

"You know, I'm just going to say it out loud."

"Yeah—maybe don't," I try.

"Stacey never appreciated a good thing when she had it in her hands. A good man. She didn't know how." Her voice goes low and lush—seductive and suggestive. "But I do. So you drop by here anytime, Connor, and I mean that. To talk or . . . so I can show you how much I appreciate you." Then she winks. "Think about it."

Wow.

I've gone out with women since the divorce. I've had sex with women. Good sex. Repeat sex. Seconds and thirds.

And while Joyce and Stacey always had that messed up, competitive mother-daughter relationship—she's still her *daughter*. Who I was *married to*. For *years*.

Doesn't that make me son-adjacent or something?

All I can manage is, "Sure thing. Bye, Joyce."

Then I grab my keys and the four of us head out the door and into my truck.

My brothers and I are grown men with successful careers. Timmy's a firefighter who runs into burning buildings, Garrett is a teacher and football coach shaping young minds, Ryan's a fucking cop.

But when we're all together and something bizarre happens that's in any way related to sex? We turn into twelve-year-olds.

"That. Was. *Awesome!*" Timmy cackles from the rear passenger seat.

"I don't want to talk about it." I shake my head.

"Dude, your mother-in-law wants your dick. Badly. And she's *hot*."

"Ex-mother-in-law," I croak. Because I feel so dirty.

"Still—I say you get on that *immediately*." Timmy advises. "Sex with older women kicks ass, and sex with Joyce?" He groans and bites his fist for emphasis. "Are you kidding me? She definitely knows her way around the tantric."

"I'm with Tim," Ryan says oh-so-helpfully. "You're both consenting adults and Joyce is a good-looking woman."

"Wait a second." Garrett—my apparently only non-deviant brother—pins Ryan with his gaze. "So are you saying you'd bang Angela's mother?"

Ryan met my sister-in-law Angela when he was sixteen. At this point, her mother practically *is* his mother.

Which brings this conversation to a whole other level of freakish.

"Angela's mom doesn't look like Joyce," Ryan replies. "Angela's mom looks like . . . the Italian grandma on a jar of spaghetti sauce."

Garrett's brows rise. "But if she looked like Joyce, you'd do it?"

Ryan thinks it over.

Then he shrugs.

"Probably."

Timmy cracks up.

Garrett grunts. "Dude, you are a twisted bastard."

Timmy turns to Garrett. "So I guess that means you wouldn't nail Mrs.—"

"Don't! Don't fucking say it!" Garrett barks.

Because Tim was about to ask if he'd sleep with his mother-in-law—Mrs. former hippie, chain smoking at seventy, and still going strong Carpenter.

"That's not an image I want in my head."

Garrett squeezes his eyes closed and groans.

"Goddamn it—now it's in my head."

"Look." Ryan brings it back full circle. "I say go for it. It's not like you owe Stacey anything—that ship has sailed and it turns out it was the *Titanic*."

Tim waggles his tongue like an immature dog.

"And then you can answer the burning question on everyone's mind: Who's better in bed? The mom or the daughter? That's right up there with the chicken and the egg, my man."

"Holy shit," I snap. "I am *not* banging my kids' *grandmother*! Now for fuck's sake stop talking about it—it's weird."

They stop talking.

For about three minutes.

Because this story is epic and it makes me uncomfortable. Which means my brothers will bring it up again and again—at Thanksgiving, birthday parties, Easter.

That's how family works.

As we pull out of the development, Timmy starts to sing "Stacey's Mom Has Got It Going On."

And it's just too much to hope that Garrett and Ryan don't know the words. So the three of them spend the ride home serenading me.

And I spend it thinking about how cool it would've been to be an only child.

CHAPTER
Two

Connor

BEFORE WE HEAD BACK TO MY HOUSE, WE MAKE A PIT stop at ShopRite so Garrett can pick up diapers for his and Callie's one-year-old daughter, Charlotte. Their three-year-old, Will, kissed the pull-ups goodbye last month.

In a small town like Lakeside, the ShopRite parking lot is kind of like the town square—you're almost guaranteed to run into someone you know. The four of us are just about to enter the store when Michelle McCarthy and her foster son David Burke come walking out, pushing a cart full of groceries.

Miss McCarthy is the principal of Lakeside High School. She was the principal when I went there—she'll probably be the principal when my grandkids go there—zipping around the halls on a mobility scooter, beeping and scowling at the teachers and telling the sagging-jeans-wearing kids to put on a goddamn belt.

"Hey, Miss McCarthy; hey, David," my brother greats them. David was a student of Garrett's. "How's Rutgers going?"

"It's good." The young man nods, his ash-blond hair falling over his forehead.

"Still majoring in English?"

"Yep."

"And education," Miss McCarthy adds smugly. "He's getting his teaching certificate."

"She's making me," David informs us in a tone that says this is an ongoing debate that he's resigned himself to losing. "I want to be a writer."

"You're an English major," Miss McCarthy shoots back. "Do you know what English majors become? English teachers. You can write the great American novel over summer break. Plus, with your juvenile delinquent record you'll have street cred—the kids will love you."

Before David went to live with Miss McCarthy, he did a stint in juvie for setting fire to a local playground.

Garrett chuckles. "Well, having a Plan B is always a solid idea. I mean, look at me—one minute I'm on track to play pro ball and the next I'm the greatest teacher and football coach in the history of Lakeside."

When God was passing out confidence, he gave Garrett extra.

But if you've got a big head, Michelle McCarthy can always be relied on to deflate that sucker down to size.

"Let's not push it. You *could* be the best *vice principal* in the history of Lakeside, but you prefer to stagnate in mediocrity."

She's been on Garrett's ass to take the vice principal position for a while now. But he likes the classroom—he likes connecting with the kids.

Miss McCarthy turns to me and her voice shifts from harsh to hushed in a New Jersey minute.

"Connor . . . how are you?"

It's how a lot of the locals talk to me now—like somebody fucking died. Such is life in a small town. Everyone knows everyone's business, so they heard the divorce wasn't exactly my idea. Poor Connor Daniels.

Oh, the humanity.

"I'm doing all right, Miss McCarthy. Can't complain."

"You were always my favorite Daniels, Connor."

Garrett puts his hand over his heart.

"That hurts."

Ryan pipes up from behind me, "I thought I was your favorite Daniels, Miss McCarthy."

She glowers at him, her full, firm cheeks pulling downward.

"You weren't, Ryan James."

Miss McCarthy is the only person on earth outside of my parents who automatically tacks on Ryan's middle name. There's a backstory there.

Today, Ryan's a respected, well-liked Lakeside police officer with an impeccable service record. But back in his teen years he was a jackass. And I don't mean your run-of-the-mill, clueless adolescent kind of jackass. I'm talking hardcore obnoxious, noogies to freshman skulls, cherry bombs in the toilets, mooning the opposing football team across the field at halftime type of jackass.

Until junior year, when a curly-haired, Brooklyn-born girl named Angela Caravusio moved to Lakeside and started dating him.

I remember it like it was yesterday. The day Angy stood in our living room in front of my parents and brothers and told Ryan in that Carmela Soprano–ringer of an accent, "I'm not goin' out with a frigging jackass, Ryan. Grow up!"

I think that was the day my brother fell in love with her. It was the day we all kind of fell in love with her.

Because that was the day Ryan stopped being a jackass.

"All right—my ice cream is melting; we gotta get going," Miss McCarthy says. "Garrett, I'll see you Monday, bright and early. Connor . . ." and her tone drops back to funeral-lite, "Keep your chin up. Being single has its benefits. Just look at me."

Yep. Super. Living the dream.

"Thanks, Miss McCarthy. That's comforting."

After we go inside and grab diapers for Charlotte, a

just-in-case-they-need-it gallon of milk for Ryan, and a pack of protein bars Tim has been dying to try, we check out and head back toward my truck.

When we step outside, the sun's at that low, dipped angle that feels like it's aiming its blinding orange light directly into your pupils. So it takes a second for my vision to clear.

But when it does, I see someone. Someone I know.

A few feet away, pushing her cart across the parking lot toward her powder-blue Volkswagen Beetle convertible in denim cut-off shorts and a tiny white T-shirt. Her chocolate-brown hair is in a high, long ponytail—the soft, wavy strands lifting gently in the spring breeze.

At work, it's crucial to keep hair out of the way—confined by the tight elastic band of a mask or twisted into a secure bun at the top of the head. I've never actually seen her hair down. But I've thought about it, imagined it—long and loose, thick and silky—more times than I'll ever admit.

Ryan bumps into my back. "Is this your first day walking?"

But Garrett follows my line of sight.

"Who's that?" he asks.

"Violet Robinson. One of the nurses from the hospital."

Timmy stands beside me, looking where I'm looking.

"She's cute."

"Yeah," I reply with an involuntary sigh.

Because the truth is, Violet Robinson is so much more than cute.

She's gorgeous—in that easy, effortless way that says she's clueless about it.

And she's a rock-star nurse. Solid, sharp under pressure, intelligent, and indispensable. I'm pretty damn quick on my feet, but I once saw Vi fly across the room to perform the Heimlich on a choking patient before anyone else had taken a single step. And she had great technique—strong hands, firm pulls.

In my book, a woman who gives good Heimlich is every bit as sexy as one who gives good head. Possibly sexier.

Now all four of us stand there watching her, but Violet doesn't notice. It's like she's lost in her own little world as she hops onto the handle of the shopping cart—bracing her midsection against the bar, feet off the ground, so she can coast playfully across the lot.

It's a move I would probably tell my kids not to do—but with her endless toned legs stretched out long and lithe behind her, she reminds me of a ballerina.

Elegant and graceful.

I raise my arm. "Hey! Hey, Vi!"

She turns in the direction of my voice, and there's this slow motion moment when our eyes meet. There's a spark of warm recognition in hers, and her lips start to curve into a sweet smile.

But then they stop.

And she goes down hard.

Smacking the pavement when her shopping cart crashes into the light pole she never saw coming. The cart tips on its side, her groceries spilling and rolling across the pavement.

Maybe *graceful* was too strong a word.

Violet's . . . occasionally clumsy. Occasionally a lot.

Not when she's working, but in those in-between real-life times when she's eating or walking . . . or breathing.

"Shit." I jog over with my brothers right behind me.

Because like I said: gentlemen.

I offer her a hand up from her knees.

"You okay?"

When she's on her feet, she lets go, brushing dark gravel specks off her knees and shins.

"Yeah, I'm all right." She lifts her face to mine, her pretty cheeks flushed and pink. "Nothing broken but my dignity."

I chuckle. *Too fucking cute.*

Ryan rights the shopping cart while Tim and Garrett pick up the scattered bags and groceries.

I spot a box under the green Lincoln beside us and crouch down, scooping it up and handing it to her.

"Here you go."

It's a box of tampons. Forty-eight count, regular and super absorbent—for those heavy days.

"Thanks." She smiles. "Would've sucked to not have these when I needed them."

"I bet." I nod.

It's pretty much impossible for emergency department staff to get embarrassed. About anything. We're too desensitized to nakedness, blood, bodily fluids, colorful cursing, and the inventive ravings of both the mentally ill and derangedly intoxicated.

We've seen it all, heard it all . . . smelled it all.

"You working this week?" I ask casually.

"Yeah, I'm on days starting Tuesday."

Nurses work in twelve-hour shifts, three days on, then three days off.

"I'm on Tuesday too—days."

She nods, smiling—her big brown eyes sparkling like two dark diamonds in the sun.

At work, I rarely have the opportunity to really look at anyone. It's too hectic, too busy. Every minute is too important. But I look at her now.

I soak up the view of her heart-shaped mouth, the soft slope of her cheeks, the delicate arch of her brows over her wide, unguarded eyes, and the long line of thick lashes that fan out over creamy skin every time she blinks.

Christ, she's pretty.

"We'll be working together on Tuesday, then."

"Yeah," I agree. "We will."

There's a loud pause, and without any more small talk left, I hook my thumb over my shoulder.

"Well, we should probably get going."

"Yeah, me too." Vi gives a little wave—managing to make the benign gesture cock-twitchingly adorable. "Bye, Connor. Bye, Connor's brothers."

Garrett and Ryan lift their chins while Timmy replies in his distinct pickup tone, "See ya around."

Violet walks past us to her car and I force myself not to turn and watch her go like some kind of weirdo staring creeper.

Timmy lets out a wolf whistle when Vi's out of earshot.

"She single?" he asks.

"Yeah, I think so."

For clarification: I know so.

Among my many talents, I'm kick-ass at listening to conversations around me while appearing completely preoccupied by something else. It's a gift. Also a handy skill when keeping tabs on what teenage kids are really up to.

"You ever ask her out?" Timmy asks as the four of us start walking back to my truck.

"No."

"Would you care if *I* asked her out?"

My expression and tone go hard, shutting that talk right the fuck down.

"Yeah, I would."

"Why *wouldn't* you ask her out?" Ryan wonders.

I shrug. "We work together."

"So?" Garrett says. "Callie and I work together. And there's nothing about it that's not awesome."

"That's different."

Garrett and Callie were serious all through high school. They broke up during the college years and the decade after, then Callie came back to Jersey from California taking a temporary job teaching theater at the high school while she took care of her parents. A temporary job that became permanent when she and Garrett got back together, got married, and decided to stay in Lakeside.

"Violet's . . . young." I explain.

"How young?" Ryan asks.

"Thirty."

"Thirty's not young," Garrett says.

"Speak for yourself, old man," Timmy objects. "I'm thirty and I'm still as young as a babe in the woods."

"You're an immature dumbass who still gets Mommy to do his laundry for him," Garrett counters. "There's a difference."

Timmy flips Garrett off. Just like the old days.

Ryan takes the diplomatic approach.

"Thirty's not young. It's just . . . younger."

Being my only single brother, Tim was my wingman after the divorce. We'd hit the bars on the weekends, he gave me pointers on dating apps, a few times we went out with one of his hookup friends and her friends.

The problem was, everyone Tim knows is thirty, like him, or younger. The girls were great to look at . . . but boring as dirt. We weren't on the same page or in the same book—we weren't even in the same library.

One time, at dinner, they didn't have the beer I liked, so I joked around "'I am Jack's disappointed liver'"—and the girl asked me if Jack was one of my other brothers.

I mean, who doesn't get a *Fight Club* reference? Apparently, twenty-eight-year-old girls.

After that I instituted a thirty-five-and-up policy that hasn't steered me wrong.

"I should take advice from the guy who just admitted he'd do the dirty with his mother-in-law?" I ask Ryan.

He laughs. "I said *probably*, douchebag. And don't tell Angy—she'll think I'm a freak."

Timmy knocks Ryan's hat off. "You are a freak, dude. The mother of your children deserves to know."

Ryan picks up his hat and punches Timmy in the arm as they climb in my truck. But Garrett's hanging a few steps back—watching the rear lights of Violet's car as it pulls out of the parking lot.

"Hey, you coming?" I call.

His expression is intense for a moment. Deep in thought. It's the same look he gets when he's staring at the whiteboard, inventing a new play for the football team.

Then he blinks, and it's gone.

"Yeah." He jogs over. "I'm getting right on that."

CHAPTER
Three

Violet

T HERE'S SOMETHING WRONG WITH GUYS MY AGE.
They're so self-centered. So wishy-washy. Soft.
So . . . *young.*

It's like they missed a rung on the developmental ladder. Or somewhere around high school, just decided to stop climbing. And voilà—thirty became the new eighteen.

Take Evan, sitting across from me in this gleaming Formica-accented, trendy-and-it-knows-it restaurant in downtown Redbank, New Jersey. We're on our first date—a blind date. His mom is the cousin of my coworker's brother's best friend's sister.

Try saying that three times fast. It's like six degrees of setup separation.

I used to partake in the dating sites—hoping their algorithms were the magic brick road that would lead me to my perfect match. But I've sworn off them for a while now. Too many jerks and possible serial killers. Like the guy who was into mouse taxidermy and wanted to bring me to his attic to show off his collection.

From that point on, it's been human-to-human setups only.

And Evan's not bad as far as blind dates go—he's five foot ten, with dark-blond hair, good personal hygiene, smooth hands, and a gentle smile.

It's just . . . well . . .

" . . . and then I said to myself, if I'm going to be studying there for three years, why not double major and make it five?"

He's still in school. Working toward his doctorate in philosophy and ancient languages. You know, like Latin and Sanskrit—the practical stuff.

And though I value education and think it's commendable he's pursing this—he still lives at home with his parents. In a room above their garage. I bet he's still on their cell-phone plan too—he has that "family share" look about him.

Evan hasn't really started life yet. There are so many experiences he hasn't had—like apartment hunting, buying his own vacuum cleaner, paying rent.

I've been paying rent since I was nineteen. Going to school while working full-time since I was twenty. Balancing doctor appointments and teacher conferences while taking care of my younger siblings.

Evan's only ever taken care of himself. He's never even had a goldfish—I asked.

So it's hard to be interested in someone who looks like a man and talks like a man . . . but for all intents and purposes, is still just a boy.

Put an Xbox remote in his hand and I bet he could talk shit with all the other twelve-year-olds.

And it's not just him. There are a lot of Evanses out there these days.

I'm pretty sure I've gone out with most of them.

"So, Violet, you're an emergency room nurse?"

"Correct." I nod.

He raises his glass. "The noblest of professions. Tell me

about your most intriguing case. Any snake bites or flesh-eating parasites?"

Lakeside is a small town. If the hospital just treated the locals, the majority of cases would be sports injuries, allergic reactions to beestings, fishhook impalements—maybe an occasional heart attack. Or a vengeful food poisoning courtesy of a wife who's been unappreciated one time too many.

That actually happened last month. Mr. Learner forgot his and Mrs. Learner's 30th wedding anniversary *and* he called last minute to ask her to cook a big dinner for him and his fishing buddies after a long, hard day of chasing the bass around the lake.

It was ugly.

Mrs. Learner made Mr. Learner a "special" dish—just for him. It didn't kill him, but for the couple hours he had to be treated for dehydration, he was wishing it did.

"We're a level two trauma center," I tell Evan. "So we get our share of car accidents, compound fractures, stabbings, head injuries, infections . . . and people with stuff stuck up their butts."

Evan's glass pauses halfway to his mouth.

"You're joking."

"Not even a little."

From beer bottles to Barbie dolls, you would not *believe* the things people attempt to stick up their asses. And then can't get back out again.

It's called vacuum suction and word needs to be spread about it, far and wide.

For all our sakes.

I put my napkin on my empty plate. "But probably the most unique case I've ever seen was a patient who came in with twisted testicles."

"Twisted? Is that . . . is that even possible?"

"Sure—it's called testicular torsion." I form a fist with one hand, demonstrating. "One testicle wraps itself around the scrotum, cutting off the blood supply. It typically presents in adolescents and is extraordinarily painful . . ."

"I bet." He grimaces.

"But this patient was in his forties and the crazy part is—he didn't feel anything at all. It was a medical anomaly. Dr. Daniels—he was the attending on the case—thought it was due to how the nerve was compressed from the swelling."

Evan gulps. "Swelling?"

"Oh yeah, they were like grapefruits. And getting bigger by the second. We were able to do a manual detorsion, otherwise the scrotum could've split right down the middle."

I slice my hand down—and that's when I notice my date's skin has a mint-chocolate-chip-ish hue—pasty pale and slightly green. But I've gone too far to stop now, might as well finish the story.

I lower my hands to my lap. "But it was only a temporary fix. When the surgeon got in there, she had to—"

Evan turns away, cutting me off midsentence. Then he lifts his finger toward our waiter.

"Check, please."

And *that* is how I end up back home alone. Before 9 p.m. On a Saturday night.

It's becoming a trend. And I don't really care. Sometimes I worry that I probably should care, because I'm in the prime of my life with my biological clock tick-ticking away. Blah, blah, blah.

But then . . . I just don't.

In my defense—my house is the fucking bomb, and there's no place else I'd rather be. It's a completely adorable one-bedroom cottage, next to the lake with ivy up the south wall and these arched doorways and built-in shelves, with a stone fireplace that's straight out of a storybook. It's like living in Snow White's cottage without the burden of the seven dwarfs. I got a pretty decent rate on the mortgage, all things considered, and in twenty-nine short years, this baby will be all mine.

And though I live alone, "lonely" is not in my nature.

I set my wineglass on the kitchen table next to my laptop, pull up the FaceTime app with the tap of a few buttons, and the beautiful faces of two of my closest college friends—Aubrey Stewart and Presley Cabot—appear.

I was only at Boyer University for my first year before I had to go back home to Delaware when my mom got sick. I transferred to a local community college and ended up going into nursing—but the months I spent tucked away in Port Hudson, New York, were some of the best of my adolescence.

I was a member of Ladies Who Write—a sisterhood of girls, like a sorority, who loved writing. After college, Presley, Aubrey, and Libby Warren formed LWW Enterprises, a multimedia corporation based out of Port Hudson. We've all stayed in touch—our friendship strong.

Aubrey's hazel eyes scan over the navy-sweatpants, gray T-shirt-wearing, braless wonder that is me.

"Why are you home so early?"

I shrug, sipping my crisp, very alcoholic beverage. "It was a bust. There was no chemistry."

Presley glances at her wrist. "You were out with . . . what was his name? Brad, Chad?"

"Evan."

"Close enough. You were out with Evan for barely two hours. That's not enough time to tell if there's chemistry."

"It was for us. He felt it too. He didn't even ask if I wanted coffee or dessert. It was the main course and wam-bam-check-please."

Her eyes narrow perceptively.

"You told him the twisted ball story, didn't you?"

"Not again, Violet," Aubrey groans.

"It's a good story!"

"We talked about this." Presley's thick dark hair sways on her shoulder as she reprimands me like the big sister I always wish I had. "You're self-sabotaging. Pushing these guys away before they get a chance to know you and using swollen testicles to do it."

"Discussing a patient's scrotum splitting open is not first date material!" Aubrey adds.

Nolan, Presley's boyfriend gets up from the couch behind them.

"And on that note, I'm going to see what's taking Knox so long in the kitchen."

From off-screen, Knox's voice calls out, "Babe, not the nut story again."

Aubrey calls back, "That's what I said! See," she tells me, "even Knox nixed the nut story, and that man isn't shy about anything."

"He asked me about interesting cases!" I defend myself. "And Connor said he'd never—"

"And there it is." Presley points at the screen. "There's your real problem. Connor Daniel-itis strikes again. You've had it for months. *Years.*"

I moved to Lakeside two years ago for a full-time emergency department nursing position at Lakeside Memorial. Except for those few months at Boyer, it was the first time I'd lived outside Delaware. I didn't know anyone. Didn't know anything about the town—not where the grocery store was or which gas station had the lowest prices or if the local pizza parlor had thin crust or regular.

My first day at the hospital wasn't easy. Everything seemed too bright, too cold—different and uncomfortable.

And ED nurses aren't exactly known for being a sunshiny welcoming group.

I mean, they get there eventually—the friendships, the camaraderie—and when they do, there's no one else on earth you'd want having your back. But it takes time. Because you need to show that you have what it takes to do the job, that you can be depended on. And the truth is, most of the time nurses are just too damn busy taking care of our patients to put in the extra effort to be nice.

By the end of my first shift, a bitchy doubting voice in my head was telling me I'd made a terrible mistake. That I should scurry back to my hometown like a mouse to its hole. Because that was the safe option, the easy option.

And I almost believed her . . . until I turned around.

And ran smack into a wide, firm chest that would rival Superman's. Every version of him.

I bounced back and would've fallen on my ass—but he caught me. Gripping my arms with big, strong hands in a hold that was firm but perfectly gentle at the same time.

He looked down at me with velvety dark-brown eyes and asked if I was okay.

And then Connor Daniels smiled at me.

He has an amazing smile. Warm and easygoing, sure and steady—just the right amount of cocky—and more sexy than should be allowed.

His smile is like sunlight—it makes you feel better, lighter, just because it's aimed at you. The kind of smile that lets you believe everything *is* okay, or it will be, because he can make it that way.

And it's like I imprinted on him or something.

Because ever since that moment, Lakeside has felt like home.

And I've been hopelessly crushing on Connor Daniels—moronically so.

"Connor Daniel-itis?" I ask Presley. "Did you just make that one up all by yourself?"

She sticks her tongue out. "I am nothing if not creative. Have you told him you want in his scrubs yet?'

"No."

"Have you told him that you like him?" Aubrey asks. "That you find him attractive? Asked him out for coffee after work like a grown-up?"

My throat tightens at the thought.

"Of course not! What if he said *yes?* I'd probably end up spilling hot coffee on his crotch and then he'd need skin grafts. I turn into a total klutz around him—a danger to myself and others."

It's humiliating. Normally I'm quite graceful—or at least functionally coordinated. But the second Connor is in my orbit outside of a work-related interaction, my limbs and brain go haywire . . . everything short-circuits.

Case in point:

"Speaking of Connor, I ran into him and his brothers in the ShopRite parking lot today."

"Really?" Presley asks, her eyes wide and intrigued.

"Really. He said hello in that deep, perfect voice and *I* . . . proceeded to crash my cart, fall on my face, and scatter my groceries all over the parking lot like confetti at a ticker-tape parade."

"Oh no." Aubrey flinches.

"Oh yes." I nod. "They helped me pick everything up, which was nice. Connor touched my tampons—grabbed the box out from under old Mrs. Jenkinsons's car and handed it to me."

Presley presses her fingers to her forehead. "Yikes."

I don't tell them the box in question is currently sitting on a shelf in my bedroom. Or that I'm going to save it the way some people save concert tickets or corsages . . . because even among friends, that detail is one crazy-bridge too far.

"I guess a small part of me is hoping that now that he knows I menstruate, he might actually realize I'm alive. That the janitorial staff doesn't plug me in at night to charge my battery in a storage closet in the hospital basement."

Despite Connor's friendliness today, he's never shown any actual interest in me as a person. A female. A young, healthy, hot-blooded woman who would jump on him like a pogo stick.

To him, I'm a nurse, a coworker, an asset that's effective at my job who helps him do his job.

Like . . . the ultrasound machine.

I take another drink—two big gulps, right down the hatch.

"And on top of that, your blind date was a bust." Aubrey says gently. "No wonder you're happy to just veg out with us and a glass of wine."

I lift the long-stemmed glass and gaze at the sunny-colored liquid.

"You'll never let me down, will you?"

"Yeah, that's healthy," Presley remarks.

Then her voice brightens. "You should write a poem about it. Were you going to write a poem about it?"

Presley is head of publishing at LWW—literature in any form is never far from her mind.

And I write poetry. Not *good* poetry or the kind that should ever be seen by human eyeballs. It's just for my own enjoyment and sanity, and the amusement of my closest friends.

"About the date with Evan? Probably."

"Oooh—write it now." Aubrey claps her hands. "I want to hear it, and you're fun when you freestyle."

Why not? I clear my throat. "Okay . . . here goes:

> *There once was a boy named Evan*
> *Who learned a valuable lesson.*
> *If you have a weak stomach few things are worse*
> *Than going to dinner with an ED nurse*
> *And asking about the cases she's assisted in*
>
> *The ED nurse learned something too*
> *When hoping for a night of romance and woo*
> *Don't go out with a boy no matter how tall*
> *'Cause it takes a real man to hear the words twisted balls*
> *And still want the date to continue*

31

Now poor Evan's alone
And the nurse is at home
Drinking her wine
With her friends on FaceTime
And writing this terrible poem."

I take a bow in my chair. "I'm going to call that one 'The Story of My Life.'"

Aubrey and Presley laugh as they applaud, making me feel giggly and good as I refill my glass.

Who needs men when you've got friends and FaceTime and copious amounts of wine?

Not this girl—no way, no how.

Although . . . penises are really nice.

Right on cue, a particular penis immediately comes to mind—on the epic day the owner of said appendage forgot to pack an extra pair of compression shorts to wear beneath his scrubs after his morning run to the hospital. How the outline of it pressed against the thin green fabric, slightly to the left, thick and long even at rest, with a heavy handsome shape.

It was a thing of beauty. The Chris Hemsworth of penises.

I wrote a poem about it.

Because it was perfect—just like the rest of him. Maybe that's why I turn into an idiot whenever Connor is around. It's hard to be close to someone you admire so much and not feel small and silly and intimidated. At least it's hard for me.

"You have to let me publish you one day!" Presley begs. "You could write a book of poetry for all the single ladies. It would be hilarious."

"Yep, that's me." I smile. "Funny all day without even trying."

CHAPTER
Four

Connor

"**I** DON'T UNDERSTAND WHY I NEED TO LISTEN TO HER."
It never fails. And it never ceases to amaze me.
"*I'm* a doctor, *she's* a nurse."

Interns. First-years. Short-coats. Newly graduated medical students who are technically doctors—but not really. They rotate through the different hospital departments working under the supervision of senior residents and attendings. They have a tendency to be jackasses. Pumped up by their shiny new medical degrees, with just enough knowledge, plus confidence, to make them dangerous.

"I shouldn't be taking orders from her."

But there's always one in the group who stands out. With balls of hubris. Arrogance to spare. Gold-medal-level annoying.

"*She* should be taking orders from *me*."

And every single year, they bring the same terrible question to the minds of the doctors who supervise them: *Dear God, was I this much of an asswipe when I was an intern?*

The cold, hard, truthful answer is: *Probably.* The answer

we tell ourselves is: *No. I couldn't have been. The nurses would've killed me.*

"Stop talking." I tell the dark-haired, twentysomething, emptyheaded grasshopper in front of me.

I think his name is something like Jamie or Jonathan or Janas.

"First of all, you're not a doctor yet. Not in this building, not on your own. We're being nice letting you hang around hoping our knowledge sinks into your thick, high-on-your-own-supply intern skull."

I walk down the hospital hall as I talk, because I'm busy and I have to set this kid straight before things get out of hand. Jackson shuffles along beside me, dodging orderlies and gurneys.

"Number two, Marisol has been a nurse longer than you've been alive. If she tells you there's a problem with one of your patients and you need to see them—it's because *there's a fucking problem* with one of your patients and you need to see them. Immediately.

"Third, nurses don't work for you—they work *with* you. You're a team. It's a vital symbiotic relationship in the ecosystem of the emergency department. If they hate you—and make no mistake, they all frigging hate you right now—it will make your job harder than it ever needs to be. Are you getting this?"

"Yes, but—"

Johannesburg is not getting it.

I stop abruptly and look directly into his eyes. "They will *kill* you. They know a thousand different ways to do it without leaving a trace of evidence behind. They're probably in the break room planning it right now."

The gravity of his situation finally registers. He gulps.

"Really?"

I roll my eyes. "No, not really. They will make you cry, though. I've seen it happen—and crying is worse."

"Worse than death?"

"Absolutely."

"What should I do?" he asks, in a low, hushed, appropriately panicked tone.

"Crumb cake."

"What?"

I scribble out an address on the pad from my pocket and shove it against his chest. "After we examine Mr. . . . ." I grab the chart from the bin on the wall ". . . Wilson. You're going to go to Polowski's Bakery and get a crumb cake. Full sheet, the high-end stuff, now is not the time to scrimp. Bring it back to the nurse's station, with an apology for Marisol. It's your only hope, padawan."

He looks at me helplessly. That's a good start.

"Who?"

Jesus, do they teach kids nothing these days?

I wave his question away. "Just go. *After* we look at Mr. Wilson."

I give the door to Exam Room 1 two raps, then breeze in with Jacques the intern trailing behind like a less knowledgeable, less good-looking shadow.

"Good morning, Mr. Wilson, I'm Dr. Daniels."

Mr. Wilson, a medium-build eighty-year-old man with thick gray hair and a frowning disposition, sits on the table wearing a hospital gown and black shin-high socks. The tear of Velcro rips through the air as Violet removes the blood pressure cuff from his arm.

"156 over 98," Vi tells me.

High BP, I mentally note as I scan the blood work on his chart.

"What brings you in today?"

I could read the triage notes, but it's always better to hear it from the patient.

"The wife," he grumps out, glaring at the petite elderly culprit sitting in the corner chair.

"The wife?"

"That's right. She nagged me here. Wouldn't stop until I came in."

"I see." I nod. "How's your health in general?"

"Excellent," he replies with a surety that only a true bullshitter could pull off.

"The wife" confirms my suspicions when she stands up and announces, "He has atherosclerosis, high cholesterol, diabetes, and glaucoma."

"But other than that," Mr. Wilson insists, "healthy as a horse."

Mrs. Wilson's eyes swing around to the ceiling.

"Show him your foot, Melvin."

"There's nothing wrong with my foot, woman!" Mr. Wilson grouches. "I stubbed my toe a few days ago, Doc, and she's been on me about it ever since."

Here's a fact for you: if one half of a couple drags the other half to the hospital kicking and screaming—especially if the kicker and screamer is an old man? There's definitely a serious problem happening.

"Well, you're already here, Melvin," I say reasonably. "Might as well let me take a look at the foot—if nothing else, the nagging will stop."

After a moment Melvin nods, still grumpily, but he reaches down to take off his sock. While he does, I offer Mrs. Wilson an apologetic look for the nagging comment, but she seems to understand we're on the same team.

And then I get a look at the foot.

Hello gan-fucking-grene—long time no see.

I snap on a pair of latex gloves and examine the foot more closely, poking and prodding the damaged flesh. Then I listen to his heart, his lungs, check his eyes for jaundice and his lymph nodes for swelling.

"You've got an infected foot ulcer here, Melvin, heading quickly toward gangrene. Another day and you'd be losing that toe—a couple more days it'd be the whole foot."

Melvin nods. Because he already knows this—he just didn't want to believe it.

"We're going to get this cleaned up, get you started on IV antibiotics, and I'm going to admit you so we can monitor your blood sugar and adjust your insulin if needed. Then I'm going to write you a very strong prescription . . . to listen to your wife sooner next time."

He grunts out a chuckle. And when his wife moves beside him, he takes her hand in his, giving it a squeeze.

"Will do. Thanks, Doc."

I nod. "I'll be back."

I cruise out the door with Jamestown hot on my heels. Out in the hall I glance at my watch and tell him, "Get me the vitals on the asthma attack in Exam Four; they should be done with the nebulizer treatment. Then come back here and I'll demonstrate the debridement procedure for a diabetic, and then you can scurry off to the bakery."

"Yes, Dr. Daniels."

I pause then, and give him some of the most important professional advice he'll ever hear.

"If you want to go into emergency medicine, your most vital relationships are not going to be with the surgeons or the cardiologists or other residents or the chief of staff. It's with your nurses. They have to respect you—and they're only going to do that if you respect in return. In most situations they're all you're going to have—and more times than not, they're all you're going to need. Don't screw it up again."

He looks at the floor, his face contemplative.

"Okay, Dr. Daniels. Thank you."

I pat his shoulder before he heads down the hall.

Then I turn around—and stop short. Because Violet Robinson is standing there, staring up at me with those round, heartbreaking eyes.

This morning, I overheard her talking to one of the other

nurses—Cooper Palmer—about a date he set her up on with his cousin or something. She said the guy was *nice*. That the restaurant he took her to was *nice*. That they had a *nice* time.

Which is frigging fantastic—because I was married for fifteen years. I know *all* about *nice*.

It's the kiss of death.

If you give her flowers, and she says they're nice? She's not impressed.

Jewelry is nice? It means she hates it.

And when it comes to guys? *Nice* means she's flat out, never-seeing-you-again not interested.

I get a dirty thrill every time I hear about one of Violet's dates going down the drain. I realize this is wrong on every level. I've heard Vi talking relationships, maybe marriage, at some point in the future. If I'm not planning to make a move, I should be wishing her a long, happy relationship with some other worthy guy.

But . . . I'm just not that good of a person.

"That was kind, what you said to him," she tells me softly. "About nurses."

"No—it was just the truth."

Her hair is up in a bun today, a thick russet knot, with gentle wavy wisps escaping behind her ear and at the nape of her slim neck. And I just can't stop myself from wondering what those tendrils would feel like, what her skin would smell like, if I brushed my lips across that exact spot.

"You're good with them—the first-years. You have a way of making them want your approval, not because they're afraid of you . . . but because they admire you. And I think that's better. Better at bringing out the best in them."

My heartbeat picks up, pounding rough and sudden against my chest.

"Well, that's the job."

"Yeah," she says with a smile and a soft nod.

A moment later, my tone shifts, becoming clipped and formal.

"I need to debride Mr. Wilson's foot."

Violet's voice mirrors mine—all business.

"Right. I'll prep him and get the cart."

"Good."

I hold out the chart, and when she takes it, my fingers brush the back of her hand.

There are three thousand touch receptors in the human fingertip, and every single one of mine focuses on Violet's skin. How baby soft it is, smooth.

The hospital temperature is set at a steady sixty-six degrees to reduce the spread of bacteria. It's why stethoscopes and doctors' and nurses' hands can feel like ice cubes. But Violet's hand isn't cold or callused from washing or the harsh rub of hand sanitizer.

It's warm, silky . . . achingly feminine.

It's not something that should register in my mind; it's not professional. I have no memory of what any other nurse's hand feels like—because I've never noticed.

But hers . . . I do.

When I was eleven, the tire on my BMX bike blew out after I jumped the homemade ramp the kid down the street constructed. I landed hard, then walked to Kmart by myself, bought a new tire with my own money, replaced and inflated the tire, and still managed to finish my paper route on time.

Because I'm a Gen X-er. My brothers and I weren't latchkey kids, but even with a stay-at-home mom, my generation was basically raised to survive a zombie apocalypse.

On our own.

I try my best to pass those life skills—self-sufficiency,

responsibility, independence—onto my boys. Aaron doesn't work during the school year, because he plays football and keeps his grades up, but in the summer he has a part-time job as a lake lifeguard. When Brayden turns fifteen, he'll find a part-time job too—probably as a junior counselor with Lakeside's summer rec program.

And when I'm on days at the hospital, I've gotten the boys in the routine of coming home from school, doing their homework, and getting dinner started. Nothing fancy or complicated—but I trust that they can manage soup and sandwiches or mac and cheese and a salad—without burning the house down to the ground.

"Dad, please stop buying the crappy fabric softener," Brayden says, folding his laundry at the opposite end of the kitchen table where I'm currently eating a roast beef sandwich for dinner. "It sucks."

Parents don't have favorites—we'd cut open a vein for any of our offspring. But some kids are just easier. Low maintenance. Generally happy and don't mind doing what they're told.

They're not our favorites . . . but they sure are nice to be around.

"I didn't realize there was a crappy fabric softener, Bray."

Brayden is my easy kid. It's unusual for a middle child, but no less awesome. He picks up the ice cubes when they fall on the floor instead of kicking them under the fridge, he's always liked vegetables, he does his own laundry—and occupies himself so well, most of the time I don't even know if he's in the house.

"Good fabric softeners have names," he explains, looking at me with his mother's eyes. "Downy, Snuggle, if it just says 'fabric softener,' it's the crappy kind."

A smile tugs at my mouth. "Got it."

"Rosie, come iiiinnnnn!" Spencer bellows from the backdoor. Then he bellows at me, "Daaaad, Rosie's chasing the squirrels again!"

"Just leave the back door open—she'll come in when she's ready," I call back, before quietly adding, "And hopefully alone."

Because our German Shepherd is the unholy terror of the backyard woodland animals' lives. She doesn't mean to be. She just wants to play with them; she thinks they're her friends. But it never ends well.

"We should put in a doggie door," Aaron says as Spencer slides into the seat next to him and starts tapping away on his Nintendo Switch. "With a bell, you know . . . to warn them she's coming."

"We'll do it this weekend." I nod. "And speaking of this weekend, I need you to stay home Friday night."

Aaron's head snaps up from his phone.

"I'm supposed to go over to Mia's."

Mia is the girl Aaron's been dating the last few months. They're not true-love serious like Garrett and Callie were, but she's nice and they're going to prom together next month.

"Well, have Mia come here."

"It blows when we hang out here! Brayden and Spencer won't leave us alone."

Aaron is not my easy kid.

"Be that as it may," I tell him reasonably, "I'll be out, so I need you to keep an eye on your brothers."

"They're old enough to stay home by themselves! You baby them so frigging much."

Brayden's fine on his own during the day and he's responsible enough to make sure Spencer doesn't jump off the roof or destroy the furniture. But he gets spooked at night—either from covertly downloading the latest *Saw* movie or reading one too many articles about real-life horror stories on the internet.

"It is what it is, Aaron. Friday night, you're home—end of discussion."

But for a seventeen-year-old, the discussion never ends. It just goes on, and on, and on . . .

"So I have to change my plans because you're going out to get laid?"

I toss my napkin on the table.

"A—knock it off. Now. B—I have a D.U.H. meeting on Friday and then I'm going fishing for Dean's bachelor party with your uncles."

Garrett's best friend, Dean Walker, is like a fourth brother to me and he's getting married in a few weeks. Dean had more than his share of wild, stripper-filled evenings—and days—before he met his bride-to-be, Lainey. So he opted for a guy's night out of fishing and beer on a party boat instead.

"I need you here because I'm going to be out on a boat and I don't want your grandparents having to drive over in the dark if the boys get scared. C—when you're paying for my car and my car insurance, then I'll change my plans for you. Until that happens, it's the other way around."

This wouldn't be an issue if Stacey and I were still married, because two is better than one and she'd be home with them. But while living out the Brady Bunch song—four men living all alone—wasn't what I pictured for them when we had them, I still think we're doing okay. Better than okay.

Aaron lowers his head, giving in, but not happy about it.

"The worst part about this divorce is I got stuck being the nanny."

Spencer gives his brother a lip-curled sneer. "We don't like you either."

Spence is my sweet kid. He has a gentle soul—as far as insults go, that's about as vicious as it gets.

Brayden picks up the slack.

"Yeah—dick for brains."

"Douche-canoe," Aaron shoots back.

"Guys!" I snap. "That's enough."

A begrudging silence descends, but Aaron gets in one last grumble, because he just can't resist.

"Still blows."

And a part of me feels for him—the part that didn't think my brothers following me around all over town was such a great time either when I was his age. That's the circle of life.

"I'm sure it does. But you'll live."

"And then Paul told me he just wasn't attracted to me anymore. That forty pounds and fifteen years had turned me into someone he didn't want to be married to." The woman sitting in the wooden folding chair covers her face with a tissue, sobbing. "And the worst part is he's right! I *have* let myself go. It's all my fault."

Her name is Karen, the newest member of the Divorced, Unattached, and Happy support group—also known as D.U.H. or "duh."

They really didn't think the acronym all the way through.

We meet in the rec hall basement the first Friday and third Sunday of every month. We used to meet on Wednesdays after Sex Addicts Anonymous, but that wasn't the best mix. The sex addicts kept falling off the wagon with the divorcées.

"There, there, boo-boo. You go right ahead and let it out."

Delilah—a deeply religious, curvy redhead who separated from her husband last fall after twenty unappreciated years because, and I quote, "her field of fucks was barren and she had not a single one left to give"—puts her arm around Karen's shoulder and pulls her in for a side hug.

"But while you do, know that Paul is unworthy to drink from the chalice of your inner beauty. I know it doesn't seem like it now, but the day will come when you will believe that, I promise you."

Some may think group therapy for long-term relationships that have met their maker would be depressing . . . the sob stories, the loneliness, the heartbreak, the betrayal.

But it's kind of a riot. Uplifting.

Mostly because every person sitting in this circle is a character and a half. They're honest, unique, determined, and funny—and that's when they're sober. Get a few drinks in them and group therapy turns into toga night at the frat house.

"Paul deserves a smackdown with extreme prejudice." Lou says.

Lou's in his sixties and originally from North Jersey. I'm pretty sure he's in the mob.

He and his wife used to own and operate a bowling alley, but after their three kids moved out of the house and they sold the business to retire, she came to the realization that they had nothing left in common.

Carl the dentist and Maria the dog groomer nod their agreement.

"Violence is never the answer," Dr. Laura Balish, the blond, bespeckled therapist who runs this group of misfit toys, admonishes gently.

"Well, sometimes it is," Lou insists with a shrug. "Never say never, amiright?"

Laura gives Lou a disappointed third-grade teacher look that would cow a lesser man, then addresses the group.

"Thank you for sharing, Karen. Remember, we can't control the feelings of others. We can only control our reactions and focus on finding happiness with ourselves."

Dr. Laura was Aaron, Brayden, and Spencer's therapist in the months after the divorce, because I wanted to make sure they were handling the transition all right.

"Would anyone else like to share?" Laura asks. "How about you, Connor? Where have your thoughts been lately?"

The "sharing with the group" thing was weird at first. Exposing. Once I realized that no one in this room actually knows what the hell they're doing—that we're all just winging it and hoping for the best—it got easier.

"I've been thinking lately that . . . maybe I'm not meant to have another relationship."

I think about how, at this point in my life, I just want to be me and enjoy fun times and shared interests and fantastic sex with a woman who's comfortable being her.

A relationship that's simple, beautiful, easy, *good*.

It doesn't sound like a tall order. But after two years of setups and hookups, and stupid fucking swipe left apps—it's starting to feel like the unicorn at the end of a rainbow who shits gold coins. A myth.

I shrug and continue, "Maybe some of us only get one chance at bat."

Tikki clicks her tongue. "Oh, baby, that's just not true. Love is like a river; it keeps flowing and moving your whole life. You just haven't found the right stream to run off with yet, but she's out there."

Tikki's been married nine times. And divorced ten. While she obviously has experience in relationships, I don't know if she's the best person to take advice from on relationships that last.

Stewart the mattress salesman, who at the last meeting shared that he was dating someone new, nudges me with his elbow.

"Careful, man—talk like that's almost a dare. Then when you least expect it, love smacks you over the head and makes you its bitch."

"From your lips to God's ear, Stew," Delilah says.

"There's actually something to that," Dr. Laura says. "Sometimes it's referred to as the not-looking-for-love phenomenon. It applies not just to relationships but efforts to get pregnant, sports performances. Essentially, it states that by attempting to find love or conceive or hit a baseball, we put too much pressure on ourselves, which keeps at bay the things we want most. But if we let go, release the pressure, if we stop swinging so hard for the ball and just have fun . . . those things we want end up coming to us."

"So you're saying I should go with the 'I'm destined to be alone until I die' line of thought?" I ask.

Dr. Laura holds out her hands, shrugging.

"It can't hurt."

CHAPTER
Five

Violet

RAISING MY BROTHER AND SISTERS WHILE GOING TO nursing school wasn't easy—or cheap. Life is expensive. When you don't have a lot of pennies coming in, every one counts.

One day, when I was walking my sister home from school, we passed a yard sale with an almost-new-looking sewing machine and a how-to booklet for five bucks. I scooped it up, thinking I could save some cash mending the kids' clothes or buying oversized clothes that I could take in, then let back out, so they'd last longer.

But the sewing machine also turned into an unexpected money maker. Once word got around that I had sewing skills, I was tailoring clothes, making custom curtains and Halloween costumes for the neighbors.

I remember sitting beside my mom on one of those endless, rough nights as the steady hum of the sewing machine seemed to soothe her. Not lulling her to sleep—in the end, she was never able to sink into a full sleep—but the sound settled her into a quiet calm that I was grateful for.

Sewing is also I how I found one of my friend groups in Lakeside: Lainey Burrows's sewing circle.

Lainey Burrows is a social media influencer with a blog called *Life With Lainey*. The whole reason she moved to Lakeside was to renovate and redecorate a lake house for Facebook. That's how she met her fiancé, Dean Walker—who was her teenage son's math teacher at Lakeside High School.

Dean and Lainey are getting married in two weeks in their backyard, beside their lake. She's doing all the decorating and planning herself and showing her followers how she's doing it without breaking the bank. The sewing circle sewed the little pink and silver roses on all the table linens.

Lainey put together all the festivities for her bachelorette party too, here at the local bar, Chubby's.

"Hey, Vi!" Effie, one of the nurses from Labor and Delivery, pushes through the crowd, greeting me with a hug and a shout above the music. "How are you doing?"

Effie's about my age and in the sewing circle too. She was one of Lainey's nurses when she gave birth to her and Dean's daughter, Ava, last year. It was a natural delivery—God bless Lainey's little masochistic heart.

"I'm good. This place looks amazing!"

Silver ribbons hang down from rose-colored balloons that cover the ceiling, and a huge Congratulations, Lainey banner is draped above the shaded windows. The movie *Father of the Bride* plays with subtitles from all four of the big-screen corner televisions and "It's Raining Men" pours from the speakers—even though there aren't actually any men, raining or otherwise. Lainey and Dean agreed to separate stripper-free parties. Outside, four chauffeur-driven, white stretch limos wait to drive the soon-to-be-plastered guests home.

"Gurl, you haven't seen the half of it! Lainey went all out! Come on, I'll show you."

After doing a lap of the large room, I can tell Effie told no lies. It's the ultimate girls' night extravaganza.

There's a neck masseuse in one corner and two manicurists doing mani-pedis in cushioned, throne-like chairs in the other. There's a straight-out-of-Candy-Land candy table, and trays of cupcakes and vegetable platters within reaching distance no matter where you're standing. The cupcakes are white with pink wrappers, and pink chocolate penises stick up from them like birthday candles. The carrots, cucumbers, and zucchinis on the vegetable platters have been carved into bite-sized penises too. There's Never Have I Ever bingo cards with homemade fruity-scented body scrubs for prizes, a Truth or Dare champagne fountain, and a Wheel of Fortune-Teller shot glass table near the back door.

Two hours later I'm convinced Lainey should quit Influencing and become an event planner—she'd conquer the industry in her very first year.

When Effie and a few of the other girls head off to the bathroom, I walk up to the shot glass table. Small glasses filled with every color of the rainbow pack the table in front of a tall, elegant woman in a black dress and jade scarf. Long, sparkling emeralds dangle from her ears. Behind her is a big wheel—like one of the games on the boardwalk—sectioned off by large words: MONEY, HEALTH, LOVE, ADVENTURE.

"Would you like to spin the wheel of fortune?" she asks with a red-lipped smile.

"Sure, why not?"

She gives the wheel a turn and it spins dizzyingly fast before ticking down to a standstill.

Landing dead center on LOVE.

And like his penis before him, one handsome face pops directly into my brain.

The woman claps her hands. "Love! Glorious love." She plucks a shot glass from the table. "Drink this, then say the name

49

of your dearest love, loud and strong, and you will have a lifetime of joy and happiness."

I don't put any stock in this hokey, mumbo-jumbo, mystical stuff—but it's a party. Where else can you let go, have fun, and let yourself believe in the patently unbelievable?

I peer into the cloudy-liquid-filled shot glass.

"What is it?"

For my twenty-first birthday some college friends bought me almost an entire bottle worth of tequila shots. I was sick for days and haven't been able to touch the stuff since.

The North remembers—and so does my stomach.

The lady shields her mouth with her hand and says, "Vodka with a dash of lemon."

Vodka works.

I lift the glass, then down the contents. After the liquid scorches a path of fire down my throat, I close my eyes and declare in a loud, clear, fearless voice, "Connor."

Mere moments after the two syllables slip past my lips, a wind-chime pleasant voice pipes up from behind my shoulder.

"Connor who?"

A voice I realize with growing Michael Myers in the background level horror belongs to Callie *Daniels*. The woman married to Connor's brother, Garrett. They both teach at the high school. They're like the prom king and queen of the whole town.

Ermahgerd!

"Did you mean Connor Daniels?"

Slowly I turn, hoping with every fiber of my being that I'm wrong. My hope dies a quick but painful death when I come face-to-face with Callie Daniels's friendly green eyes.

I force a swallow down my panic-narrowed throat and wave a sweaty-palmed hand as nonchalantly as I can manage.

"No. Not Connor Daniels. Definitely not. I meant another Connor."

Callie's light-blond brows furrow and her blond head tilts in curiosity.

"Oh. Another Connor?"

Lying isn't a skill I possess. So, I literally say the first thing that pops into my head—it's my only defense.

"From Tacoma."

I never said it would be a good defense.

Callie squints. I don't blame her.

"Connor from Tacoma?"

"Yes."

"Like, Tacoma, Washington?"

When I was twelve, my neighbor, Noah Jarvis, convinced me to run across Highway 9 to the Dunkin' Donuts on the other side. Halfway across the southbound lane, Noah panicked, turned around, and tried to run back.

He got hit by a Range Rover and spent the whole summer in traction.

Moral of the story? The only way through is forward—always stick with the plan.

"Yep . . . that's where Tacoma is."

"Really?" she asks, like she absolutely doesn't believe me but is too nice to say so.

And that's when I cave. Because lying is just too exhausting. The inconvenient truth tears out of me in a rapid-fire burst.

"Okay, no—*not* really. I meant Connor Daniels. But for the love of God, you can't say anything! To anyone!"

Callie says nothing for a few seconds. She just stares at me, looking me over, a slow, sly smile sliding onto her pretty face.

"This is fantastic!"

"*No one!*" I stop short of screeching—but it's close.

"Connor is my brother-in-law. I could introduce you."

I rub my hands over my face—because she's not listening to a word I'm saying.

"Violet works at the hospital. She's a nurse."

Lainey Burrows has entered the chat. Coming up beside me and Callie—and she's not helping either.

Because news of my occupation just delights Callie Daniels even more.

"That's *perfect!*" she says. "So you and Connor must know each other already?"

I grab their arms and drag the three of us into a tighter triangle in the corner, to keep the sound of our voices contained and knowledge of my mortifying crush drowned out by the beat of the music.

"Yes, we know each other. We work together. So you have to swear to me—woman to woman, Girl Scout pledge, sisterhood of the traveling vagina level swear—that you won't tell anyone what you have learned here tonight. Especially *NOT* your husband. And it can't be one of those '*Oh, honey, I'm going to tell you something but you have to promise not to mention it to your brother*' kind of things that I know all you married people do, because it never works! He's a man—he'll talk."

"It's true." Lainey says, slurring a little behind the big silver straw in her giant pink-concoction-filled Bride goblet. "Garrett came over to the house the other day so he and Dean could have a 'strategy session' for the upcoming football season. But all they did was gossip about which of their players was dating who and which one of them was most likely to get dumped before the first game. They were like little old ladies."

"See! You can't say anything, Callie. You don't understand."

"No, *you* don't understand!" Callie says with a vehemence that takes me back a step. "You haven't seen the women Connor has gone out with." She ticks off each one on her newly manicured hand. "There was the girl with the dragon tattoo . . . on her face. The woman who would only eat foods that started with the letter G. The one we found out later was on the FBI's Most Wanted list—and they're just the tip of the shitshow. Connor's a relationship guy, a family guy—he's not meant to be alone. He's going to keep searching for his better half and who knows what kind of disaster he'll stumble across next. But you're gorgeous! And you know Lainey and you seem normal . . . and you're a nurse! I mean, Jesus, if Connor made his perfect woman in a computer—you are what would come out!"

A sudden heaviness weighs down on my me, crushing my tone into a whisper. A sad, truthful whisper.

"He doesn't even see me. We've worked together for two years and he barely knows I'm there."

Callie puts her hand over mine, squeezing. "What if you're wrong? I can't believe that Connor wouldn't notice someone like you. What if he *does* see you? Or what if he just needs a little nudge to see you? Guys can be really stupid. Sometimes they need help."

Lainey waves her pointer finger at Callie like it's a magic wand.

"Also true."

I let myself think about it—to imagine being set up with Connor. How he would pick me up at my house, maybe bring flowers. How easy our conversation would flow—about life, work, his kids, my brother and sisters.

I picture what it would feel like to make him smile, make him laugh, or even better—to make him groan. To have him look at me with heat and hunger in his eyes . . .

And I want it so much my heart throbs and my mouth goes dry and my vision swims.

But just for a moment.

Because then I come back down to earth . . . to reality. My reality.

"That's not a chance I can take. I love this town, I love the hospital, I love my job. If Connor had any clue that I have feelings for him and he didn't feel the same way—I don't know how I would ever be able to look at him again."

Callie's face goes soft with sympathy. Maybe pity.

"My life is in your hands, Callie. Please promise me you won't say anything."

Her features tighten with hesitation, like I'm dragging her over a line she doesn't want to cross. Then she sighs. "Okay, if that's what you really want . . . then I promise."

Blessed relief blooms through my chest cavity.

"Thank you."

Callie loops her arm through mine. "Come on—let's get a drink."

"Yes, your hands are empty," Lainey says like she's only just noticed. "No empty hands allowed, ladies!"

I walk over to the champagne fountain with them, secure and settled that my secret is safe and nothing will change.

But here's the thing about Callie Daniels. She may seem all sweet and undevious, but deep down . . . she's a lying-liar who's not above lying when she thinks it's for a worthy cause.

Because even though Callie raised her left hand solemnly when she made me her promise—her other hand was behind her back. With her fingers crossed.

Classic loophole.

But I wouldn't find that out until later.

After it was already too late.

CHAPTER
Six

Connor

I'M BACK ON DAYS AT THE HOSPITAL. IT'S A SLOW THURSDAY morning, but that's the thing about the Emergency Department—it can turn on a dime, and like Forrest Gump's box of chocolates, you never, ever know what you're gonna get.

Not all doctors like that aspect of the job—the unpredictability—but I do. It keeps me sharp and in constant learning mode so I can stay on top of my game.

At 11:30 I get nine occupants from a three-car accident.

None of them are seriously injured, thankfully, and a few sutures, a dozen X-rays, two slings, and one neck brace later, I send them on their way with prescriptions to take it easy for the next few days and ibuprofen for muscle pain.

We have lunch breaks built into our schedule, but our schedules are more of a suggestion than a rule.

So I don't make it down to the hospital cafeteria, where Garrett and Dean are waiting, until two hours later. Garrett texted me on Monday that he wanted to meet up for lunch when I was free.

I grab a sandwich from the counter and take a seat across the square table from Garrett and Dean.

"Hey. Sorry you had to wait for me."

"No worries," my brother answers. "The chocolate pudding here kicks ass. I remember it from when Charlotte was born—made the wait worth it."

I take a bite of my sandwich. I eat sandwiches a lot these days—they're quick, filling, generally healthy, and require little cleanup—basically the ideal meal for a single guy.

"So what's up? Why did you guys want to meet for lunch?"

"Does something have to be up? Can't I just want to visit my older brother?" Garret asks. "We had a few days off this week."

"Gotta love those unused snow days," Dean adds, his blue eyes scanning from the door of the cafeteria, across the room, then back again.

"O-kay . . ." I look back and forth between them, because something seems off.

Shady.

Before I can push the issue, Dean's attention darts to the doorway.

"Hey, look, there's Violet."

I turn around in my chair. We worked on two of the car accident cases together, but this is the first time I've actually looked at her.

Vi stands in the doorway, her eyes drifting around the crowded room behind a pair of sexy as hell, black-rimmed librarian glasses she doesn't often wear at work.

She's also wearing the bunny scrubs today—dark blue and dotted with little white rabbit faces. Scrubs look good on Violet—which is a feat in and of itself—but *those* scrubs are something else entirely.

They remind me of pajamas.

And that makes me think about what Vi wears to bed. Lacy, sheer lingerie or barely there cotton ensembles that are as translucent as a wet T-shirt on spring break. And *that* makes me imagine Violet *in* bed, wearing nothing at all. Laid out bare, with that long dark hair spilling over the pillow and those bedroom eyes beckoning.

And that pretty picture almost always turns me on.

I haven't had a public erection since I was a teenager, but if I let myself contemplate Vi in those Peter Cottontail scrubs long enough—that'll do the fucking job.

"How do you know Violet?" I ask Dean, still watching as she navigates the food line.

"She's in Lainey's sewing circle."

"Lainey has a sewing circle?"

I thought sewing circles were for rocking-chair sitting, gray-haired ladies in the 1800s.

Dean lifts a shoulder. "If it involves making something awesome out of absolutely nothing, Lainey does it. It's like witchcraft. Hot, modern-day witchcraft."

He cups his hands around his mouth and calls across the room. "Hey, Vi!"

When she doesn't hear him over the thunderous chatter of the cafeteria, he presses two fingers to his lips and whistles—making Violet jump before her attention shifts our way.

Dean waves her in. "We have an open seat here—come sit with us."

For a quick second, Violet's gaze vacillates warily from me to Garrett, but she quickly flashes a bright smile and takes a step toward us.

And then she trips.

Over nothing but air.

Momentary panic stabs me in the chest, but she recovers! Catching herself in a half turn around an occupied chair, lifting her tray over the head of the person sitting in it, while still managing to keep a single thing from spilling, with an agility that's goddamn impressive. Especially for her.

"Hey, guys," she says when she reaches us unscathed, sliding into the open chair beside me. "Thanks—this place is a madhouse today."

Vi takes a drink of her iced tea and makes small talk with Dean about the upcoming wedding.

"I can't wait to see how the table linens look," Violet says.

"You're going to Dean and Lainey's wedding?" I ask.

"Yeah."

"Hey," Dean says, leaning forward. "I just got an idea, just this second sitting here. The seating arrangements have been driving Lainey a little cuckoo for Cocoa Puffs. Some of the tables have an odd number of chairs and she likes even numbers, you know?"

I've met Lainey Burrows . . . she's almost as laid-back as Brayden. There's no way she suddenly has a rabid obsession with symmetry.

But Violet nods, like that's a totally normal thing to say.

"Right. I mean, who doesn't?"

"Exactly," Dean continues. "So, since you're coming solo to the wedding, Vi, and Connor here isn't bringing a date either—would it be okay if we sat you two together?"

And my brother and Dean's need to visit me here at the hospital suddenly becomes so clear.

For a few seconds, Violet says nothing.

And I don't say anything because I'm too busy waiting to see what she's going to say.

"Ah . . . yeah, sure," she eventually stammers out, the way people do when they're not sure. "Connor and I know each other—it'll be fun. It's not like I'll knock the candle centerpieces over and set the table on fire." She barks out a harsh laugh, then adds under her breath, "Hopefully."

My brother's lounging back in his chair, balancing on the two rear legs—a habit my mother tried and failed to break him of. But now he leans forward, bringing the front two legs to the floor with a decisive smack.

"I have an even better idea. Since you guys are already sitting together—why don't you just go to the wedding together?"

"Good thinking, D," Dean says smoothly. "That *is* a better idea."

"Connor, you could pick Violet up. I mean, that's one less car in the parking lot and it's going to be packed, right, Dean?"

Dean nods. "And it would help reduce the carbon footprint of the wedding."

"We all have to do our part," Garrett tells us solemnly, like he's been possessed by Al Gore.

Violet's eyes dart back and forth between my brother and his best friend—like she's the deer and they're the headlights. Her voice is breathy and high-pitched as she tries, "I . . . uh . . . well . . ."

In order to be good at my job—and I'm very, very good at my job—I sometimes need to assess a patient's status based on body language alone. If they're in pain, and if so, how much pain. They can't always tell me, so I have to read it on their faces.

Violet is unguarded, charmingly honest. Everything she feels is always right there on the surface.

At the moment her expression is awash in hesitation—swirling with uncertainty, doubt. Not because she seems particularly opposed to Garrett's suggestion . . . but because she doesn't know if I am.

And not knowing if a guy is willing to take you out after it's already been suggested in front of him comes with a hefty heaping of awkward. Ask anyone who's ever been set up by their no-longer-gives-a-shit grandma or their meddling Aunt Jean.

Embarrassment spreads across Violet's face like strawberry jam, painting her pretty cheeks a shameful pink.

And that really doesn't work for me.

Because Violet is awesome and beautiful—and she doesn't deserve to be embarrassed about anything. Ever.

So I sack up.

"I think it's a great idea."

She turns my way sharply, lips parted in shock and awe.

"You *do?*"

When my eyes meet hers, it's like the air particles slow down around us. Insulating us from the cling and clang of the cafeteria, and it's just us in this quiet, secluded moment together.

"Yeah, I do."

I can sense Garrett and Dean watching us with rapt attention from across the table.

"I would love to give you a ride, Violet."

And the moment is broken.

Dean snorts, his shoulders jerking. My brother coughs, smothering a laugh.

Because they just can't help themselves. They're surrounded by adolescents all day, so at least half their brains still function at a teenage boy level.

And if I'm being honest, I might not be much better.

Because when I try to fix it, I end up saying, "I would love to give you a ride, in my car."

And now a litany of X-rated Dr. Seuss lines are rolling through my head.

On a train, on a plane, in a box, beside a stuffed fox—I would ride Violet here or there I would ride her anywhere.

I ball my napkin in my fist.

"I would love to give you a ride to the wedding, Vi. I mean . . . if that's okay with you."

Violet

Is that okay with me?

Is that *okay* with me?

Is he *joking?*

He might as well have asked me if I'm okay with my deepest, wettest, bestest, fantasy coming to life before my eyes.

"Yeah," I manage to reply in a slightly squeaky, but still casual tone. "I'm okay with it. That'd be . . . good."

I can't let go of something Callie said to me last week. About how Connor hasn't had any luck dating. About how he's not the kind of man who's meant to be alone.

That he needs someone.

Why can't that someone be me?

What if Connor did see me clearly—and he liked what he saw?

Stranger things have happened. The Pentagon announcing UFOs are real and no one caring, Kanye running for president . . . people actually liking bubble tea.

And we're talking about a wedding here. An outdoor lakeside wedding surrounded by candles and the soft glow of string lights, and dancing and warm, fuzzy love songs.

It's the Mount Rushmore of romance!

"Cool." Connor smiles, deep and real.

For the first time I notice the perfect, lickable dimple on his left cheek. And my head goes so light I almost fall out of my chair.

Eating lunch after this is simply not possible. So I stand up, ready to make my way to the trash bin in the front of the square column behind me to dump my tray.

"So we'll work out the details later?" Connor asks. "Exchange numbers and what time I'll pick you up and all that?"

"Yeah." I slide my chair back carefully—out of tripping range. "That sounds perfect."

I force my voice to be steady—to not betray the all-caps-worthy elation bubbling through me because I HAVE A FREAKING DATE WITH CONNOR DANIELS!!

I'll scream and jump around about it later, in the privacy of my own home—as decorum demands.

Right now, I need to be calm. Dignified. Alluring with a hint of mystery and sophisticated detachment. All I have to do is walk out of the room. Glide away and make a smooth, polished exit.

I can do this. I've been walking almost my whole life . . . I'm a pro.

"So . . ." I inch back carefully, holding my tray while keeping eye contact with him for as long as possible. Connor has great eyes. "I'll talk to you later."

"Yeah." He nods warmly. "I'll see you later."

And then I proceed to turn around . . . and walk right into the motherfucking wall.

Forehead first.

Catching the sharp, ninety-degree corner with my face.

The only thing louder than the contents of my tray clattering to the ground is the sound of three deep male voices speaking in unified cringe behind me.

"Shit."

"Ouch."

"That's gonna leave a mark."

I bounce backward, propelled by the sudden stoppage of my previous forward momentum. Pain explodes in my head—but it's drowned out by the absolute humiliation that pounds through me with every beat of my horrified heart.

Then Connor is there—right beside me, a heavy, steadying hand on my shoulder.

"Are you okay?"

I evade, backing away from him with my palm covering half my face, doing my best to act like what just happened totally didn't.

"Fine—I'm completely fine."

It's a damn, filthy lie. But I throw in a hearty laugh to conceal the pulsing in my skull and the mortification shriveling my heart into a dried prune.

"You hit the wall pretty hard," Connor says, moving nearer, looking closer.

I retreat another step.

"I'm good. All good. Everything's good."

P.S.—I'm bleeding.

My palm is slippery with the warm life-liquid, because head wounds are always so dramatic when it comes to the bloodletting. Fucking divas.

Connor notices the blood—it's kind of hard to miss with the way it's now seeping down the bridge of my nose and all.

"No, you're not." His strong brow dips low with concern, and his voice slips into that commanding doctor tone that says refusal is not an option. It never fails to make him exponentially hotter. "I need to look at that. Right now. Come on, let's go."

And that is how I end up flat on my back with Connor Daniels above me.

Not in any way I've dreamed or fantasized about—but, I'll take what I can get.

We're in an exam room, I'm on a gurney and he's seated behind my head. The lights are off and it could be kind of romantic . . . if it weren't for the shining spotlight aimed directly at my face, singeing my retinas and probably putting every line and imperfection on full display.

But I'm not going to let that yuck my yum.

Instead, I'm going to bask in the yum—drown in it. And allow myself to enjoy having Connor all to myself. His undivided attention, the feel of his touch on my skin . . . latex covered though it may be . . . and the closeness of the two of us alone in a room together.

"If it's any consolation," Connor says, "that wall came out of nowhere. You never had a chance."

God, he's adorable. Without even trying. It's always fascinated me that he's a man that can go from rivetingly sexy one minute to womb-achingly sweet the next. I don't know how he does it—I'm just grateful I get to be in his orbit when he does.

"That makes me feel so much better," I reply.

"That's what I do."

In my peripheral, I see the business end of a Novocain syringe in his hand.

"Just a little prick," he warns.

I close my eyes, joking, "That's what she said."

Connor's chuckle floats between us.

"Not to me," he teases back.

Every inch of my skin tingles and my palms grow damp, because . . . is he flirting with me? I think he's flirting with me. Or it's possible I hit my head a lot harder than I thought.

The pinch of the needle bites into my skin and I gasp at the sting.

"Sorry," he says in rough, regretful tone.

"It's okay."

And then . . . brace yourself . . . Connor Daniels *blows* on me.

And I almost orgasm on the spot.

The soft wisp of his breath is cool and clean with a faint hint of mint. It soothes the hurt of my forehead and makes me ache deliciously everywhere else. The muscles in my lower stomach clench and throb in time with my pounding heartbeat, and a little moan slips out that I can't contain.

"What was that?" Connor asks.

I wet my dry lips, fidgeting my hips and crossing my ankles. This moment will live in infamy in my masturbation fantasies from now until the end of time.

"Nothing," I'm able to manage shakily.

We're both silent after that—our hushed breaths the only sound—as Connor closes my wound with steady hands and smooth strokes and an unwavering, intense gaze.

In the immortal words of Old Rose from *Titanic*, it's the most erotic moment of my life.

I just can't tell if that's fantastic or sad.

When he's finished, he looks down at me. There's a tenderness in his eyes that fills me with liquid warmth from the top of my head to the tips of my toes.

"You good?" he asks.

"Right as rain." Connor helps me into a sitting position, turning me so my legs dangle over the side of the gurney. I steal a glance at my reflection in the silver metal of the spot lamp. "Pretty nice work, big guy. You could join the sewing circle—let me know if you're interested and I'll hook you up."

He smiles but sticks to business, watching my eyes as he holds up his pointer finger in the center of my line of sight.

"Follow my finger."

He moves his hand left, then right, checking for signs of a concussion as my eyes track the movements.

"Good. Are you seeing two of me?" he asks. "'Cause that would be pretty awesome."

"Har-har. You're funny today."

He lifts one broad shoulder. "I try."

Connor snaps his gloves off, tosses them in the waste bucket, and moves to the sink to wash his hands.

"Listen, Vi—about what Garrett said in the cafeteria . . . it's okay if you want to back out on the wedding. It's not a big deal."

It feels like I walked into the wall again. But harder this time. Worse.

I'm glad his back is to me. Glad he can't see me. I don't think I'd be able to hide the crush of disappointment that's on my face right now.

By the time he does turn around, drying his hands with a paper towel, my expression is blank and emotionless. It's a countenance I've perfected when speaking to the family of patients who we know aren't going to make it.

"Don't feel like you have to go with me just because we told them we would."

He's smiling at me as he says it. Like I should be pleased. Like he's doing me a favor.

And it pisses me off.

"Right." I nod sharply. "I see how it is."

He's confused by my response. Or bothered—or both.

"Wait a second. What do you see?"

"You were just being polite—of course you were."

Stupid hopes, stupid dreams. Stupid, stupid, stupid.

"I didn't say that."

"Then what are you saying?"

"I'm saying I don't want you to be uncomfortable. Or feel . . . pressured to go to the wedding with me because of my brother and Dean."

I uncross the arms I hadn't even realized I'd crossed—lifting them out on my sides.

"Jesus, Connor, I'm not some wilting flower."

"I know that."

"Do you?" I snap. "I have a mouth, you know."

"Trust me," now he's snapping too. "I'm keenly aware."

"I can speak my mind if something is bothering me."

"I know you can, Violet. I . . . I like that about you."

"And it's just a wedding. We might actually have fun to-gether, did you ever think of that? And . . . and I happen to be a fantastic dancer."

Connor watches me for a moment, not saying anything. And then he chuckles, rubbing the back of his neck—that gentle, teas-ing tone slipping back into his words.

"I'll believe that when I see it."

"Just keep any sharp objects or scalding liquid ten feet away from me at all times and we should be fine."

The left corner of his mouth lifts. And somehow it's beau-tiful. *He's* so beautiful.

"Was already planning on it."

"Okay, then."

"Good."

"Great."

His voice goes fainter—a feather-brush whisper I'll hear in my dreams tonight.

"Good."

Then he gives me his hand and helps me down from the gurney.

"I want you to head home now. Take the rest of the day off."

My face is too sore to roll my eyes, so I infuse my voice with gooey eye-rolling goodness.

"Connor, I'm fine."

"It wasn't a suggestion, Violet. You've got four stitches in your head."

"And no concussion," I counter.

"But I bet it hurts like a bitch."

I open my mouth to argue—and then close it. Because it does hurt like a bitch. And because it feels good . . . to have someone looking out for me. Concerned about me.

To have *him* concerned about me.

I've never had that before.

"Don't make me bring Stella into this," Connor warns lightly. "She scares me."

Stella Brine is the head nurse of the Emergency Department. She's a no-bullshit, effective, steel spine of a woman—like a nonpsychotic, less brutal version of Aunt Lydia from *The Handmaid's Tale*. Navy SEAL drill instructors would acquiesce to her.

"Stella scares all of us. I think it's in her job description."

"Right." He grins. "And you know the drill with the stitches—the wound will heal fully in seven to ten days, the stiches will fall out on their own. Until then . . . it's too bad it's not closer to Halloween—you'd make an awesome Frankenstein."

"Well, it's only May—there's plenty of time. God only knows what the fall will bring."

He laughs again—a deep, lovely rumble from his chest. A chest I might feel under my cheek next weekend if we dance.

On. Our. DATE.

"Take it easy today, okay?"

"Yeah, I will. I'll probably just take a nap. Or maybe a bath."

He glances toward the wall, his eyes sort of glazing over a little.

"Connor?"

He lifts his head, shaking it. "Sorry. I got distracted thinking about . . . something." He clears his throat. "Make sure to keep those stitches dry when you're in your . . . bubble bath."

I never mentioned bubbles—but now that he's mentioned it, the thought is enticing. A long, warm, luxurious soak in some creamy suds with my favorite pear-scented candles lit all around me and Dionne Warwick singing on my record player is exactly what the doctor ordered.

Literally.

Connor glances at a message on his phone and gestures toward the door. "I've gotta get out on the floor."

"Okay, I'm heading home now. Bye, Connor."

Before he heads for the door, he moves to me—close and sudden and so near I can feel the heat radiating off him. Then he offers me his phone.

"Do you want to give me your number now?" A new contact page is pulled up with my name on it. "So I can text you about the wedding stuff?"

"Yes! Right, of course."

I add my number, save that bad boy, and hand the phone back. Connor taps the screen for a moment.

"I just sent you a text, so you have my number too. If you need it."

And then he puts his hand on my right shoulder, giving it a gentle, quick squeeze.

"Bye, Violet. Take care."

He turns around and walks out so quickly that by the time I answer, the door is already swinging closed behind him.

"I will," I say to an empty room.

It's not a big deal. Connor is a friendly guy, a confident guy. Easily affectionate—I've seen him hug some of the other nurses—on birthdays or when a family member passes or new babies arrive.

It probably doesn't mean anything and that's totally okay.

Still . . . I press my hand to my shoulder, covering the spot Connor touched that's still warm and tingling. And that's when I decide that cracking my head open like a melon and looking like a moron doing it?

Totally worth it.

CHAPTER
Seven

Connor

Y OU'D MAKE AN AWESOME FRANKENSTEIN???
It's a weird feeling walking around wanting to punch
yourself in the face.

But that's exactly how I've felt all week—every time I think about the stellar compliment I gave Violet the last time I saw her.

Frankenstein . . .

Dumbass.

Vi and I aren't on the same schedule at work for the next few days, so I kept checking my phone, figuring once the full realization of my idiocy sunk in, she'd send a polite but uncomfortable text message bailing on the wedding.

But the text never came.

So here I am.

Outside her quaint, stone, hobbit-cottage of a house—which was the servants' quarters back when this property was owned by the first mayor of Lakeside—wearing my gray suit and burgundy tie, to pick her up for Dean and Lainey's big day. The sound of my truck door closing bounces off the lake beside her house and echoes in the air. I straighten my jacket and rub my palms on the sides of my pants. Because . . . I'm nervous.

And I don't get nervous. I don't really know why I am now. It's just a wedding, like Violet said—just two coworkers and semi-friends going together for the sake of convenience and seating arrangements. It shouldn't be a big deal.

But it feels like it is.

Or that it has the potential to be.

Halfway up the cobblestone walk to her house, the wooden front door opens and Violet steps out onto the front stoop.

I stop and stare—a dazed, automatic whisper slipping from my mouth.

"Even better than the bunny scrubs."

Her hair is down and finally seeing it in the flesh puts my imagination to shame. It frames her face in glossy, russet waves that fall over her shoulders and down to the middle of her back. Her bangs gently brush her eyebrows, highlighting her delicate features—big innocent eyes, her dainty nose, her pert chin, and perfectly rosy, high cheekbones.

A simple, strapless merlot-colored dress molds perfectly to her body—putting the swell of full breasts, her slim waist, the rounded curve of her hips that would be fucking perfect to hold onto, and the toned length of her endless legs—on naked display. A single, round diamond hanging from a thin silver chain rests below her clavicle, just inches above a teasing crease of cleavage.

"What did you say?"

"Nothing." I swallow roughly. "You look . . ."

I search for a word that fits. *Exquisite? Stunning? Edible?* They all fall short.

". . . almost too good to be true."

Vi's eyes dance and her lips curve into a bright, immediate smile.

"Thank you." She scans me over, taking in my thick combed hair, then trailing down my torso and thighs before coming to rest on my shined dress shoes. I've been checked out by enough women in my life to know that Violet likes what she sees.

That knowledge melts away my nerves—and my heart pounds a little faster, my lungs squeeze a little tighter, with the pleasant zing of anticipation.

"You look pretty unbelievable too." Her dark eyes alight on my tie. "We match."

I glance down, picking up the silk fabric.

"We do."

She lifts a pair of maroon, open-toed sandals with beading on the front and about three-inch heels. "I figured it was safer to put these on once we're there. Didn't want to risk busting an ankle or a kneecap before we even make it through the door."

"Way to think ahead." I move up the walk, watching how the light catches in her hair, making it shimmer like sunlit ripples on the surface of the lake.

Vi glances beyond my shoulder. "Are your boys coming to the wedding?"

"They are. Aaron is taking his own car—picking up his girl-friend—so Spence and Brayden wanted to ride with him. He's a lot cooler than I am."

"Right," she laughs. "So it'll just be us on the drive over?"

I nod. And I can't stop looking at her.

"Just us."

I hold out my arm, to be sure she doesn't trip on the way to the truck and because it's the gentlemanly thing to do, and . . . because I want to be closer to her.

"Ready?"

Violet takes a breath, then exhales slowly. I catch the scent of strawberry—the mouthwatering, addictive kind—like sweet, sugary bubble gum that never loses flavor.

And she slides her arm into mine.

"Ready."

I like to think I'm a sensitive guy.

I'm in touch with my feelings, I go to group therapy—I vacuum on a regular basis. Being married for a decade and a half trained me to notice things like a new hairstyle, a change of curtains, the difference between a comforter and a duvet.

But I'm still a guy.

Unless it's a cool Indy stripe on a classic muscle car or a set of sweet new rims—floofy, purely decorative touches don't really impress me.

Until now.

Dean wasn't kidding when he said Lainey practiced modern-day witchcraft—because when Violet and I walk into their backyard, it's been transformed into a magical wedding wonderland—and I'm damn impressed.

Every surface and corner are accented with bunches of pale-pink roses, swirling silver ribbons and tall glass-encased white candles. The pristine lake is a stunning backdrop for a long, rose-petal-strewn path, with a dozen rows of white wooden chairs on each side, each with an elegant pink seat cushion and a gossamer bow tied in back. The aisle ends at the mahogany-stained dock with a tall wooden wedding trellis laden with soft pink roses and twining green ivy.

A section of violin, harp, and cello players—that I know is comprised of students from the high school orchestra—warm up their instruments on the emerald grass to the right of the dock. Closer to the house is a huge open-sided white tent with a square oak dance floor in the center. Surrounding the dance floor are round light-pink cloth-covered tables with tall rose-filled silver vase centerpieces, shiny silver place settings, and a long buffet table of chafing dishes that extends across the entire back. Strings of clear bulbs hang overhead and unlit, wrought-iron tiki torches and firepit basins frame in the whole area.

Even the weather is perfect—a cloudless, robin's-egg blue sky, with a gentle crisp breeze off the water that keeps the sun from feeling too hot.

"Holy shit," I say to Garrett, who meets us at the end of the aisle wearing a sharp black tux. He's in the wedding party, an usher, because Dean ended up asking Lainey's teenage son, Jason, to be his best man, as Garrett thought he should be.

My brother nods, eyes scanning the yard. "Damn skippy."

Then he gives Violet a peck on the cheek—the same way he'd greet my sister-in-law or one of Timmy's long-term girlfriends if he ever actually has one.

"Good to see you again, Vi. You look beautiful."

"Thanks, Garrett. It's good to see you too. This place looks incredible."

"Yeah, Lainey really kicked ass and took names. She told Dean her posts on the wedding preparations are the most viewed on her blog ever, and she's gotten a bunch of sponsors and advertising offers."

"Well deserved."

Garrett nods and points at the chairs on the groom's side.

"Why don't you guys sit down? The show's going to get on the road soon."

In the first row, in the seat of honor, wearing a purple gown and matching hat, is Grams—Dean's petite firecracker of a grandmother who raised him. Beside her, looking blond and too young to have a son in his thirties, is Dean's mom. They're not super close but Dean was happy when she said she was flying in from Vegas for the wedding.

I tap Garrett's shoulder. "I'll see you later."

We find seats in the same row as my parents, Tim, Ryan, and Angy. The place fills up quick—half the town is here and all of the high school faculty. I keep an eye out for Aaron, his girlfriend, Mia, and Brayden and Spencer. When I spot the four of them walking into the backyard, I lift my arm, waving them over to the last of the empty chairs beside me. Once they're seated, I tip back in my chair, gesturing to Vi.

"Guys, this is Violet. Vi, these are my boys—Aaron, Brayden, and Spencer."

The introductions come with an unashamed ring of pride—because raising good kids is hard, being a good kid can be even harder, and I've seen enough to know that I'm damn lucky to have three good ones I get to call my own.

Violet leans slightly over me, sending another hit of that delicious strawberry bubblegum scent my way. It makes me want to attach my mouth to the thrumming little pulse point in her neck for a deeper taste.

"It's nice to meet you," she tells them warmly.

Early on, I set a rule for myself that my sons wouldn't meet a woman I was dating unless it was getting serious. Stability is important and I wouldn't want them getting attached to someone who may not stick around. I don't want them thinking it's normal or expected for people to fade in and out of each other's lives. Despite my current situation with their mother, I want them to have the chance to believe that love can last a lifetime.

I told them I was bringing a friend from work to the wedding, so they reply to Violet with a nod, a wave, and a "hi," respectively, without thinking anything more of it.

The musicians tee up their instruments and begin to play. Dean, Jason, and Garret are stationed at the trellis on the dock, beside Lainey's sister Judith who got certified online to officiate the wedding.

Lainey's mother walks down the aisle beside one of her sons-in-law, followed by her two other sisters wearing matching short-sleeved, light-pink gowns, escorted by their husbands.

Dean and Lainey are outgoing people, so it makes sense that their daughter, Ava, is unbothered by the hundreds of eyes trained on her as she wobbles down the aisle, throwing rose petals from her basket with chubby hands, her baby-soft blond hair pushed back from her smiling little face with a pink-and-white polka-dot band.

Once Ava gets a kiss from her dad and is seated next to Grams, the bridal march begins and all the guests stand. Lainey walks down the aisle on her father's arm, her hair flowing around her in loose, golden ringlets. She's wearing an ivory, form-fitting, beaded, backless gown that, judging by the look on his face, knocks Dean's socks off. He has an elated expression of pure adulation and devotion. Like he can't quite believe he's the guy who gets to have her, hold her, and keep her, forever.

I remember that. The hope and love and thrilling eagerness of starting a new life with someone, for all the beautiful moments and memories you'll make together.

I miss it sometimes in a way I can't really describe. The bonding and sharing—the knowing that even if everything else falls apart, you'll still have each other.

After Lainey's dad gives her a peck on the cheek, he shakes Dean's hand and turns away toward his seat—wiping his eyes with a handkerchief the way older, tough guys do.

Then Dean and Lainey only have eyes for each other as they stand beneath a flowered arch and become husband and wife.

Dean and Lainey decided to outsource what I personally think are the most crucial parts of any wedding—good food and good music. She hired a professional DJ and a white-gloved catering and bar service to keep her guests entertained, well-fed, and happy.

Throughout the cocktail hour, mounds of hors d'oeuvres are consumed, thousands of pictures are taken, and the drinks flow like water. I'm on my way back to Violet from the bar, carrying a white wine for her and a Jack and Coke for me, when I'm intercepted by Dean.

I set the drinks down on the table and give him a back-pounding hug.

"Congratulations. I'm proud of you."

His smile is so big it almost hurts to look at him.

"Thanks, man. I should stop off for some lottery tickets on the way to the honeymoon—it doesn't get any luckier than me right now."

Then he slips out a set of keys from his pocket. Aaron's keys.

"So listen, the bartender's not carding and Aaron asked me if I was okay with him and the girlfriend having a few drinks. I told him it was fine with me as long as it was good with you. And I told him he had to give up his keys."

I take the keys from Dean.

"Yeah, that's fine. Aaron won't get stupid."

One of the most lethal things in the world to kids is curiosity. I think it's vital to let teenagers have some experience with alcohol before they're let loose onto a college campus. They should know how a few drinks affects them and—more important—what their limit is.

Once the cocktail hour concludes, we take our seats at our assigned tables. I hold Violet's glass and pull out her chair as she sits down. There are champagne toasts from Jason and Garrett and Lainey's oldest sister.

Then Dean and Lainey dance their first dance to "I Am Yours" by Andy Grammer.

It's a good song—it fits them.

After Lainey dances with her dad and Dean takes Grams for a few spins around the dance floor, the salad and pasta courses are served.

While Violet and the boys dig in, I glance across the room and spot Garrett and Callie talking to another couple. My brother's arm is draped across Callie's lower back, his palm on her hip, his fingers mindlessly stroking as he speaks. They were always like that, even when they were kids in high school—holding hands, arms entwined, leaning against each other, fingers hooked. I don't think they even realize they're doing it. It's just natural for them to be connected.

Stacey and I were never like that. Even in the early days, we were never . . . effortless. Our relationship took work and thought and sometimes brute patience. I used to think it meant something—the fact that we were both willing to put so much energy into staying together.

But now . . . I just think it never should've been that hard. Loving someone, making a life with them, should feel easier.

"What happened to your head?" I hear Brayden ask Violet, when the breeze off the lake brushes her bangs to the side, revealing the neat row of black stitches.

"I walked into a wall."

Bray nods. "Been there."

He points to the thin white line that extends from his upper lip to the base of his nostril. "See this scar?"

She nods.

"When I was nine I was walking and drinking from a water bottle and I tripped. Jammed the bottle right into my lip and split it open. That's a mistake you only make once."

Spencer joins in the ceremonial trading of war stories.

He lies across Brayden's lap and dips his chin to show Vi the back of his head.

"There's a patch back here that will never grow hair. I hit it on the corner of a drawer that Aaron opened without telling me while I was getting something out of the bottom cabinet."

"You should've been more careful." Aaron smirks, sitting beside his girlfriend across the table.

For that comment, Aaron gets a tongue stuck out at him.

"What about you, Connor?" Violet asks. "Any battle scars?"

I shrug. "A couple on the knees I'm pretty proud of. Old football injuries from high school."

"And he's got a bite mark on his butt," Brayden volunteers helpfully.

Violet's eyebrows go high.

"Dog bite?" she guesses.

I shake my head.

"A patient bite."

She snorts out a laugh, covering her mouth.

"No!"

I grin sheepishly. "Exam Room Three. I got in between a drunk woman and the boyfriend she'd just discovered was screwing around. When I turned around to tell him to wait outside, she went in for the kill. Thankfully, the rabies test came back negative. But I have the scar to remember it by. Upper left cheek."

Violet laughs again, her cheeks flushing prettily.

"That must be . . . something to see."

While the waiters clear the plates away, the DJ temporarily shifts from an elevator-music-type playlist to classic pop staples. When "U Can't Touch This" starts playing, Violet bounces in her chair—making her breasts jiggle phenomenally.

"Ooh! This is a good song. We should dance!"

Before I can explain that Daniels men go by a strict slow-dance-only-when-sober code, Brayden answers for all of us.

"Dancing isn't really our thing."

Vi is undeterred.

"That's the beauty of weddings! It's the chance for everyone who can't dance to dance anyway, because it's the one place no one cares that they can't. And this is a great song. I've liked MC Hammer ever since my eighth-grade formal, when it was down to me and Annie Burgler in the big dance contest and '2 Legit 2 Quit' put me over the top."

"Who's MC Hammer?" Brayden asks.

Violet whips around to give me an accusing look.

"Your kids don't know who MC Hammer is?"

"I . . . guess not."

"You have failed as a parent."

I chuckle, while Violet's shoes get kicked off again and she stands up, moving a few yards back from the table.

"MC Hammer is a singer," she tells the boys. "And this is the MC Hammer dance."

She spreads her feet, bends her knees, and holds her arms out to the sides, wiggling her shoulders while shuffling her feet left to right and back again. In the middle of the third circuit, she jumps, crisscrossing her feet in front, then back again, before continuing the shuffle.

Spencer is impressed. Brayden . . . not so much.

"Yeah, I'm not doing whatever that is supposed to be."

"Wise choice, Bray," Aaron tells him. "Wise choice."

"I'll do it." Spencer shoves his chair back.

"Atta boy." Violet gives him a high five. Then she points at the rest of us. "Chickens. All of you."

"Bok-bok," Spencer clucks, for good measure. Then the two of them take to the dance floor.

I stand up from the table and turn around to watch them, sipping my drink. For someone who has a hard time walking in a straight line, Violet moves surprisingly well. She gyrates her hips, shaking her sublime ass from side to side in steady, confident swivels.

My dick comes alive imagining how she could look like that while straddling me. How her hair would sway and her breasts would be right at mouth level—perfect for licking and nibbling—all sorts of fun.

But then Vi varies the dance, introducing Spencer to the Roger Rabbit and the Running Man—and he just about doubles over from laughing so hard. When I see the way his face lights up, the sheer joy that Violet put there . . . I feel something else entirely.

There's a very specific kind of happiness when you walk through the door after a never-ending day. Your chest loosens and your shoulders lighten, and it's like your entire soul eases.

Because you know, at last, you're home.

That's how it feels watching Violet and Spencer right now. A soothing, exquisite contentment—like those first steps through the door.

And isn't that fucking terrifying. It's been years since I felt anything close to it and . . . we all know how that turned out.

I toss back the remainder of my drink in one mouthful and sit down. Violet and Spencer are still laughing when they come back to the table.

I give them the applause they deserve. "Nice moves."

"I told you I was good." Violet curtsies quick and cute. And she doesn't trip—which is nearly as impressive as her dance moves. She scoops her purse off the table. "I'm going to run to the bathroom."

"Okay."

And yes, after she brushes by the back of my chair, I turn my head . . . and watch her go.

Cliché as hell? Sure—but I just can't help myself.

One chair over, Spencer takes a long swig of his Shirley Temple. Then he looks up at me, breathing hard.

"She's fun."

"She is," I agree.

"Do you think she could be our babysitter? She's a lot prettier than Aaron. And I bet she wouldn't say I look like a toe."

I chuckle. "Vi's not a babysitter, Spence. She's a nurse."

"That's even better. If I fall down the stairs or Rosie tries to get Mr. Malkovich again when he's delivering the mail—she'll know just what to do! You should ask her, Dad."

"We'll see."

I'm the frigging GOAT at the "we'll see" delivery. Honest tone, sincere expression . . . sometimes I even believe myself.

Dinner is served—surf and turf for the adults, chicken tenders and fries for the kids. Aaron falls somewhere in the middle, eating his steak but passing his lobster tail to Mia because he's not a fan of seafood.

When Violet finishes her wine with dinner, I get us both another round from the bar. I'm just sitting back down when Spencer points at a bird flying like a shadow in the darkening sky above the lake.

"Hey, look, it's a bald eagle!"

"There's a nest by the high school too." Violet says, resting her chin on her hand. "I saw it when I was running around the track the other day."

"Why do you run at the high school track?" I ask. "There are some gorgeous running trails on the property right by your house. Why don't you jog there?"

"Do you remember after the first week I started at the hospital I had to take the next week off?"

At this point I'm lucky if I remember what I had for breakfast this morning—I don't even want to think about what fifty's going to look like.

"No, I don't remember that."

"Well, I did. And it was because I had gone jogging on one of the trails by my house. A couple of miles into my run, I stepped on a ridiculously big rock that had no business being on the trail—and I twisted my ankle. Badly. I couldn't put any weight on it, so I sat on the side of the trail waiting for someone to come by and help me—but no one ever came. I ended up crawling back to my house, in the dark, and getting feasted on by mosquitoes. I swear every bloodsucker in this town has had a taste of me."

And who could blame them?

"Ever since then I don't like to jog in the woods alone."

Like a human crane, Spencer lowers a cherry from his Shirley

Temple by the stem into his mouth. Then, chewing with his mouth open, he tells Violet, "My dad jogs too. Sometimes he leaves early for work so he can run to the hospital."

Violet smiles at him warmly. "I've noticed that."

And I wonder, what else Violet has noticed about me?

"Hey, Dad, why don't you run with Violet?" Brayden suggests. "Then you could run on the trails and she won't have to jog alone."

"Yeah," my youngest concurs, "and then, you know—if things go good, you and Violet can be F-buddies."

The Jack and Coke I hadn't quite finished swallowing goes spraying out of my mouth.

At the same time, Violet coughs, choking on her wine.

"We could be what?" I rasp.

Spencer blinks innocently.

"Fun buddies. Mrs. Goober pairs us up into fun buddies every week so no one gets left out at recess."

Oh." I nod, clearing my throat. "Fun buddies, right, got it."

I glance at Violet at the exact moment her gaze lands on me. And when our eyes meet—there's this spark, a connection, that feels heated and sweet . . . and intimate.

"What'd you think I meant?" Spencer asks.

Brayden, who knows exactly what I thought Spence meant, tosses his head back and cackles.

"Well . . ." I scratch my eyebrow, trying to come up with something when the DJ announces, "Ladies and gentlemen, the dessert table is now open. Please help yourselves."

Spencer's head whips around like a dog spotting a bouncing tennis ball.

While he and Brayden rush over to make the front of the line, I lean toward Violet, "That was well-timed."

"Yep." She gives me a thumbs-up. "Sugar saves the day."

That's when the party really gets started.

After dinner, after dark, when all the torches and firepits have been lit and the music is loud and the dance floor is packed and laughter echoes all around. Aaron's dancing with his girlfriend and the boys are running around somewhere with Lainey's nieces—probably down by the lake. Vi danced for a while with Callie and the bridesmaids and a few girls she knows from work who are here.

But now it's just the two of us. Sitting relaxed and comfortable at the table, while the glow of the candles paints pretty dancing shadows across Violet's face.

"So, do you and your ex get along?" she asks me.

I think it over for a minute before answering.

"You could say that. I mean, as long as we don't have to talk to each other or actually agree on anything—yeah—we get along great."

Violet chuckles. "Sorry. I shouldn't have asked."

"No, I'm glad you did. A lot of people around town talk to me like I'm the walking wounded. It's nice for someone to just ask without smothering me in sympathy."

"My parents split up when I was a kid," she explains. "And then they got back together. And then they split up again. It was like they couldn't bring themselves to quit each other, but they couldn't live together either. And my dad had never wanted kids. Which was weird, because it seemed like he'd come home and they'd get back together just long enough for my mom to get pregnant. And then he'd take off again."

"Did they end up together in the end?"

"No. She died. Breast cancer." Violet takes a drink.

"I'm sorry."

She nods gently. "He wrote her a letter when she got

sick—said he wasn't coming home because he couldn't handle watching the love of his life wither away and die."

"So, he left you to watch instead." There's a sharp bite to my words—because Vi's dad is a selfish fucking prick.

She glances down at the table, smiling sadly.

"Pretty much."

"How old were you?"

"I was twenty when she passed away."

"Were you tested for the BRCA mutation?"

It's a very personal question—but I just can't turn off the part of my brain that knows these things. That women with a family history of breast cancer before the age of fifty and those who have mutations in the BRCA1 or BRCA2 genes have a significantly higher risk of developing aggressive breast cancers.

"I was—I'm negative. My younger sister, Chrissy, was positive for the BRCA2 mutation. She got a double mastectomy for her twenty-secomd birthday."

"Jesus."

"But she's good now—there's a comfort in knowing what happened to my mom will never happen to her."

"Is that why you became a nurse?" I ask.

"One of the reasons. I mean, by the time she went on hospice, I already knew how to start a line, monitor her blood pressure, administer her meds. And even during chemo it was always the nurses who helped her the most. They really . . ."

"Made a difference," I answer for her.

Because I've seen nurses in action—and that's what they do.

"Yeah."

"Did your dad come back to see you? After?"

"No. I haven't seen him since I was . . . seventeen? Like I said, he was never really into kids. I think to him we were just a side effect of loving my mom. Something he sort of had to put up with. Once she was gone, in his mind, so were we."

I can't fathom it. Not any part of it. I know there are men out there like Vi's dad—probably a shit-ton of them—but trying to relate to their way of thinking is like trying to get into the mind of a male frog who fertilizes the eggs and just hops the fuck away.

I'll never understand it.

I put my hand over hers on the table, brushing my thumb against her skin. "I'm sorry, Violet."

She lifts one shoulder. "It's okay. It was a long time ago. At least it feels that way most of the time."

Violet looks away, staring over at the orange flame of one of the firepits. When she turns back to me, her voice is more upbeat. Cheerful.

"Wow—am I a fun date or what? I'm sorry to be such a downer."

"No—you're not."

Her head tilts with disbelief. "Sure, I'm not. Abandonment, cancer, death—all the fun-time topics."

I laugh, shaking my head, debating if I should tell her that she's the best date I've had in years. And it's not even close.

But then Tom Waits comes out of the speakers—playing a guitar and singing in his gravelly voice about how he hopes he doesn't fall in love.

So instead I say, "We should dance. Do you want to dance?"

Violet's eyes lift to mine.

"Yeah, I do."

"Good." I stand up, holding out my hand. Without hesitation, she slips hers into mine and I pull her to her feet. "Come on, fun buddy."

Vi tips her head back, laughing beautifully and lighthearted and so fucking sweet it makes my chest constrict.

"I swear, my heart stopped when Spencer said that. It was hilarious."

"That's my kids." I lead her toward the dance floor, still holding her hand. "Always a barrel of laughs."

The ride back to Vi's house is different from our drive to the wedding. Before it was just her and me, with the music playing low on the radio, our easy conversation filling the cab, covert looks and quick stolen glances.

On the way back, it's her and me . . . with three teenagers jammed in the back and one ten-year-old squeezed in the front seat between us. Plus the bickering, the complaining, the almost constant changing of the radio station and blasting of the air-conditioning.

All that's missing is Rosie the barking dog.

Then Brayden decides to slip off his shoes and socks, stretching his legs out and resting his bare feet on the rear center console.

And all hell breaks loose.

"What the shit is this?" Aaron yells. "Dude, your feet reek!"

Mia covers her mouth and nose with her hand, which outrages Aaron even more.

"You're making my girlfriend nauseous—put your frigging shoes back on."

"I've got to air the boys out," Brayden explains while passive-aggressively wiggling his unusually long toes. "Let 'em breathe."

Meanwhile, Spencer is smiling and staring at Violet in a way that's starting to feel *Children of the Corn*-ish creepy.

"Did you have fun at the wedding?" he asks her.

"I did," she answers. "It was great."

Then he dives headfirst into the sales pitch . . .

"You could be our babysitter, you know."

. . . while Aaron and Brayden are threatening to kill each other in the backseat.

"My dad doesn't mind spending money when it comes to us. It could be a pretty sweet deal for you. You should think about it."

"You're not the boss of me, butt-munch! I can take my shoes off wherever I want."

"Keep talking, wonk-donkey—the minute we're home I'm kicking the crap out of you."

"Oooh, I'm so scared," Brayden says in a high-pitched, mocking voice.

Followed by the inevitable, "Oww! Daaad—Aaron stepped on my toes!"

I have zero chance with this woman.

Not that I really did before. She's young, gorgeous, carefree— she has the world at her feet and could have any guy she wants by the balls. When we get to her house, Violet should run for her life in the opposite direction of wherever I am.

"That's enough!" I tell the animals in the back—not shouting, but close enough to shouting to get their attention and bring the arguing to an instant end.

"Aaron, do not stomp on your brother—you're too damn old for that. Brayden, have some consideration for the other people in the car and put your socks and shoes back on until you get home."

When I glance over at Vi, she's not looking at me with the horror I expect. She's watching me with something like amazement on her face. Like she's deeply impressed.

And then she impresses me right back.

When she tells Spencer, "It does sound like a sweet deal," and she pats his knee. "We'll see."

And her delivery is almost as good as mine.

After I pull into Violet's driveway and kill the engine, she says goodbye to the boys and slides out before I have the chance to open the truck door for her. But I walk beside her up the stone path to her door, to make sure she gets in okay.

"I had so much fun tonight," she says softly.

"Me too."

"Thank you for taking me. And for letting me hang out with your boys—I can't remember when I had such a good time."

"Thanks for coming with us. They had a great time too."

And me. I had a fan-fucking-tastic time. But I keep that part silent.

Once we reach the front step, in the halo of the yellow lantern light hanging beside the door, I say, "So, I guess I'll see you at work."

"I guess so."

"Good night, Vi."

She takes a breath and gives me a smile.

"Good night."

I turn around and take two steps toward my truck.

"Connor?"

I turn back.

"Yeah?"

"Were you serious about us . . . running together?"

"Oh, yeah. Absolutely. They're great trails—you shouldn't miss out on them. I'm up to go running anytime you are. You could text me . . ."

"Yes! That would be awesome." She bounces a little—seeming both relieved and excited.

And again . . . her boobs jiggle fantastically. It's almost hypnotic—I could stare at them all day long.

"Perfect," Vi continues. "I'll text you and we can figure out when we're both free this week?"

"Sounds great." I smile, drifting back toward her like I'm being magnetically pulled.

"Good," she says with a nod, slightly breathless.

If this was a real date, with a normal woman my age, this would be the moment when I'd go in for a good-night kiss. Maybe a simple brush on the cheek, maybe something near the corner of her mouth—a feeler kiss—to see if she was open to the real thing.

And if she was . . .

I would skim my palms up her hips and slide them around her back—holding her gently and pressing her close. So she could feel how tightly wound I was, so she would know how much she's wanted. Desired.

And then I would lean down and press my mouth against hers, so soft at first, to relish the velvet feel of her lips. And when she was stretching up on her toes, pushing her breasts and stomach against me, craving more—I would taste her. I'd take my time and delve into her warm, tight mouth, again and again—drowning in the sweetness and sensation—until we were both weak-kneed drunk.

"Daaad, come *on*!" Spencer whines out the window of my truck. "You're taking forever and I gotta go home and take a poop!"

I sigh. Tilting my head up to the starry night sky, to laugh, and ask God why.

"And on that note, I should probably go."

Violet covers her mouth, laughing behind her hand.

"Okay—good night, Connor."

"Night, Vi." I get in one long, last look of her before turning toward my truck. "Sweet dreams."

CHAPTER
Eight

Violet

I DON'T THINK I'VE EVER TRULY UNDERSTOOD THE EXPRES-
sion *on cloud nine* before. But now I do. Because in the weeks
after Dean and Lainey's wedding, I'm walking on cloud nine,
ten, *and* eleven.

There's a floatiness to my steps, a sparkling fizzy sensation
beneath my skin, and a constant current of happiness swirling
in my stomach. The sun is shinier, colors are more vibrant, the
air seems cleaner, fresher.

Because not only are Connor Daniels and I meeting up to
jog together on a regular basis . . . we're also officially texting. And
that's only one letter away from sexting.

Granted, most of the time it's about jogging:

Free tomorrow morning?

They're calling for rain on Wednesday, don't forget your jacket.

How's Sunday evening looking for you?

But after a few days we start to have inside jokes, experiences
that only the two of us can relate to.

"Hey, Vi," Connor catches me in the hallway one Tuesday afternoon when we're on the same shift at work. "I think I spotted

Horny in my yard this morning. He was sneaking out of a tree at the crack of dawn looking guilty as hell."

He's referring to the nickname we bestowed on a fat, furry, squirrel we saw humping a rock on our run two days earlier.

I shake my head, grinning. "I told you he was a player. He's probably got a different girl squirrel in every tree in town thinking she's the only one he shares his nuts with."

Even my clumsiness around Connor begins to improve— *thank God*. Although when we're jogging I still devote at least fifty percent of my attention to not colliding with a tree or plunging down a ravine . . . just in case.

"If you had to describe your sense of self in only one adjective, what would it be?" I ask him halfway through a sunset jog on a Friday.

Because we also talk as we run. Nothing complicated or deep, but short, light conversations in between breaths that I replay in my head afterward over and over.

"Studly," he answers automatically.

I roll my eyes. "I'm being serious."

"Me too. Ask anyone—studly isn't just what I do—it's who I am. Some guys are just born with it."

"Okay, Maybelline," I tease.

We get closer. Comfortable. We get to know each other better. And the more I get to know Connor, the more I like him. And I really didn't think that was possible.

"Is this one of those personality quizzes from Facebook that's supposed to reveal your inner Disney character?"

"Maybe it is," I reply. "Do you want to revise your answer? You don't want to end up with Gaston. He was studly—and a dick."

We joke with each other. Tease. There are even a few exchanges that could be considered flirtatious—as well as a whole bunch of covert sniffing on my part.

Because the man smells delectable. Seriously. Even his sweat smells good—masculine and outdoorsy—like the scent of freshly cut wood and warm flannel.

The synchronized rhythm of our thudding feet on the dirt path echoes through the trees as Connor considers the question.

"Successful."

I glance at him jogging beside me—at the broad, toned, shape of him—powerful but poised. The kind of man who's careful because he's aware of his own strength. And I think about how he is at work . . . not testy or snappish the way some doctors can be . . . but always confident, firm, and commanding.

"That's important to you? To be successful?"

He shrugs. "I mean nobody wants to be *un*successful. But I'm a dad, a doctor—people depend on me. It's important to me that I don't let them down."

Connor lifts his chin toward me in that sexy, alluring way that makes me imagine him reclining in bed—naked, with one muscled arm tucked carelessly behind his head—inviting me to hop up and take a ride.

On him.

"What's your word?"

I give him the first answer that pops into my head.

"Sensible."

And I immediately want to take it back, because—could I be any blander?

"That's not very exciting, is it?"

"Exciting comes in many forms, Vi. It changes as you get older."

"Regardless, I'm going to go with . . . practical. Final answer. Practical is still boring, but slightly better."

His brow ruffles. "No, practical isn't boring at all. It's focusing on what matters. What's important. When shit goes down and things gets real—practical is exactly what you want right there beside you."

Like I said, cloud nine, ten, *and* eleven.

One hot Saturday afternoon in June, Connor and I make plans to go jogging a little before dusk. He pulls into my driveway while I'm on the front lawn limbering up.

I spend an embarrassing amount of time choosing my clothes for our outings. Obviously, I want to look good in a way that gets his attention—but I don't want to look like I'm *trying* to look good.

It's a delicate balance.

Today I'm wearing black Lycra bike shorts that accentuate my legs and a cute oversized zip-up white hoodie. As Connor rounds the front of his truck, looking good enough to eat in a gray short sleeved T-shirt that hugs his biceps and black basketball shorts, I unveil the pièce de résistance of today's outfit.

I unzip my sweatshirt and tie it around my waist—leaving me in nothing up top but a new teal sports bra that goes great with my tanned summer skin and pushes the girls together fabulously, without strapping them down.

Connor takes one look at me—and trips over his feet.

Excellent.

Oh, how the tables have turned.

"You okay there?" I ask playfully.

"I'm good." He nods. Then he clears his throat and gestures to me. "That's ah . . . nice top."

"Thanks." I smile. "I have it in white too."

I'm tempted to mention that you can see my nipples through the white one—but I think that would be overdoing it.

We head out on the path that starts behind my house and winds through the woods around the lake in a serpentine pattern. We fall in step beside each other, the rhythm of our strides matching, in a comfortable silence. The air is warm but it's cooler on the trail beneath the trees.

I love this time of day. How the fading sun glows deep orange through the branches and the shadows slowly descend, turning everything tranquil and secluded.

Two miles in, we stop for a water break. I brace my foot on a boulder and tighten my loose shoelace. A few feet away, Connor tips his head back and takes a drink from his Lakeside Memorial water bottle.

I stand with my arms at my sides, watching his throat ripple as he swallows and a little wet drop slides down from the corner of his mouth to his chin. He's got an awesome chin—the kind you want to scrape your teeth against and bite. Move over, John Travolta, there's a new chin king in town.

Connor glances at my empty hands.

"Where's your water?"

"I left it on the front table." I swipe my arm across my forehead and lick at my parched lips.

And I feel his eyes on me—on my mouth—like the secrets of the universe are tattooed there.

He holds out his bottle. "Do you want some of mine?"

His voice is deeper than usual, rough . . . like he's asking me one thing, but thinking something else.

That happens sometimes, but I never know if it's just my imagination, if I'm projecting and hearing emotions in his words that aren't really there.

Connor's easy to talk to but he can be guarded—difficult to read. At least for me. I'm kind of a mess when I'm near him. There are just too many wonderful, thrilling sensations surging through me, making my head light.

But every once in a while, I think he feels it too.

The pull between us. The magical, breath-stealing magnetism that says we could be outstanding together.

We could be everything.

But I can't ever be sure. And I can't afford to be wrong.

This time I get to spend with him is too sweet, too precious to me. I can't risk misinterpreting him, reaching for more and ending up falling on my face in front of him, like I have so many times before.

My tongue pokes out again, tasting salt on my upper lip.

"Yes, please."

Connor walks up to me and passes the bottle, standing so close I have to step back to take a drink. As I bring the bottle to my lips, he doesn't move, I'm not even sure he breathes.

He just watches. And it's different from how he's looked at me any time before.

His jaw is taut and his eyes seem to grow darker the longer he looks. The muscles in his forearms are strung tight and straining. Like he's holding himself back . . . but only just barely.

I like how he's looking at me. No—I love it. It makes me feel beautiful and needed. Craved.

Then he says my name. It comes out on a low breath, hushed but sharp—like a warning.

"*Violet.*"

But it only makes me want him more.

"Yes?"

My chest rises and falls but I can't catch my breath.

And we stand there, just inches apart, gazes locked. And it would be so easy for him to dip his head and kiss me.

I'm right there—waiting and wanting and already his.

All he has to do is want me back.

But then a sound tears through the air, streaking through us, making our heads turn in its direction.

"Did you hear that?"

"Was that a—"

And it was—it was a scream.

I know because it comes again, piercing and terrified.

"Help! Help me!"

"That way," Connor says, and we both take off running without another word.

Sprinting off the path, into the foliage, kicking up leaves

and jumping over fallen branches, heading downhill toward the lake. Once we clear the trees, we have an unobstructed view of the water. There are people on the other side, a fishing boat anchored far off in the distance—but the shoreline closest to us is rockier, less popular, and empty, except for a single square blanket bunching in the breeze.

In the water, I see a hot-pink tube, the kind little kids wear around their waists. But this one is empty, just bobbing with the waves on the surface of the water.

And there, toward the center, there's a flash of orange. A bright orange bathing suit, on the still form of a small girl. She's floating, facedown.

"Help!"

The scream comes from another girl—I can't tell her age—swimming with furious splashes toward the child.

We run down the hill. Connor kicks off his sneakers and tosses me his phone.

"Tell 911 we're at the east dock. Mark the time."

You only have minutes to start CPR on a drowning victim, to stave off the damage from lack of oxygen and circulation to the brain and heart. Icy water can buy extra time, but this water isn't cold enough. The longer a victim is down, even with CPR, the less likely it becomes that anything you do will bring them back.

Connor pulls ahead of me, his long legs propelling into a blur. He crosses the dock and dives off the edge into the water.

One of the first things I learned after moving to Lakeside is that the lake at the center of town is shallow around the edges—but just a few feet in, it drops off.

And it drops off deep.

Like a cold black hole, it's deep enough that you can't touch the bottom and make it back to the surface on one breath. And there's debris down there—fallen trees and tangled brush and thick snagging branches that rise up in spots—trapping your feet and making it feel like some sinister force is grabbing for you and trying to pull you down.

By the time I'm off the phone with 911, Connor is carrying the prone child, who looks maybe three or four years old, from the water, with the other, older girl a few feet behind him. She's twelve or thirteen, and I inanely wonder if she could be a classmate of Connor's son, Brayden.

"I was counting to see how long I could stay under at the dock," the older girl cries. "She was right there! But when I came up she was gone. I went under to find her but it was too dark, I couldn't see her. And then she popped up but she wasn't moving!"

Her face collapses into a sob as I move her back.

"Here, honey, stand over here while we help her. What's her name?"

"Serena."

Connor lays the little girl on her back on the dock, rubbing her chest and shaking her shoulder.

"Serena! Can you hear me?"

She's unresponsive.

He presses two fingers to the carotid artery in her neck, checking for a pulse, while turning his head and leaning his cheek close to her mouth and nose—so he can feel if she's breathing and see if her chest is moving.

But she's not.

He tilts her head back to open her airway and pinches her nose, covering her mouth with his and delivering two steady rescue breaths. Then he checks for respiration and a pulse again.

He lifts up. "No pulse, no respiration—starting compressions."

His voice is robotic, the same tone he uses in the trauma room. It's why repetition is an essential part of medical training—we have to go through the steps automatically. There's no time for thinking or feeling when seconds make the difference between life and death.

Connor folds his hands on the little girl's chest and pushes down with straight arms—pumping her heart for her. The CPR ratio for a child is fifteen compressions to two breaths when multiple rescuers are present. I move to her other side, down on my knees to take over the rescue breathing. Because in real life, CPR isn't like in the movies. It's hard work, taxing, and we have to work together if we're going to last.

As we start the second cycle of compressions, a woman yells in the distance and races up to us.

"Oh my god, what happened?"

From the horror on her face and the terror in her voice, I assume she's the girls' mother. She has a canvas bag in her hands that she drops on the ground as she crouches beside the teenager near us, wrapping an arm around her shaking shoulders.

They were probably having a lovely day, down at the lake—a picnic and a swim that would tire the little one out before bedtime. The mother probably went to the car to get forgotten towels, maybe a snack—just a quick trip. It should've been fine. Everything should've been all right. And now she's here and her whole world hangs on a razor's edge.

Life is a bastard sometimes.

"She slipped out of her tube," the teenager sobs. "I didn't see her—I'm so sorry, Mom."

The mother covers her mouth with her hand, watching Connor and me work.

"Is she . . . is she gonna be okay?"

"An ambulance is on the way," I tell her in a level voice. "I'm a nurse and this is Dr. Daniels. We're doing everything we can to help Serena."

Because that's all the assurance I can give.

We keep going. Mechanically repeating the movements. A police officer arrives on the scene—not Connor's brother—but since he doesn't have a defibrillator and we're already performing CPR, there's not much for him to do but watch.

After the second round of five cycles, I tell Connor, "Hold compressions."

And I lean down to check for a response.

When I lift up seconds later, I meet his gaze.

"Nothing."

"Fuck!"

Frustration slices in his voice and burns in his eyes. Because despite all of Connor's knowledge, without the proper equipment and medicine, his options are limited. Restrained.

Like Superman without his powers—he's just human now—like the rest of us.

"Resuming compressions," he snaps, and begins a new cycle.

"Do you need to switch?" I ask.

"No. How long?"

He's asking me how long she's been down. I glance at his phone on the ground beside me.

"Five minutes."

He bites back another curse.

"What's EMS's ETA?"

"911 said seven minutes."

He nods sharply, focusing his attention on the little girl in front of him.

And then he whispers quiet and low and in time with the compressions.

"Come on, baby. Come on."

I don't know if he's praying or begging or willing the life back into her—I'm not sure if he even realizes he's speaking.

"Come back, baby, come back. Come on, come on, come on . . . "

When you work in the emergency department, death is a part of your job. That's just how it is. It becomes a part of your day, a part of your life. Sometimes you don't even feel it—there's no shock or sadness—when it's predictable or expected.

And sometimes, even when you know it's inevitable, it's devastating. It brings you to your knees.

"Come on, baby, come back."

And I know right then, if we lose her—if *he* loses her, because that's how he'll see it—it will stay with Connor forever. He won't show it, will probably never talk about it . . . but it'll be there.

This one will hurt him.

"Come back, come on, baby, come back . . ."

And like the snap of the universe's fingers, like the flip of a switch—it can happen like that—Serena comes back.

Water sputters from her mouth and she shudders hard with coughing. And then crying.

And crying is *amazing*. The best sound in the whole world.

Because it means she's breathing.

"There you go." Connor croons, gentle with relief. "That's it, sweetheart."

Our hands cover each other's at her back, lifting her slightly to help clear the fluid from her lungs and turning her to her side. "Okay, that's it. You're okay. You're okay now . . ."

The sounds of an ambulance siren pierces the air as Serena's mother moves closer, reaching for her crying child.

"Thank you! Oh god, thank you so much."

It's dark by the time Connor and I make it back to my house. We walked back on the trail together silently, using the flashlights on our phones to light the way, the only sound between us was the deafening chirp of crickets.

I flick on the hall light after we walk through the door, leaving the rest of the house shrouded in black shadow. I lay my keys on the table, beside my forgotten water bottle. It's only been a little over an hour that we've been gone—but it feels longer. Further away, somehow.

And that's when I notice my hand is shaking.

And I'm not the only one who does.

"Violet?" He's beside me, his voice steady and deep. "Hey ... you okay?"

Connor takes my hands and presses them between his palms, rubbing his warmth into them.

"Your hands are freezing. And you're trembling."

"No, I'm fine. Really." I shake my head. "It's just—"

"Yeah, I know."

It's the aftermath. The buildup of stress and adrenaline. We block it out, lock it down, shut it up, but once a crisis has passed, it has to come out somehow.

"Come here."

And I'm pressed against Connor's chest, his arms around me, holding me, surrounding me in his scent and warmth. I let myself sink into him, pushing my face against his sternum.

"Your shirt is damp. Do you want me to—"

"The shirt's fine, Vi. I'm fine." His hand strokes up and down my spine. "Everything is okay."

He speaks in lulling, calming tones—because he gets it. And it's so nice to be understood, without needing to say a word. The thrum of his heart beats beneath my cheek, and that's comforting too.

"What if we weren't there?" I ask in a small voice.

"We were."

"She's just a little girl. It's would've been so awful if—"

"I know." I feel the press of his mouth against the top of my head, the warmth of his breath in my hair. "It's all right, Violet."

"What if we didn't save her?"

It's normal for fears to follow even after things turn out good. *What if I screwed up? What if I forgot what I was supposed to do? What if I forget the next time?*

It's a part of the process, part of dealing and carrying on. Because there's always a next time—and you don't know when it's coming or what it will be—but it could be worse. Harder.

And you could fail, you could let down the people who need you when they need you the most.

"We did save her." Connor squeezes me tighter. "She was laughing with EMS when they pulled away. She's going to be fine—kids bounce back really well—you know that."

I nod, letting his words flow through me, calming me.

"You did so good, Violet. We did good together. We make a really good team."

I smile against him. "Yeah, we do."

Then I raise my head, looking up. Connor smiles gently down at me.

But then his expression stills, and something shifts in his eyes before they drop down to my mouth. My heart speeds up and my breaths quicken as Connor brings his fingers to my chin, his thumb stroking, tilting my face up to his.

And then he lowers his head and presses his lips to mine.

His mouth is so warm and soft. The pressure of his lips a coaxing, seducing weight that makes me reach up on my toes to press back against him, feel more of him. My arms slide around his neck and his arms wrap around my lower back. Connor angles his head, changing direction—sparking a simmering heat that builds in my pelvis, when the tip of his tongue slides slowly across my lower lip. I open for him, gliding my tongue into his hot mouth at the same time that his slips into mine. The wet, stroking caress is so erotic I moan, and Connor's fingers grasp at me, digging into my skin needily. He slants his mouth over mine again and again, our noses brushing until I encase his upper lip, sucking gently.

Then he dips his knees and lowers me to my feet, leaning back but keeping his hands splayed across my hips. We breathe deeply, staring in shock at each other for a long moment, waiting for one of us to say something.

But neither of us do.

When I remember it later, I'll never quite be able to work out in my mind how it happened—who moved first. But I think we move together.

Because in the next second our mouths crash together, tongues clashing, and he's crushing me against him—chest to chest, stomach to stomach, hips grinding heated and hard. Our hands tear at each other, touching and tugging at too many annoying clothes—like we want to crawl beneath each other's skin.

It's wild and rough, crazed and desperate.

We kiss like the world will end if we stop.

And it's perfect. The most perfect second kiss that ever existed.

He grips my hips and yanks me up. I wrap my legs around his waist and squeeze for all I'm worth. And then I gasp, open-mouthed, at the rock-hard erection wedged between my legs, covered only by the light, thin fabric of his shorts.

Connor's lips drag across my jaw and down my neck, sucking and scraping with his teeth. He groans against my skin when I rotate my hips, riding him through our clothes, the friction so sublime I could come on him just like this.

He swings us around, pushing my back up against the wall beside the foyer table. Something clatters to the ground—my keys or the water bottle or maybe the whole damn table. I don't know and I don't care, because his mouth is on mine and it's glorious.

He kisses like he wants to consume me, devour me, pumping against me on the wall like he wants to merge us into one person. He holds onto me like he covets not just my body—but my heart and my soul too.

And I'd give them over to him happily. Because I want him the same way.

"Violet, wait." His voice scrapes up his throat and I can barely hear him over the rushing in my ears. "Wait, wait, wait. Jesus, look at me."

My lips feel bruised and swollen as his words register and I open my eyes to his searching, hungry gaze.

Connor sucks in a breath, panting more than he has on any of our runs.

"Are we really doing this?" he asks. "Is this what you want?"

I have no thoughts in my head. There's no plan, no doubts—no *after*.

There's only Connor and me and the need that's thick and scorching between us. Fusing us together like molten metal and begging for more.

He runs his thumb down along my hairline to my jaw. His touch so tender. And such a shocking contrast to the heavy, hard, pushing cock that's pressed between my legs.

"You need to tell me, Violet. I want you to be sure."

There are moments in life that require you to tread carefully, bide your time, be prudent. And then there are times when you just say fuck it—and jump off the cliff. And whatever is waiting for you down below—warm waters or jagged rocks? It doesn't matter anymore.

Because the rush of the fall will make it all worth it.

"I've wanted this for so long, Connor. Please don't make me wait any longer."

It's like he's a barrel of gasoline and I just lit him on fire.

My cute sweatshirt? Gone.

My new teal sports bra? Ripped over my head, off my arms, and thrown on the floor—probably too stretched out to ever wear again.

And I love it. I love his harsh movements, like he can't get to me fast enough. I love how he stares at my bare breasts for two solid beats and then groans crudely.

I love how he pins me to the wall with his hips, palms my

breasts with both hands and lurches down to lick and lave like a starving man—sucking the hardened points of my nipples into his mouth and flicking with his hot tongue until I see stars.

And then I'm whimpering, tugging at his hair and rubbing mindlessly up and down against his cock—because it's not enough.

I need him closer—inside—hard and full and pounding.

I don't have to tell him . . . Connor already knows.

He kisses me deeply, cups my ass in his hands, and carries me down the hall, kicking open the door to my bedroom on his first guess and laying me on the bed.

In my mind, I hop up and go full she-hulk on his clothes, shredding them off his body.

In reality, I lean back on my elbows and watch as he tugs his shirt over his head, kicks off his shoes and socks, and slides his shorts and boxer briefs off to the floor.

And my eyes have seen the glory . . .

Connor's body is all man—strong and rugged and fit. And every inch of him beautiful.

A smattering of dark hair dusts his chest and lower on his stomach. His torso and thighs swell with taut muscle and tanned skin. His erection protrudes proudly—thick and long—the broad head smooth and crimson. He's bigger than I imagined, even bigger than he felt—large enough that when Connor takes his wallet out of his shorts and slips out his own condom, I'm relieved . . . because the standard-size box in my nightstand drawer wouldn't have fit.

He puts one knee on the bed and leans over me. I run my hands all over him—everywhere I can reach—loving the hard, silken feel of him. His watches me with sensuous, heavy lids as I wrap my hand around his shaft and slowly stroke him, reaching between his legs to cup the soft, weighted sack—massaging and giving a gentle tug that makes his eyes drag closed.

Then I go in for a taste—licking and kissing along his ribs, making his breath catch. I intend to go lower, but he grabs me by the nape of the neck, dragging me up to kiss me, his tongue plundering.

I'm not a virgin. I've had hookups, boyfriends, even what you could say were "lovers," though I'm not that fancy. Some of the guys I've been with were good in bed.

But with each of them there was a tangible undercurrent of selfishness in all the thrusting and flipping around and hair tugging. It's not that I didn't enjoy those things—but they never felt like they were for me.

About me.

It was always all about them. What they wanted to do, feel, try—how and where and when they wanted to come.

With Connor—every move he makes, every whisper and touch—feels like it's all for me. To worship me, please me, make me gasp, make me quiver. Holy god, it turns me on.

And he *knows* things.

When he peels my shorts and panties off and slips his hand between my legs, his movements are bold and sure. But when he pets me there, sliding the pads of his fingers back and forth on my clit, his touch is delicate and sensual, applying just the right pressure.

He knows how to kiss me, when to hold my head still and spear his tongue roughly into my mouth—making me take it—and when to pull back to a teasing stroke and make me chase him for more.

And what he doesn't know—he asks—and that's hot too.

The rasping, hushed whispers in my ear. *Here? You like that? More?*

It makes me so wet—heated, slippery, moisture clings to the apex of my thighs.

But there's no embarrassment or shame. He likes how wet I am. I know because he tells me.

You're so slick for me, Violet. Fuck, you're making me so hard.

He spreads my knees and nudges between my thighs, giving me a front row seat as he rolls a condom on with sure hands. He lines himself up and slides up and down against my soaked opening. And then thrusts inside—going in full and smooth and to the hilt.

My back arches and our moans echo through the room. I lie back and watch his face above me.

He runs a thumb across my parted, panting lips.

"Are you okay?"

I clench my muscles, clamping down and squeezing all around him—pulling a filthy groan from his throat. Because he feels so good. So big and hard and hot—every inch of him stretches me, fills me in the most delicious way.

"I'm perfect."

Connor braces his weight on his hands beside my head.

"You are, Violet. You're so perfect."

He leans down and kisses my breasts, my neck, before taking my mouth in a tongue twining, lips sucking, head spinning kiss that never ends.

And then he rides me—rocking his hips forward and back, surging in and out in a practiced, steady rhythm. He fucks me deep, his cock rubbing against my clitoris with every perfect stroke.

It's constant and miraculous and catches me off-guard with how quickly an orgasm begins to build. I'm not a fast comer—I don't really know how I compare to other women—but it usually takes me enough time to get there that I start to worry if it's taking too long.

But not now, not here, not with him.

The cresting pleasure swells higher and higher with every thrust. The room fills with the sounds of our moans and heavy breaths. And then, when Connor's deepest inside me and his pelvis presses up against me, he drags his hips in a tight, slow circle.

Over and over, round and round.

And *boom*.

I go off like a rocket to Mars. Soaring, shooting, bliss sends me flying fast and high, making my muscles go tight and lights swirl behind my closed eyelids.

And I want to tell Connor how good it is. That it's never been like this. I want to tell him he's amazing, and a god, and, yes, maybe even that I love him.

But it's so intense, the sensations wrack through me so hard, words aren't possible. Breath-catching gasps and high-pitched whimpers are the only sounds I'm capable of as I shudder in his arms.

But even without the words, Connor seems to know that too.

He stays buried inside me, not moving, making love to my lips with his mouth as I come back down to earth. Then he pulls out and turns me on my side—settling in behind me—his chest warm against my back and his wet cock sliding between the cleft of my ass.

He nuzzles my nape with his lips, peppering my skin with kisses. And then he's touching me everywhere—and from this position there's nowhere he can't reach.

He palms my breasts and pinches my nipples, he sucks at my earlobe and licks my neck. His hand slides down my stomach, between my thighs, and his fingers spread my outer lips so he can rub my clit slow and soft.

And the bliss starts building all over again.

There's a distinct possibility I won't make it out of this alive. Death by orgasm . . . what a way to go.

Connor lifts my top leg, bringing my knee to my chest—and he nudges my opening with the head of his cock, before pushing back in.

His groan is gorgeous gravel in my ear. And I'm clenching him again, loving the feel of him inside, wanting him to stay right there forever.

The heat of his chest leaves my back as he leans away behind me—gaining the leverage to thrust deeper, harder—faster—his big hands holding me still as his hips snap up against me.

My awareness fades—all of my focus settling on where Connor moves in and out of me. Frantic words seep from my throat—*yes*, and *God*, and *please, please, please*.

Then he's back against me again, his arms a tight band around me, his thrusts losing their rhythm—turning uneven and wild. He takes my hand and presses it between my legs, rubbing myself with my fingers.

"Fuck, fuck . . ." he grinds out behind me. "Violet . . ."

I cross the orgasm point of no return and push back against him, coming and moaning and reaching back to dig my nails into the hard bulge of his thigh.

The grip of his fingers bite into my hips and the hiss of his breath heats my shoulder as a low growl rumbles through his chest. I feel Connor's cock twitch inside me, jerking in time with his groans.

I've never really been into semen. Swallowing it or rubbing it in various places—it's always just been one of the messy parts of sex.

But I want to taste him on my tongue. Swallow him. I want to feel his come on me, in me, trickling out of me—anything he wants. Everything he wants.

I go boneless on the bed, my nose pressing into the sheet, breathing in the scent of sex and cotton. Connor kisses my shoulder softly and withdraws. The bed jostles as he climbs out of it and I force my eyes open to watch as he walks across the room to the bathroom. His ass is a firm, perfect work of art in the silver light shining from the window.

He's wonderfully still semi-hard when he walks back in, wearing a grin on his lips that's both savage and satiated. I roll to my back and he glides on top of me, cradling my head in his hands, kissing and nibbling my mouth languidly.

And we stay just like that, for I don't know how long. There are no words or conversation—only kisses and touches, deep gazes and twining together.

Eventually, things heat up again—what with him naked between my spread legs and all. Connor has a second condom in his wallet that we put to excellent use.

It's slower the second time, gentler and longer—and somehow even more intense.

After Connor takes care of condom number two, we lie in bed facing each other, exhausted, spent, and satisfied—my leg hitched over his hip and his hands holding my ass like a security blanket.

If I was thinking clearly, if my mind wasn't clouded by all the orgasms, I might be concerned by how deeply I feel for him. How ruined I am already.

But I'm too resplendently content. Too happy. Joy takes up all the air in the room; there's nothing left for worry.

So instead, I sleep.

We both do.

It's sunny when my eyes creak open. Still early, probably before 7 a.m., but late enough that there's a robin on my bedroom windowsill pecking at his reflection in the glass.

I breathe deep and stretch—a little stiff—sore in all the good places.

I fully intend to make a sneaky dash for the bathroom to

brush my teeth and untangle my hair, but first . . . I want to know what Connor Daniels looks like when he's asleep.

Is he a boyish, peaceful slumberer? Is he a devilish sleep-smirker in the midst of a stupendously dirty dream? I hope so.

I want to memorize Connor's sleep face. Sketch it in my mind so I can transform it into poetry later.

So I roll over in his direction. And blink.

Because the bed is empty beside me.

Connor is gone.

CHAPTER
Nine

Connor

"**A**ND THEN I LEFT."

I'm smiling as I give the D.U.H. group an update on the latest developments between me and Violet the next day. Well, the G-rated version of the updates—because only scumbags kiss and tell.

I haven't stopped smiling since I left her house. Literally. It might be an undiscovered medical condition—some kind of Joker syndrome, an overdose of endorphins—and if it is, I don't care. I'm just that fucking happy.

The other members of D.U.H. look at me like I'm an alien. An asshole alien.

"What do you mean, you left?" Stewart asks.

"Like . . . you left to get her bagels?" Lou guesses.

"You left her a heartfelt note thanking her for a beautiful night and telling her you can't wait to see her again?" Tikki hopes.

"You left to buy her coffee and pick her flowers from the neighbor's yard?" Maria tries.

"Nope, I just left. I got out of her way—let her get on with her morning."

And they still look confused.

"What was in your mind when you made that decision?" Dr. Laura asks.

"Well . . . I'm into Violet in a big way—so I have to play this just right. I can't be stupid. I don't want to scare her away. And she's young."

"How young?" Karen asks.

"Thirty."

Lou shakes his head, "Thirty ain't that young."

"It's young enough to have a whole different outlook. Girls like her don't want some old dude who's clingy. They want freedom, they want to do their own thing with a man who's capable of doing his own thing. Sex is the first step. I read that in a dating book—compatibility is huge. If you're not good together on the screwing front, there's no point in going forward. That's how thirty-year-olds think. And our sex was fucking earthshattering, so we've passed the first hurdle. Now I need to back off and show her I'm not going to smother her. That's how this works."

They still seem concerned.

Dr. Laura adjusts her glasses and seems to choose her words with care.

"Connor, are you sure this is the way you want to handle this? Best-case scenario, it's very presumptuous. Are you certain this isn't an excuse to keep Violet at arm's length? To protect yourself from forming an emotional attachment to another woman, and possibly being hurt again?"

I think about all those careful words. For five seconds.

"Yes, I'm sure. It's not any of that."

The D.U.H. posse is unconvinced.

Delilah raises her hands to the sky and prays.

"Jesus, take the wheel. And make it a convertible, Lord, so you can smack Connor upside his stupid man head with a low-lying branch."

There's a few muttered amens around the circle. Lou makes the sign of the cross.

"Connor," Dr. Laura tries again. "What you're talking about sounds dangerously close to playing mind games. Acting in a way that doesn't reflect what you truly feel, but as a manipulation to achieve a desired outcome. Those maneuvers tend to end badly for everyone involved."

I shake my head. "I'm not playing mind games. This is how committed relationships get started now. This is the foundation. Honesty comes later; right now I just have to keep her interested. It's like the Mandalorian says: this is the way."

"Fuckin' Mandalorian again," Carl snarls.

And everyone groans. Because ever since the new crop of movies came out, he's deeply resentful of anything Star Wars related. Don't even get him started on the Jar Jar Binks conspiracy.

"That helmeted bastard could be leading you all off a cliff and you'd follow him saying, *This is the way, this is the way.* Like zombies."

"Let's not digress, Carl. We've talked about this." Laura says.

"Disney is the Empire, Dr. Laura! Mickey is Palpatine. It's been there in front of us the whole time!"

Tikki covers her eyes. "Oh my God."

"Shut up, Carl!" Maria yells.

"We're supposed to be helping Connor," Stewart says. "And he, like, really needs it."

"Look, guys." I hold up my hands. "I appreciate your concern, honestly. But I've got this. I'm awesome! I know exactly what I'm doing—everything's going to be fine."

If this were a movie, now would be the time when the narrator's voiceover comes on and informs the audience that I did not, in fact, know what I was doing and nothing—*nothing*—was going to be fucking fine.

Violet

Maybe I snore.

Or talk in my sleep.

Maybe I kicked him and thrashed around. No one's ever told me that I'm a restless sleeper, but it's possible.

Oh God—what if I *farted* in my sleep? It's a normal bodily function and Connor's not the prissy type, but maybe it's too early in the relationship for nocturnal gassing?

These are the thoughts that run through my mind all day Sunday as I obsessively check my phone, waiting for a text or a call.

That doesn't arrive.

I go over every moment in my head searching for the reason Connor bailed and is now ghosting me. But nothing stands out. No hint of hesitation on his part, or indication that he was anything but supremely into everything we did.

That he liked it, liked *me* . . . every bit as much as I did him.

I don't understand.

And that's the hardest part. The not knowing. If I was clear on what I did wrong, I could deal with it, and figure out a way not to do it again. But not having any clue about where it all went wrong is torture. Making me replay the day and night on repeat, again and again.

Reliving every look and touch and kiss, every pant and breath and blissful orgasm in slow motion until I'm in a perpetual state of horniness and depression.

It's not a fun place to be.

I consider texting him. Something casual and lighthearted. *Hey* could work.

Or something direct and bold. Inviting him to come back

over for round two ... or four ... if we're getting technical. Or the simple, one-lined burning question of *why did you leave?*

But every time I move to type the words—they sound too pathetic. Too needy. No man likes needy.

The cold, plain truth is if Connor wanted to talk to me— he would. He'd reach out or he never would have left in the first place. And if I'm being honest ... he never made any promises to me.

Not once.

So I force myself to do nothing. To wait until I see him at work tomorrow. When I can see his face and hear the inflection in his voice and watch his body language ... and understand what the hell went wrong.

In the meantime, I put on a record, one of my favorites, and blast "Always Something There to Remind Me" by Dionne Warwick through my house. The lyrics are sad but the melody is upbeat—a perfect reflection of the clash of emotional titans going on inside me.

I write a poem to purge my feelings. It's terrible, even for me—it doesn't even rhyme. I cross out and rewrite so many words, it just ends up looking like a giant ink smudge on the page. So that's what I title it: "Smudge."

And I put it in my mother's old jewelry box on my dresser, with all the others.

I take a calming bath and drink chamomile tea, even though I hate the taste of it. And I give myself a manicure. I need to keep my nails on the short side for work, but I clean up the cuticles, buff my nail beds to a high sheen, and paint them with a simple lavender polish. To feel pretty.

To try and feel happy again. Like I was yesterday.

But in the evening, when the sick, churning confusion refuses to ebb, I call my sister, Tuni. Chrissy's the dreamer, the romantic. But Tuni's the logical, straightforward twin. If anyone can help me sort myself out, it's her.

She picks up on the second ring.

"Hey, Vivi! What's up?"

With dismay, I realize I'm holding back tears. I'm a hard crier. Sloppy and sobby like a dam that bursts and drowns any living creature below it in a deluge of hiccups, unintelligible words, and snot.

"Am I like Mom?" I ask her in a thick, clogged voice.

It just comes out. Not something I've been dwelling on, but I realize now it's at the heart of my worry. Because my mother was warm and wonderful and for her whole life she loved a man who didn't stick around. Who slipped out the door in the middle of the night when she was sleeping. Who never loved her back the way she deserved.

"What?" my sister asks, the previous joy in her tone evaporating like dry ice in the air.

"Am I like Mom?"

I hear the scraping of a chair in the background, and a shuffling, like she recognizes this is a sitting down sort of conversation.

"You are definitely like Mom. And you should take that as the compliment it is."

I pick at my newly dried nail polish.

"No, I mean—do you think I'm like Mom when it comes to men?"

"Well, Mom only had a taste for one man—and it wasn't the healthiest choice in the pantry."

"Exactly."

"But Dad loved her."

"Did he, though? Did he really?"

"I like to think he did, for her sake. I remember watching them together, and I know he made her happy when he was around. I think he loved her as much as he was capable of loving anyone."

"But that's not enough, Tuni! She loved him with her whole

heart, and it broke her when he didn't come back. I saw it break her."

Would I love Connor that much?

I think I would—eventually. I think one day I could love him so deep and so hard that I'd let him shatter me . . . as long as I still got to keep a piece of him.

"It wasn't right," I insist.

"No, it wasn't right." Tuni concedes softly. "But she could've chosen differently, Violet. She was strong enough to do that. But he was who she wanted—warts and all. Just because you're like her doesn't mean you'll choose the same."

Her words bring me back down, soothe my aching heart and ease my panic.

"Yeah," I sniffle. "I guess that makes sense."

"What's going on with you Vivi? What's the story, morning glory?"

Even though I was head of the household after my mother died, we don't have a parental sort of relationship. I was the adult, but it was still a situation where the four of us were in it together. So now that Tuni's all grown up, she's my beloved sister, but also on my level—my dearest friend.

"There's this guy . . . that I work with." My voice lightens, the way it tends to whenever I talk about Connor. "He has three boys and he's divorced and he's gorgeous and funny and an incredible father. He's perfect and I've liked him forever. And we got close . . . we became friends. Then we slept together—and it was *amazing*. More amazing than I could ever tell you."

My heart expands with the sweet memories. And then it squeezes, like it's being crushed in a stainless-steel, high-end juicer.

"But afterward, he didn't react like I thought he would. He left while I was asleep and I haven't heard from him since. I don't know why and I don't know what to do."

Tuni's quiet for a few moments.

Then she says, "Some men are complicated fuckers."

I laugh, for the first time today.

"You said he's divorced?" she asks.

"Yeah."

"Well, maybe he was overwhelmed by the power of your enchanted vajayjay? He could be gun-shy if he's been burned before."

I didn't know Connor when he was married. His divorce was finalized before I moved to Lakeside. Though I know he's dated—nurses talk—he hasn't been in a serious relationship since his marriage ended. And according to Callie, even his one-off dates haven't been experiences to write home about. Could it be that he's just out of practice on post-sex etiquette?

"That's true."

"Or maybe something's going on with one of his kids? He got the call and had to rush out the door without leaving a note. You know how that can be."

I once had to rush out in the middle of a night class because Chrissy accidentally set the kitchen curtains on fire when she was cooking dinner. She'd put the fire out with the fire extinguisher, but I still had to get home to talk to the fire department and make sure everything was okay.

"I didn't even think of that. I hope everyone is okay. The boys are great kids, but they're still kids—definitely a handful."

Slowly, the weight of being blown off by Connor starts to lift from my heart.

"He mentioned he was on at the hospital tonight, so I can go in early tomorrow morning for my shift and talk to him before he leaves."

"There you go," Tuni says. "Now you know what you're going to do. And whatever happens, Vivi, just remember that you are a treasure. You're so good at loving the people you care about—anyone who's worthy of you is going to see that, feel it, and want to give all that love right back to you. It's the law of balance—it's science."

I laugh again. "I love you, Petunia. Thank you."

"I love you too, sis. Anytime."

Early the next morning, I find Connor in the doctor's lounge, at his locker.

Though his back is to me, I stand in the doorway for a moment, soaking in the sight of him. Because now that I know what he feels like above me and behind me—now that I know how the planes of his shoulder blades and his waist feel beneath my palms, his taste and his scent and his tantalizing sounds—I'm drawn to him even more. Like a sugar craving, an addiction: having a little just makes you want more.

I move up toward him as his fingers deftly turn the combination lock. My breath catches at the remembrance of what those fingers are capable of—how they stroked and teased, pinched and rubbed so exquisitely.

But I shake off the lust-fog and step up beside him.

"Hi, Connor!"

Inside, I cringe at the high-pitched cheeriness in my voice.

"Hey Violet," he replies smoothly, the warm timber of his voice threatening to call forth another round of salacious memories.

But I push them away, asking, "How are you?"

"I'm good." He smiles. "Terrific. It was a slow night. Just an infant with an ear infection, a couple sutures, and one case of chlamydia that was taken care of with a trusty shot of penicillin."

"Super."

"Yeah."

Even though we're alone in the room, I move closer and lower my voice.

"So . . . I wanted to talk to you about the other night."

His gorgeous smile stretches wider and his eyes warm. "What about it?"

"Well, I mean, I woke up and you were just . . . gone."

"Yeah." He nods like it's totally fine, totally expected. "I had to get home to the boys and you were sleeping, and I figured you'd have stuff to do. I didn't want to be in your way."

Okay, that makes sense.

Kind of.

Except for the whole not waking me up to say goodbye after sharing one of the most intense and intimate sexual experiences of my life. And the not calling or texting afterward. That's still pretty shitty.

Then a crushing thought occurs to me. Maybe it wasn't as mind-blowing for him? Maybe he was . . . disappointed? Is that what he's trying to say?

"But you . . . you had a good time, right?" I ask, my cheeks flushing with the heat of Mordor's Mount Doom.

Finally, he quits digging through his locker. He stops purposefully and turns, his dark eyes delving deeply into mine.

"I had a *great* time, Violet."

And the anxiety that's been strangling my lungs loosens its grip. Because Connor's looking at me with sincerity and affection and pure, infinite tenderness.

"It was fun."

Hold the fuck on . . .

"Fun?"

And now I sound like a parrot. A stupid, stupid parrot who's about to get her heart pulverized into dust.

"Yeah," he says, closing his locker with a metallic clang. "We should do it again sometime. If you're free and I'm free. You know, whatever."

What. Ever? Is he serious right now?

With my thoughts spinning and my soul dying, I nod like a robot on the very last of its battery power.

But then, as he slides the strap of his bag onto his shoulder, there's a slow flicker from deep inside my gut. An orange ember just beginning to ignite, that builds and grows—feeding off my disappointment and humiliation and converting my heartache to incandescent rage.

Rage is so much easier.

Burning, wild, scorned woman fury.

Fuck you, Connor Daniels! I don't say it out loud, but I'm shouting it from the rooftops inside, because seriously—fuck him.

Fuck him gently with a whole shed of chainsaws.

How dare he turn out to be just like every other asshole on the planet when I have idolized him for years!

Fuck his beautiful voice and his flawless, awesome personality. Fuck his sexy arms and his phenomenal penis. Fuck his brilliant doctor mind and his gentle, magnificent dad soul.

"Sure, whatever." My lips press together in a smile so tight I think they split. But he doesn't notice because he's not looking at me. "That would be swell."

For the record I never say *swell*. I picked it up off a *Madmen* episode and since we're now operating at that same level of epic dickbaggery—I figure it fits.

From now on that's all he gets—the fake me.

Connor doesn't get to have any piece of the real me. Not my smile or my laugh or my words . . . definitely not my heart.

Not anymore.

He squeezes my shoulder.

"Cool. Have a good shift, Violet. I'll talk to you later."

And he walks out the door.

CHAPTER
Ten

Connor

A FTER VIOLET APPROACHED ME IN THE DOCTORS' lounge that morning, I thought things were going in the right direction. That I was handling the situation masterfully and she was right where I wanted her to be. Interested. Eager. Prepared to come back for more—again and again.

I checked my phone the whole day, expecting a text from her inviting me to her house. Maybe asking if I wanted to grab a bite to eat or even just to check in on when I was free to go jogging again.

And according to Timmy, the girls he knows like to instigate the making of plans. It's a power move—to show they're independent and in control. I didn't want to deprive Violet of the chance to do that.

But no text or call ever came. Not that day or the one after.

Once you're in a solid relationship, women get off on knowing a guy is pussywhipped. It's a confidence booster; it makes them feel secure that you're not going to go screwing around.

But timing is everything. Coming off too pussywhipped too soon is pathetic and an instant attraction killer.

But as the days progress, things between me and Violet start to feel . . . off.

Different.

Wrong.

Violet and I don't go jogging together again for the next two weeks. Eventually, I bite the bullet and text casual offers, but she declines, saying she's busy—and canceling twice on me after initially saying yes.

We don't sit together at lunch, or talk and joke around at the hospital in between cases. She seems preoccupied. Standoffish.

One morning on the way into the hospital, I stop at the corner coffee shop and grab the fancy frappé-machi-bullshit-latte thing she likes to drink.

Violet's behind the nurses' station, typing on the computer when I walk in. And I jump at the opportunity to watch her when she doesn't know it.

She's wearing her glasses today—thick, square, black frames that I imagine sliding gently off her face so I can kiss her long and deep. My tongue tingles with the fantasy, because I can still taste her. Sweet and hot and stunning. I remember how she felt all wrapped around me, her arms and hands pulling and pressing—her sexy, throaty little sounds—her pussy so tight and snug and wet, it was like I saw the face of God when I came.

One of the nurses says something to Vi that I can't hear, making her lips twitch. And a wrecking ball of longing nails me right in the chest. Because I miss talking to her. I miss her smile, her laugh. I miss *her*—period.

I grip the cup tighter in my hand and shake my head.

Pull it together, Daniels. Be cool.

"Hey."

"Hi." She smiles—but it's brittle and guarded and all frigging wrong.

I hold out the large paper cup.

"I swung by Magnifique Coffee this morning and grabbed this for you."

"That was nice." She takes the cup. "Thanks, Connor."

And it feels like a victory. A small victory, sure, but even Everest gets climbed one step at a time.

Then Violet walks out from behind the nurses' station and drops the cup directly into the garbage. It lands at the bottom with a dull, flat thud . . . like my hopes.

"But I'm trying to cut back on the caffeine."

I nod slowly. "Right."

And she walks away without looking back.

Great. Perfect.

Fuck.

A week after that, I run into her at the high school when I show up a little early to pick up Brayden from the obligatory pre-freshman-year summer tour. Spencer and I are hanging out on the bleachers when I spot Violet's unmistakable form jogging around the track.

I intercept her on the asphalt. "Hey. What are you doing here?"

She stops running, brushing her damp bangs back from her forehead, and shrugs. "I just felt like I needed a change from the trails. It's smooth pavement here, you know? No unexpected bumps or potholes to trip me up."

And she's looking at me in the way women do when they're saying one thing but mean something totally different—and they expect you to read their minds.

I didn't think Violet was one of those women . . . but I guess I was wrong.

She glances down at Spencer and her whole demeanor changes. Her eyes go from distant and lifeless to affectionate and bubbly. And her smile is genuine—suffused with her natural warmth.

"Hey, Spencer. How are you doing? It's good to see you."

"Hi, Violet! You know that babysitting position is still open. Are you still 'seeing'?"

"Yes." She laughs gently, and jealousy flays me to the bone. Jealous of my own kid—that's not messed up, is it? "I'm still seeing."

Violet lifts her face to mine—and we're back to the dead eyes again.

"Well, I should finish my run. See you around, Connor. Or not. You know . . . *whatever.*"

"Those are some serious thoughts for a Sunday morning," Tim tells me from across the kitchen table. "I can hear you thinking from here."

Garrett focuses his attention on me. Because the gang's all here at my parents' house for the traditional weekly family bagel breakfast.

"You do seem kind of . . . broody."

"Yeah," Ryan agrees, "Who pissed in your copy of *The Catcher in the Rye*, Holden Caulfield?"

Garrett gives Ryan an odd look. "That's very literary of you."

Ryan shrugs. "I was helping Josephina with her English paper last night."

"Yeah, she's got Dillinger for English—he's a total slacker. He hasn't updated his reading list since 1995."

"Hello." Angela waves at them from the other end of the table. "Can we focus, please? And find out why Connor is more sullen than my teenage daughter—and pray to gawd that it doesn't have anything to do with the cutie he brought to Dean's wedding? I liked her."

"I like Violet too," Callie adds, because my love life is always

127

up for a family vote. "You two seemed like you really hit it off, and she was great with the boys."

I sigh and resign myself to spilling my guts. My sisters-in-law are the best, but their interest is like the jaws of a rottweiler—once they latch on, they never let go.

"It *is* about her, actually. Things were going good after the wedding. We were jogging together, texting, I thought we were on the same page. But now . . ."

I leave out the sex part. Sitting at my parents' kitchen table discussing my sex life is too weird.

" . . . she's not really talking to me anymore. Like, at all."

"Maybe she's playing hard to get," Tim suggests. "She knows you took the bait so now she's jerking the line to set the hook deeper. You should ignore her. Or insult her—insults would be better."

"Insult her?" I ask, like he's lost his mind.

"Definitely. Negging works like a boss."

"No. Violet's not like that."

"They're all like that, bro." He thinks about it further. "Could also be she's actually blowing you off. Girls do that all the time—it's the nature of the beast. She's probably been 'jogging' with two other guys on the side."

"Hold the phone." Angy puts out her hand. "Why are you taking advice from Timmy about dating? Or . . . anything?"

"I resent that," my youngest brother says.

"He's the same age as Violet," I tell her. "And he's single. None of you have been single for years. It's a fucking jungle out there."

Angy is already shaking her head. "Timmy has a type. He dates *girls*. Young, morally questionable, not the brightest bulbs in the box—"

"Smoking hot . . ." Tim interjects.

"—naive *girls*." Angela finishes. "Violet is a woman. I knew it the minute I laid eyes on her. And no woman in her right mind would blow off a man like you for no reason."

She folds her arms—going full Brooklyn.

"What'd you do?"

"I didn't do anything," I scoff.

Ryan and Garrett laugh. Full on cracking up. Garrett wipes at his eyes.

"That's hilarious."

"You guys are kind of dicks, you know that, right?" I tell them.

Ryan gestures around the table. "Our single days may be ancient history, but if that's what you actually believe, you've been single too long."

Callie slides in with the final piece of the puzzle.

"*You* might not think you did anything wrong, Connor, but *she* definitely thinks you did something wrong."

The back of my neck gets itchy and hot under their stares.

"Well . . . there was one thing. Possibly."

"Here we go," Ryan quips.

And Angela raises her eyebrows expectantly.

"We hooked up," I admit. "And I woke up afterward and she was sleeping, so . . . I left."

Tim laughs like an ass, clapping his hands.

And I know immediately I'm screwed.

"That's great!"

"No." Callie shoots him a stern teacher look. "That's really not great."

"Legendary," Timmy insists. "She must've been so pissed off."

"What are you talking about?" I ask him. "I don't want to piss her off."

"Of course you do. Dodge and duck, leave and come back, run and she will chase. She won't be able to tell which end is up. That's how the game is played."

I look my youngest brother in the face.

"Violet isn't a game, Tim. She's important to me."

Finally, he gets it. And his face goes smooth with understanding.

"Oh." And then he looks worried. "You might have a problem, then."

Son of a bitch.

"Listen," Angy says, inching forward in her seat. "It's not that complicated. If you want to screw around and play the field, you listen to Timmy. If you want a mature, honest relationship with this woman—you only have to trust your heart. What does your heart tell you, Connor?"

My heart says Violet didn't appreciate me giving her space right after we had sex—momentous, intimate, profound sex. My heart says it was wrong to tell her the next time I saw her that we could get together and do it again sometime, like it didn't mean anything to me. Like she didn't mean anything.

My heart's telling me I'm definitely the asshole in this equation.

The question is—what am I going to do about it now?

The next day, the answer becomes clear. And it's lose my ever-loving shit, apparently.

Because Violet is going out with another guy. He's here, right now, picking her up from work.

I can see them through the glass window, in the rear parking lot near the staff entrance to the ED. He's tall with dark hair and seems on the young side, a couple years younger than Violet. She runs toward him, smiling huge and giddily—the way she used to smile at me—and throws her arms around his neck, letting him hug her close, practically lifting her off her feet.

And something tears loose inside me—snaps in half—leaving

any inclination I had to proceed with caution on the trauma room floor with the rest of the medical waste.

Even the double glass doors get the hell out of my way.

Okay—yes, they're sliding glass doors with a sensor.

But even if they weren't—they'd open for me now. Such is the raging level of my pissed-off-ness.

"You have got to be fucking kidding me."

Violet turns my way, all round bewildered eyes and puffy parted lips that make me want to kiss her and never stop.

"Excuse me?"

"You've spent weeks giving me the cold shoulder, barely talking to me, canceling on me, throwing out my coffee, and not even looking at me unless you have to for work. And now you're out here all warm and huggy with this douchebag?"

Yeah, that's right, I said it.

Doo-hoosh Ba-hag. Prove me wrong.

Holding my gaze, Violet tells doucheboy in a careful, level tone, "Darren, can you please wait—"

That's when I start to lose it.

"Darren? His name is *Darren?*! Like the husband from *Bewitched?* What are you gonna do? Are you gonna—" I make a stupid tinkling sound and twitch my nose back and forth with my finger the way the blond housewife witch used to on the old TV show.

And I take it back—it's obvious I've already *completely* lost it.

But does that mean when *Darren* decides to grow a pair and steps up to me with his chest puffed out, that I back down? Fuck no.

"Who the hell *are* you?"

I get in his face. "You want to know who *I* am?"

I'm the guy who's about to remove his head from his shoulders and shove it up his ass. I'm a goddamn physician—I know just how to do it.

He jabs a finger at me. "No—on second thought—I don't give a shit who you are. If you ever talk to my sister like that—"

Cue the record scratch.

I'm sure whatever he continues to say is riveting and impressively threatening, but the entire universe of my existence stops at the word. "Sister?"

Violet steps between us, her mouth cinched into a tight, glossy bow, her eyes shooting sparks—and if I thought she was beautiful before—good God, when she's pissed, she's stunning.

"Yes, Connor—*sister*. Aka, the douchebag—"

"Hey!" Darren objects.

"—is my *brother*!"

I fold my arms across my chest.

"Oh."

And I lift my chin, to at least try and give the appearance of dignity considering I've incinerated any shred of mine with a nuclear blast.

"Well . . . this is awkward."

A hot, growly sound comes from Violet's throat and she exhales violently out of her nose, like a pretty bull about to charge. She grabs my forearm and drags me a few steps over into the shadow of the hospital building.

"What the hell is wrong with you, Connor?"

"I thought you were dating him."

"And so what if I was?! Why do you care?!"

Shame slithers down the back of my neck like cold KY. Because I have screwed this up so bad. Frustration makes my fists clench and my words brusque.

"I care because we used to be running partners—we were friends—and now we're not. And it's messed up that you just—"

I stop myself short. Because none of that is real. It's just an excuse—just fear and defensiveness—and it's not even close to all the things I want to tell her.

The things I *need* to tell her.

"No—actually, that's bullshit. The truth is . . . I like you, Violet. I like you so fucking much. And I *miss* you."

Vi peers at me, her voice dropping to a shocked whisper.

"You do?"

"Christ, yes. That night between us was incredible and perfect and I woke up next to you, and you were so damn beautiful, and I . . . completely freaked out."

"You did?"

I nod. "Because it's been forever since I've felt about anyone the way I feel about you. So I left. And I have regretted it every second since I walked out your door."

Her head tilts and her eyes seem a little dazed.

"You have?"

"Yeah, Vi. I have."

She shakes her head quickly.

"But . . . but it's been weeks. Why didn't you say anything?"

I toss the dating book info and the website guidance and every stupid piece of advice Tim has ever given me into the mental garbage dumpster of my mind.

Because this thing with Violet—it could crush me—I can already feel it. It could wreck me if it doesn't work out. Hurt me in a way that not even my marriage ending ever did.

But . . . she's really worth the risk.

"Because you're all I think about. And if I asked you for a second chance and you said no, I didn't know what I was going to do. But if I didn't ask yet, then there was still hope that I could fix it. There was still a chance you would—"

I don't get another word out.

Because Violet grabs the front of my shirt and pulls me to her, pressing her sweet, pillowy lips hard against mine. And any thought that's not about how fucking good she tastes is gone from my mind.

I wrap my arms around her, pulling her closer, feeing her soft and supple body, finally, after so long. Our tongues slide and tangle in an almost frantic reunion, before I cup her jaw and kiss her more gently. Until we're standing, with our foreheads pressed together and our lips still touching, slowly breathing each other in.

"You're an idiot," she whispers against my mouth.

"Yeah," I agree. "It's probably better that you realize that now—just get it out of the way. It'll save us time later on."

She laughs. "When does your shift end?"

"Ten a.m. tomorrow. Then I have the next two days off."

"And I have the next three off."

She glances around, seeming to remember where we are. One of us probably should.

"Okay, I'm going to go to dinner with my brother because I haven't seen him in a year. And you really should—"

"Yes." I jerk a thumb over my shoulder. "Doctor. Patients. Medicine. On it."

"Right," she laughs again. "You're probably going to want to sleep when you get home, have something to eat, hang out with the boys . . ."

I fucking love that she thinks of them. That she automatically knows spending time with them is as essential to me as eating and sleeping. People who don't have kids don't always get that . . . but she does. *Such* a turn-on.

" . . . so why don't you swing by my house in the late afternoon or after dinner?"

"No. I want to take you out. Let's go out for dinner. Together."

Her dark eyes widen.

"Like . . . a date?"

My voice is firm, clear, and completely unambiguous.

"Totally, one hundred percent, a date."

Violet's full, pouty lips stretch slowly into a beaming smile. "Okay."

I nod, my tone going a little softer, a little relieved.

"Okay."

She drifts backward toward her brother, eyes on me. "Then I guess I'll see you tomorrow."

"Yeah, you will."

"Have a good shift, Connor."

"Have a good visit with your brother."

Speaking of her brother—I give him an apologetic look.

"Hey, Darren, listen, I'm really not usually this much of an asshole. And Darren is a great name, seriously. A classic."

He chuckles, shaking his head. "Whatever, dude. It's all good."

And then I'm heading back inside—feeling like a new man. Luckier and more on top of the world than I've felt in weeks. Maybe in ever.

"You two kiss and make up?" Nurse Stella grouches. Because she's mean and astute—and she's got the goods on every person in this department, just by looking and listening.

I spin her around, dancing to the song "Brown Eyed Girl" playing in my head.

"Life is good, Stella. Life. Is. Good."

She cackles, shoving me away.

"I'm glad you think so, cowboy." Then she presses two charts against my chest. "We've got a case of shingles in Exam Two and a bowling trophy lodged where the sun don't shine in Four."

But not even oozy pus-filled blisters from the adult reoccurrence of chickenpox or foreign objects in the rectum can bring me down.

"Fantastic. Time to cure the sick."

And I walk down the hall with one arm in the air like Judd Nelson at the end of the goddamn *Breakfast Club.*

CHAPTER
Eleven

Violet

"OKAY—HOLD UP—THIS DOESN'T MAKE SENSE. You need to clarify."

A dark lock of Connor's hair falls dashingly over his forehead and the soft glow of the lamplight overhead makes his eyes a lighter, golden shade of brown.

We're at Boccone's, a hidden-away, unpretentious restaurant I've never been to that Connor swore had the best brick oven pizza on whole East Coast. Two slices in and working my way through number three—I don't disagree.

He knocked on my door at 7:30 sharp like we'd planned, wearing navy jeans that hug his fantastic ass and a light blue, collared button-down shirt with the sleeves rolled up.

And he was holding flowers. Flowers for me.

A gorgeous little bouquet of red roses and lavender. He told me I looked incredible in my short, polka-dot sundress and black wedges with my hair down but pulled back on the sides. And the way his eyes ate me up from head to toe, I couldn't not believe him.

Then Connor leaned in and pressed a kiss to my cheek, all sweet and chivalrous.

It made me want to jump his bones and tear both our clothes off right there in my foyer. Again.

He opened his truck door for me, and gave me a hand up as I climbed in, and the cab had that clean, fresh, just-taken-to-the-car-wash scent.

There hasn't been any awkwardness or hesitation that often happens on a first date. It's been only fun, simmering excitement—lingering smiles—and the easy enjoyment of each other's company.

"What do you need clarification about?" I ask, taking a long drink from my frosty beer mug and licking at the foam on my upper lip.

He gestures to me.

"You're Violet."

"Correct."

"And your sisters are Chrysanthemum and Petunia . . ."

"Chrissy and Tuni for short," I say with a nod.

"How the hell did your brother end up a *Darren?*"

He's chuckling before he finishes the question and the sexy rumble turns my insides to warm Jell-O.

"My mom loved flowers. Violets, chrysanthemums, petunias were some of her favorites—obviously." I pinch my thumb and forefinger together. "My brother came this close to being Hyacinth."

Connor flinches. "As the father of a Daniel Brayden Daniels, I feel I'm qualified to say—fucking yikes."

"But she decided to spare him the years of inevitable schoolyard torture and went with Darren instead. After her favorite uncle."

He lifts his beer in a toast.

"Your mother was a smart, kind woman."

"To Mom," I laugh, tapping his mug with mine.

"Do any of your siblings live nearby?" he asks before taking another bite of his pizza and chewing seductively. Who knew that eating could be such a raw, carnal act? But the way Connor does it—the strong set of his mouth and the rhythmic roll of his jaw—is sinfully hot.

"Nope. Darren's been stationed in Germany—he's an intelligence officer, so I don't really have any idea what he does because he can't talk about it. Chrissy is a pastry chef in a restaurant in Chicago and Tuni is a concierge at the Beverly Wilshire in California."

"What made you move out of Delaware?"

Connor doesn't ask questions to be polite or fill the silence—he genuinely wants to know the answers. I can tell by the way he leans toward me, how he watches and listens . . . he wants to know *me*. And that awareness is liberating. It makes me want to tell him every secret, show him every shadow.

Give him all of me.

"About two and a half years ago we ended up all ready to fly the coop at the same time. Darren was about to ship out; the twins had graduated college and culinary school and were set to start their jobs. The house we grew up in was too big for just me—and it was my mom's house—it never felt like mine, you know?"

Connor nods. "That's why I bought a new house with the boys even though we were staying in town. To have a something that was just ours—a fresh start."

"Exactly. So, we sold the house, paid off the mortgage, and had enough left over for each of us to make tiny dents in our student loans, and to find someplace new."

Connor's eyes drift over my face.

"And you found Lakeside?"

"I did. New Jersey was close but far, different but still kind of the same. There was a full-time ED position at the hospital and when I saw the town, I guess you could say it was . . . love at first sight."

"Lucky us." He reaches across the table and covers my hand with his own. He really does have magnificent hands—large and chiseled, but always warm, always careful and capable. Connor gives my hand a gentle squeeze.

"Lucky me."

It's the perfect Jersey June night for a walk—warm but not humid, breezy but not windy, and a sky that's a cloudless black backdrop for a zillion shimmering stars. Connor and I decide to skip dessert and walk down to the Soda Fountain—an old-timey ice cream parlor several blocks away.

Main Street is a quaint area, lined with *Singin' in the Rain*-style lampposts and awning-covered mom-and-pop stores.

"Hey, Vi, look—bubble tea—your favorite." Connor points at the pastel-colored stand that seems to be a hit with both the senior citizens and the high school crowd.

"Bubble tea is an abomination."

"Yeah," he laughs. "I know you hate it."

I stop walking and face him, crossing my arms.

"How do you know that?"

Connor inhales slowly, like he's about to unveil some deep secret. Then he puts his hands on my hips possessively and tugs me closer.

"I'm an observant guy, I notice things. I noticed you . . . for a while."

"Really, Dr. Daniels?" I ask him playfully—covering for my heart fluttering against my ribs like a caged bird.

"I tried not to, but it didn't really work. You've always been there, Violet."

There was a movie a few years ago, I don't remember the name—but the main character gained super powers without realizing it. One day she was walking along and realized she was levitating two feet off the ground.

And that's how I feel right now. Like I'm floating on air.

At the Soda Fountain, Connor gets a scoop of chocolate fudge ice cream on a sugar cone . . . and watching him lick it is literally the stuff of my dreams. I get butter pecan with rainbow sprinkles in a cup—and I don't care that it's a grandma flavor, it's my favorite. We sit at the round wooden tables beside the building, talking as we eat.

"Did you always want to be a doctor?" I ask him.

"Since high school, yeah."

"How come?"

"I was good at math, good at bio and chem. The money's great . . . and I like making an actual difference in someone's life, every day. There aren't a lot of careers that let you do that."

I stir my ice cream, considering him.

"Why emergency medicine? Why not ophthalmology or dermatology—the hours are a lot better."

"That's true. But the ED is never boring. And I like being challenged—I never know what's going to come through the doors so I better be ready for anything. I like being in charge too."

When we're finished, we walk back to Connor's truck leisurely, holding hands and falling naturally into a sort of relationship lightning round.

"Did you go out with Hanson from Radiology last year?" Connor asks me.

"No."

"I heard that you did."

I shake my head. "Just a rumor. I've never dated anyone from the hospital. Have you?"

"No." He swings our joined hands. "Present company excluded."

"Why do some of the nurses call you cowboy? Is it an inside joke? Is it a sex thing?"

Connor tilts his face to the sky and laughs.

"No, Violet, I'm not into cow kink or spur fetishes. Sorry to disappoint."

I tug on his hand. "I didn't think that."

"It's a nickname," he explains, "for doctors who break the rules once in a while, ride by the seat of their pants—that kind of thing."

"Is it true you once threatened to beat up a respiratory therapist in front of his kids?"

It was a rumor I'd heard when I'd first started working at Lakeside—and it gave Connor a bad-boy doctor edge that, surprise-surprise, I found super attractive.

"No. That's completely not true," he scoffs.

That's rumors for you—they always get it wrong.

"It was a pulmonologist. And I told him if he didn't get his ass out of bed, I was coming to his house to beat the shit out of him in front of his *wife*."

I snort out a laugh, covering my mouth.

"That's really not better."

Connor shrugs. "He was on call and we had an ARDS patient on the way and he was giving me a hard time about coming in because it was two in the morning."

ARDS is short for acute respiratory distress syndrome.

"And it worked. He showed up in record time and the patient was treated and discharged the next day."

"Did he write you up?"

"Oh, yeah." Connor smirks. "And I'd do it again in a heartbeat."

I'm pretty sure I actually sigh out loud. And start to look up at him like the hero he is—until I notice the sign above the darkened store behind him.

Retro Records Coming Soon

"Oh wow!" I keep hold of Connor's hand, bringing him with

me as I move to the big picture window to peek at the rows of boxes inside. "I didn't know a new record store was opening here."

"You listen to records? Like, actual records? Aren't you kind of young for that?"

"Good taste has no age, Connor."

"Fair enough." Connor checks the sign on the door. "It says their grand opening is in three weeks. We can come back then, if you like."

And it's such a simple thing to say, but it rocks my world. Because that's when it really sinks in. That this thing with Connor isn't a daydream or a wish, it's not the result of a concussion or a coma, it's not a friendship or a casual fuck.

It's solid, real, it's happening . . . and this is only the beginning.

My throat tightens with so much excitement and emotion, my voice goes reedy.

"I would love that."

Connor

Holy shit, this girl.

It's crazy how into her I am. How fast and hard I can feel myself falling for her.

Violet Leigh Robinson.

You get to a certain age, a certain point in your life, when you just don't think that's possible anymore. You're too adult, too cynical. You've experienced life and lust, love and loss. You have too much control over what you want, what you feel, what you know.

And then . . . *kapow.*

All those expectations are obliterated.

It's not a tumble or slide—it's a plummet, straight down—like falling into a well you never knew was right in front of you.

One minute you're standing on solid ground, thinking you know exactly where you are, where you're going, and then you take a step and you're *gone*.

Consumed in one single, swift drop.

And yet it makes perfect sense—because she's *amazing*. Smart and funny, so fucking gorgeous, so fucking sweet.

"Connor . . . *hmmm*."

Violet's ragged little moan slips from her mouth into mine. We're in my truck, in her driveway, parked behind her cute powder-blue car—making out like teenagers frantic to get off before curfew.

She's straddling my lap, wriggling around in the tight confines between my chest and the steering wheel, making me so hard my vision blurs.

I palm Vi's breast over her dress, the stiff point of her needy nipple poking my palm, taunting me. I lick her throat, tasting strawberry-flavored skin, dying to get my mouth on the rest of her.

I can't even bring myself to break away long enough to get us in the house.

She's too enticing—she feels too goddamn good.

All I can think about is laying her back on these leather seats, lifting her dress, and eating her out until her screams puncture my eardrums.

It was explosive that first night. I thought I'd be calmer this time—less desperate. But I was wrong. Now that I've had her, the way I want her is even more raw and incessant. And I'm not even a little freaked out about it—never again. It may be a full-on cliché but it's true . . . nothing this fantastic could ever be wrong.

"Connor, Connor, God . . ."

Violet chants as she writhes, her hips swiveling as much as she can—driving me crazy—her tight little pussy so hot and ready I can feel the heat of her seeping through my jeans. I suck harder on her neck, probably marking her with hickeys but not giving a shit.

She yanks at the collar of my shirt to slide a hand in, gliding her silky touch over my chest, wickedly scratching at my pecs.

And then our lips are molded, mouths fused, trying to consume each other.

Christ, I need to bring her in the house.

I need more room, more light. I want to lay her down on the bed and strip her slowly. I want to see Vi's lips parted and glistening as she gasps, watch her perfect tits bounce while I fuck her, gaze deep into her endless eyes when she comes.

And I will. I swear to God, I will.

But first . . .

I shove my hand between us, lifting her dress above her waist and slipping my hand down her panties, where she's smooth and warm and soaked. I push two fingers up inside her and she keens low and long. Her pussy squeezing my fingers so tight it almost hurts.

My other hand goes to the back of her neck, guiding Vi's mouth to mine—because the truck is filled with her scent and sounds and I need to taste her tongue or I'm going to lose it.

Violet rides my hand, holding onto my shoulders, pumping herself up and down, while my thumb presses against her sweet, swollen clit. Her breath quickens and her chin dips—her legs go stiff and taut.

"I'm coming," she whimpers. "Connor I'm coming, I'm coming. . ."

Yeah, she fucking is. And it's beautiful.

I want to plunge my tongue into her moaning mouth and swallow her cries.

But I want to watch her more.

How her neck arches back, pushing her breasts forward, and her long black lashes fan beneath her blissfully closed eyes, the way color rises sharp and light on her cheeks, but her lips go a darker, deeper shade of pink.

Violet goes limp against me, sinking her face into my shoulder, her little breaths tickling my neck. I slip my hand out from between her legs, and—yeah—I bring it to my mouth, sucking my fingers clean.

She's sweet like strawberry juice, and warm like honey. And I can't wait to have her straddling my face—so I can taste that sweetness straight at the source.

"We should go inside, baby."

Vi lifts her head from my shoulder, her pretty face lax and dazed.

"No, not yet."

I brush her hair back and massage slow circles into her neck.

"Let me take you inside, Violet. We're not done, not even close. But I want to take my time with you."

She shakes her head again and slips off my lap.

She lays on her stomach on the seat next to me, bending her legs at the knees so her feet dangle in the air and her dress rides up exposing the luscious lower cheeks of her ass, peeking out below black lace panties.

I'm momentarily captivated by the sight—I can't not grab it. So I do—feeling the soft, firm flesh against my palm and slipping my fingers under the fabric to tease up and down along her crease.

Violet tears at the button and zipper of my jeans like a woman on a mission from God. Like a vixen, an angel, a whore, and a saint.

She opens my pants, tugs my briefs down, and wraps her hand around my aching, stiff cock—pumping the shaft slow and firm.

"Violet we . . . *fuuuck me*—"

My head lolls back on my neck and words are no longer physically possible.

Because my dick is in her mouth—and it's hot, wet, and perfect.

Her lips are a tight, pillowy seal as she slowly sinks down and down, taking me all the way in. Until I'm nudging the back of her narrow throat and can feel the exhale of her breath out of her nose against my groin.

And then Violet stays right there. Just like that. Keeping me lodged in the heaven of her scorching mouth and clasping throat until I'm gripping the seat and my eyes roll back and my heart feels like it's ready to explode.

She sucks hard on the way up, dragging her tongue, leaving a glistening wet trail behind her. Vi rubs her lips against the head, licking and kissing and worshipping—like I'm a mythical Greek cock-deity and she's my supplicant servant girl.

She takes me all the way back in, sucking harder, her dark head bobbing up and down in a way that looks incredible and feels unreal.

My balls go heavy and tight with the oncoming release and my hips lift on their own accord. I start thrusting in and out of her mouth, spearing her lips—and Violet moans around me—telling me how much she likes it.

I come hard, groaning her name—flooding her mouth in thick, hot, pulses—the pleasure so intense colors burst like bombs behind my eyelids. Violet's throat constricts as she swallows, trying to keep up, even as I give her more and more.

After the jerking aftershocks subside, my spine goes slack. I don't move—can't move—the fuses of my somatic nervous system have been momentarily blown . . . along with the rest of me.

Violet gives me a final lick, then rises up, resting proudly back on her calves. Her eyes are shining and her smile is bright. She swipes her tongue across her bottom lip and runs her finger over her chin, wiping away what she couldn't swallow fast enough.

It's kind of dirty and extraordinarily hot and it makes me want to start all over again.

We're never going to leave this truck.

"That was incredible."

I chuckle.

"I'm pretty sure that's my line."

And I reach for her, draping her across me, sinking my hand into her hair and pouring every drop of affection and fulfillment that rolls through me into our kiss.

We do eventually make it into the house—into Violet's bed.

I make her come with my mouth between her legs, because I really can't get enough of her taste. And then I sit at the edge of her bed, feet on the floor, I curse and whisper crude things in her ear as she rides me hard and fast with my hands on her ass—until we come again at the same time.

And then we talk. We kiss and cuddle. We discuss in more detail how she felt when she thought I was blowing her off and I describe the torture of my confusion when she seemed so pissed, but not really, and I couldn't figure out which end was up.

Glad that's fucking over.

Violet heads into the bathroom to take her contact lenses out and I ogle her shamelessly the whole time she's out of bed.

Then we grow quiet. I press my nose to the nape of Violet's neck, breathing her in, and she wraps her arms around my forearms, holding on tight. The rise and fall of her chest evens out and I think she drifts off—so when my phone alarm vibrates at half past midnight, I kiss her neck and scrape my teeth over her earlobe.

"Are you awake?"

Vi inhales deeply.

"Yes."

I trace my finger up her bare arm because I love the smooth,

147

soft feel of her skin and she wriggles her ass back against my dick . . . and that feels pretty awesome too.

"I have to go. I don't like leaving the boys alone too late."

"I figured you were going to say something like that."

Violet turns over in my arms and kisses me slow and deep, running her hands gently through my hair.

"Will you call me tomorrow?"

"Definitely. Maybe we can grab lunch?"

"Lunch would be good."

I throw my leg over her waist, keeping my weight off her as I climb off the bed. She takes her folded glasses from the nightstand and puts them on to watch me get dressed.

With my jeans on but open and my shirt hanging unbuttoned from my arms, I bend down and kiss Violet's lips—brushing her hair back, with all the tenderness that's currently crushing my ribcage.

"I had a great time tonight, in case that wasn't perfectly clear."

Her lips stretch into a smile.

"Me too."

"I'll talk to you tomorrow, Vi."

"Okay. Good night Connor."

But just as I reach the bedroom door, I make the mistake of glancing back to look at her—and like the power of Medusa, my dick turns to stone.

She's not doing anything blatantly sensual—just lying back in that large, girly bed with those glasses on, wearing a pretty well-fucked expression and watching me with languorous eyes.

Her hair is dark as midnight in the low light—loose and wavy, splayed out in shiny strands against her skin and on the pillow all around her. The white comforter comes to her waist, but her right knee is bent, angled out invitingly, and the rosy buds of her nipples are high and tight—just begging to be sucked.

And I'm so tempted to rip this shirt right back over my head and pounce on her. To kiss her hard, stay the night. It would be so good.

But it's only a pipe dream right now. A fantasy.

Because Dad-life calls and there are three great kids who need me at home. So I grip the doorknob behind me without turning around, so I can keep looking at her, and then I back out of Vi's bedroom and out the front door.

CHAPTER
Twelve

Violet

"**S**IR, PLEASE DON'T TRY TO GET UP."

For the next few weeks Connor and I continue to see each other. We go to the movies or out to dinner, and we come back to my house for long, sweaty, sex-filled hours. Sometimes we go jogging and have sex in the shower afterward.

Sometimes we skip the jogging and just go right to the sex.

"What's your friend's name?"

And I didn't know sex could be like *this*. Playful and teasing, rough and dirty, tender and intimate. Sometimes all at once.

But always incredible. Always with an intense connection between us—drawing us together—before, during, and long after.

"What did he drink? Was it just alcohol or drugs too? You won't get in trouble but I need to know."

Sex is an amazing part of our relationship—but it's not the only part. We talk too. Flirty conversations in the car and deep, naked ones in bed. We text about our day when our schedules don't coincide—we joke and make each other smile.

Sometimes we don't do anything at all. We hang out at my house—happy just being together.

"Run a line. Start him on fluids and pump the stomach."

We . . . progress. Our relationship evolves, becoming steady and a part of our everyday lives. Our normal. I can feel it happening—not too fast, not too slow. The perfect pace.

Perfect for us.

"Whasshapenning? Wheremy? Hey, letgo. Letmego!"

At work, we keep a slightly more formal distance. I mean, everyone knows—we don't hide anything—the people Connor and I work with are our friends. And what happens in Vegas might stay in Vegas but what happens in the ED gets told to everyone else in the ED. Plus we have to report the relationship to HR because, apparently, there was a lawsuit a few years before my time and now HR is scarred for life—so any time two people in the same department are dating, that's what you have to do.

But we keep it strictly professional.

All the time.

Mostly . . .

"Jeremy, you need to calm down. I'm going to put an IV in your arm so we can give you medicine and get you better," I tell the college kid who's neck deep in alcohol poisoning—which could lead to coma and death. He was dragged in, totally incoherent, by his fellow fraternity brothers.

A lot of people don't know this, but nurses do: rage isn't the most dangerous emotion to have to deal with.

That trophy goes to paranoia, every time.

"Nah! Nogetaway!"

Jeremy starts thrashing the minute he sees the needle. I grab for his arm, trying to hold it down without sticking either of us— but panic makes him strong.

"Help! Aliens! Haaalp!"

He roars something about probes and abductions, but it's hard to make out with all the kicking and flailing.

He throws out his left elbow in the struggle, catching me in

151

the nose—snapping my head back and making my vision white out.

"Son of a bitch!" Connor shouts.

Someone hands me a cloth and I press it to my face, tasting blood in the back of my throat and feeling wet warmth on my lips.

"Restraints—now! And get security in here!"

The veins in Connor's forearms stand out as he pins Jeremey's right arm down.

Orderlies and nurses converge, strapping his struggling wrists and ankles to the gurney as he curses them out.

The second he's secured, Connor tells his resident, "Start the gastric suction when the line's in—I'll be right back." Then he's guiding me into the exam room next door. "Let me look at that."

He sets me on a stool and sits across from me.

"Connor—"

"Don't talk."

His eyes shine sharp with anger and his face is a tight mix of fury and concern as he sticks rolled gauze up both my nostrils.

Forcing me to breath out my mouth—like a caveman.

Then he presses his fingers carefully below my eyes, along the bridge of my nose, checking my teeth and jaw.

"I don't think anything's broken."

"Connor—"

"How's your vision? We should do an X-ray just to be safe."

"Connor!" I push the stool back and stand up, finally getting his attention. "Nothing is broken, I'm fine. And you can't do what you did in there just now."

He leans back, eyes narrowing.

"And what did I do, exactly?"

"You can't slap every zonked-out patient in restraints to try and protect me. Or drag me out to an exam room for every bump and scrape."

My stopped-up nose undercuts the righteousness of my speech—making my voice honky and nasally like a talking goose.

Connor stands up too—his movements harsh and uncompromising.

"I would've put that asshole in restraints, period."

"I was handling it. This is a part of my job."

"Taking an elbow to the face from an idiot frat boy is not part of any nurse's job—not on my fucking shift. The fact that you're my girlfriend is the reason I have to stop myself from walking back in there and beating the shit out of him *while* he's in restraints. Two totally different things."

I stare at him—mouth-breathing for two solid beats.

"I'm your girlfriend? Like ... officially?"

I assumed we were headed in that direction but hearing him say it out loud is different. It makes me feel all lit up inside, my heart skipping and bouncing around like I've been transformed into a human pinball machine.

"Well ... yeah." His brow ruffles but he doesn't look sorry he said it. "I mean, that's how I think of us. If it's okay with you."

I smile—and I really hope there's not blood on my teeth.

"It's completely okay with me. It's perfect."

Connor's dimple comes out to play—the corner of his mouth inching up into a smitten smirk.

"Good."

"You know, that actually brings up something else I wanted to talk to you about." I take the gauze out of my nose because this is not a conversation I'm having with tampons protruding from my nostrils.

"I have an IUD."

"Niiice." Connor exhales.

I roll my eyes.

"It didn't feel so nice going in. Buuut, I figured we should put it to good use and ..."

"... get some blood tests," Connor finishes for me. "And rely on the IUD for birth control."

"Exactly what I was thinking."

No one can ever say we medical people aren't true romantics.

"You can write up the order for the lab and Melissa can draw my blood before I head home," I say.

"God, you're awesome." Connor's eyes caress my face, softer now. "You know that, right?"

I laugh, cherishing the warmth spreading through my stomach.

"It's always nice to hear." I move toward the door. "Well, *boyfriend*—we should get back to work."

"Vi, wait." He wraps an arm around my waist, tugging me back. "You have dried blood on your face. Come here."

Connor grabs a few alcohol wipes, tilts my chin up, and gently dabs at my skin.

"I am so sexy," I tease, looking at the ceiling. "I don't know how you can resist me."

He chuckles, tossing the balled-up wipes in the trash when he's finished.

Then he leans in and kisses me on my rubbing-alcohol-flavored lips.

"You are. And I can't. Not anymore."

When my shift ends at 11 p.m., I grab my purse from the locker and head over to the desk to say goodbye to Connor. He's hunched over, looking at his phone as he curses.

"Everything okay?" I ask.

"No. Aaron's MIA—he sent me a text an hour ago saying he's arguing with his girlfriend and doesn't know when he'll be home, and hasn't answered me since. Brayden and Spencer watched some movie that spooked the hell out of them and they're sending me 911 texts that they're pretty sure there's a cult surrounding the house as we speak."

I smother a laugh. Connor rubs the back of his neck and continues.

"I could ask my parents to go over but my father will insist on driving and he's blind as a bat at night. And he's too stubborn to wear his night glasses—if he even knows where they are. Ryan is working, Angela is probably already in bed, Timmy's drunk at his apartment with his firefighter friends. I hate to bother Garrett because Charlotte is teething, so he and Callie aren't sleeping as it is . . . but it looks like he's my only option."

I smooth his hair back from his forehead—he's my boy-friend—I can do things like that now.

"Or, I could go over?" I offer.

"That's not why I'm telling you this. I don't want to put you out."

"No, you wouldn't be. My schedule's totally open. I was just going to go home to clean out my fridge."

I was also planning on writing a poem about Connor calling me his girlfriend . . . but I keep that tidbit to myself.

"Unless you think it's too soon? Or it would be weird for them?"

Connor hasn't mentioned officially introducing me to his boys as someone more than a friend, and I haven't brought it up because I have no clue what the timeline is for that kind of thing.

"It wouldn't be weird for them—they know you from the wedding and Spencer brings up the possibility of you babysit-ting like every other day."

I laugh.

"And it's not too soon, Violet," he insists. "I was thinking we could all go out to eat or something next week."

He leans in closer—close enough that I can smell his tanta-lizing male scent that not even industrial hospital sanitizer can diminish. "I would've brought it up sooner, but I've been really en-joying our . . . alone time . . . in case you hadn't picked up on that."

Images of our "alone time" dance through my head, each more sensual than the next.

"Yeah," I say breathily. "I've enjoyed it too."

"I noticed." He smirks in a cocky, kissable way.

I shake my head, clearing the seductive—and at the moment, inappropriate—memories from my mind.

"But it's really fine if you want me to stay with Brayden and Spencer."

"You're sure?" he asks. "I'll be here until nine tomorrow morning."

"I'm sure. It'll be good—it'll be great."

"Okay." Connor kisses me quickly, but tenderly. "Thanks, Vi. Really. I owe you."

And I just know the way he plans to repay is going to be mind-blowing.

And that is how I end up standing on Connor's darkened front porch half an hour later. The street is quiet and still; the only sounds in the air are the chirping crickets and wailing frogs.

It actually is kind of creepy. What the hell kind of neighborhood is this?

I knock on the door. Connor texted the boys that I was coming, but I still see the front curtains rustle and two pairs of wide boy-eyes peeking out. A moment later the front door opens a crack—just far enough for me to see Brayden's face squished into the crevice—his gaze darting left, right, and behind me, searching for a potential ambush.

"What's the password?"

"Rosie-posie."

It's the secret code Connor gave me to confirm I'm actually here at his direction, and not to kidnap them.

Brayden swings the door open and rushes me inside.

"Okay—come in quick."

He slams the door shut, locking the bolt and the chain with one hand and gripping a wooden baseball bat in the other. Rosie the German Shepherd stands beside Spencer and I bring my hand to her raised nose, letting her smell it.

Then she trots off into the house, completely uninterested. Connor said she's not much of a guard dog.

"I've decided to accept the babysitting position," I announce to Spencer.

"Niiice," the ten-year-old drawls, sounding so much like his dad I can't not smile.

"So why are you two so scared?" I ask them. "Did something happen?"

Brayden cops to it immediately.

"We watched *Hereditary*."

"Are you nuts? That's like the most disturbing movie ever made."

"It was a bad choice," he confesses regretfully.

Spencer concurs. "Especially when that old lady climbs up the wall and—"

"Nooope—don't remind me, I've seen it."

And no part of that film isn't terrifying as shit.

"All right, here's what we're going to do . . . you guys go get your pillows and blankets from your room and we'll camp out down here on the couch together for the night."

I wouldn't want to sleep in a room by myself after watching a movie like that if I were them. I'm not sure if I want to sleep in Connor's room by myself after being *reminded* of the movie.

"And we'll put a wholesome, totally non-scary show on the TV."

"Okay." Both boys march up the stairs.

But halfway up, Brayden turns back.

"Can you . . . come up with us so we don't have to go upstairs alone?"

"Please?" Spencer adds like he thinks I'd actually say no.

"Of course."

I check out my surroundings on the way up the stairs, because this is where Connor lives—where he raises his boys, where he sleeps. His essence lingers—I can feel him here—his scent, the warm strength of his presence.

And the house is gorgeous, with a long, curved staircase and oak railings, gleaming hardwood floors, and a landing at the top of the steps that looks down into an immense family room. But it's a little . . . sparse. Barebones. You can definitely tell it's home to four guy-boys.

In the upstairs hallway my phone pings with an incoming text from Connor.

If you need something to sleep in, my T-shirts and sweats are the second and third drawers down in my dresser. Help yourself.

I text him back:

Thanks. That's sweet of you.

And he replies:

My intentions aren't entirely pure.

I'm instantly intrigued, and the three dots tease for a moment as he elaborates.

I like the idea of you sleeping in my clothes. I like the idea of you sleeping in nothing in my bed even more—but my clothes are the next best thing.

Joy bubbles like champagne over my skin, and my ovaries do a little shimmy. Because Connor isn't just a hot, gorgeous guy with sex appeal to spare . . . he's also thoughtful, a man who takes care of the people who are close to him.

And if that isn't the boyfriend trifecta at the end of the dating rainbow, I don't know what is.

I type back.

Ditto xoxo

And then I follow the boys into their rooms.

Connor

There are some night shifts in the emergency department that feel endless—when the minutes drag and hours seem to take forever to pass. Other nights fly by, and you only get caught up on half of what you intended to do. There's no real rhyme or reason to it, whether the patients flood in or drip, complicated cases or simple doesn't matter. I think it's more internal than anything else.

And some nights are just a spikey, thorny, son of a bitch.

Tonight is one of those.

A thirty-two-year-old male walks in complaining of abdominal pain, and after scans and bloodwork, I admit him for a mass in his lower intestine that's more than likely advanced stage colon cancer.

An eighty-five-year-old woman with no living relatives gets wheeled in from her nursing home in acute heart failure. She has a DNR, so the only thing I can do for her is put an intern at her side, holding her hand, until she slips away.

Paramedics call in an MVA and eight minutes later they rush in, doing compressions on an intubated twenty-year-old who swerved to avoid a deer and ended up hitting a telephone pole, while not wearing a seat belt.

I let the ED resident—not an intern, but still a baby doctor—run the trauma.

"Shock again at three hundred. Clear."

The patient jolts as she shocks the heart for the third time and we look to the monitor for a miracle—to see if a rhythm appears. When it doesn't, she tells the nurse, "Charge to three sixty."

"Wait," I intervene. "How much epi have we given him?"

"Four." Skylar's tone is solemn because she's a veteran trauma nurse, so she knows where this is going too.

159

"How many transfusions?"

"Three."

It doesn't matter how much blood we give him—it's coming out faster than we can get it in.

"He's gone." I shake my head. "He was gone before they got him here."

The resident's dark-green eyes jolt up to me, then she looks down at the patient and calls the time of death.

"Is the family here?" I ask.

"There's a mom," Tanner says, turning off the monitor. "She's in the private waiting room."

"Does she have anyone with her?"

"No, she's alone."

"Goddamn it." I yank at my gown, balling it up and shoving it in the bin. "Call Pastoral Services, have them send someone down."

Fifteen minutes later, in clean scrubs and a white coat, I stand outside the door to the small waiting room with Chaplain Bill on one side and the resident on the other.

"Don't say anything," I tell her. "I'll do the talking."

There is nothing on earth that could make this conversation better—but there are things an inexperienced doctor can say that would make it infinitely worse.

I walk in the room where a petite, light-haired woman sits in a chair in the corner. When I was young and green, I would've wondered why she's here by herself. If she has a husband or other children . . . or if her son was her entire world.

I know better than to think about those things now.

"Ms. Allen?"

Her face lifts expectantly.

"Yes?"

I move forward, stopping two feet from her chair—within reaching distance.

"I'm Dr. Connor Daniels. I'm the physician who treated your son, Brandon, when he was brought in after his car accident."

"How is he?" she asks. "Can I see him?"

I look into her eyes and make it quick, even though that won't make it easier to hear.

"Ms. Allen, Brandon was critically injured when he was brought in—his heart was not beating. We gave him medicine and blood transfusions and used every tool and technique available, but I'm sorry to have to tell you that his injuries were too severe . . . and Brandon died."

It's important to use the actual words. Dead, died. It's brutal, but euphemisms breed hope and there is no room for hope here.

She blinks. They all blink at this part—in that short, hazy window of time before the words sink in and make sense—and their lives are forever changed.

"But . . . I just saw him. I talked to him. He was fine."

"I know."

She shakes her head.

"He was going to the store. He's on a new weightlifting diet and I forgot to pick up chop meat this afternoon."

"I understand," I tell her. "I'm so sorry."

"Wait. Are you—"

She tries to stand, but her knees give out. I catch her before she goes down, holding her up.

"Easy . . ."

Her fingers twist in my coat and she wheezes for breath, like I've kicked all the air out of her lungs. She lowers her head and tries to scream but she can't—only a strangled, suffocating gasp comes out.

When you do this long enough and the years go by, you forget the names. But you never forget their faces. The sounds they make when you tell them. Jagged, incomprehensible sounds filled with horror and grief.

If hell exists . . . I think this is what it sounds like.

I guide her back into the chair but she holds onto me, her eyes desperate and darting.

"Are you sure it's my Brandon? Are you sure he's really . . . that he died?"

I don't look away; I meet her gaze directly—because she needs this.

"Yes, I'm sure it's Brandon. He died. I'm deeply sorry."

Her hands fall away and the life goes out of her. She stares, unseeing, at the floor and she won't hear anything I say now, but I tell her anyway.

"This is Chaplain Bill. He's going to stay with you, and help you with the next steps."

She doesn't answer; she doesn't blink. Not anymore.

I turn and walk out the door. I don't stop walking until I'm around the corner at the end of the hallway—reminding myself to breathe.

At my elbow, the resident is on the verge of losing it—her cheeks red, her eyes full.

"Do not fucking cry," I order, sharp and mean. To snap her back—make her refocus. "Not here, not now."

She sucks in a shuddering breath, trying.

"I've never . . . that was the first time I—"

"Okay." I nod, guiding her to lean over slightly. "Bend your knees and breathe. Three deep, long breaths. Come on."

She inhales, slow and shuddering, eyes closed. Then she does it again, shaking her head.

"That poor woman."

"Don't think about it."

"How do I not?" she rasps.

"Picture . . . a safe in your mind. Thick, steel walls and one of those huge locks like the vault at a bank. And you take Ms. Allen and everything you're feeling and you put it in there—and you shut the door, lock it up. Because we have three other patients waiting. Maybe three other Brandons that you can still

162

help, three more chances to not have that *horrific* conversation. But you can't treat them if you fall apart. If you're distracted and upset and your vision is blurred."

She nods, inhaling slowly again.

"When you're home, later," I tell her. "When you're in the shower or in bed—that's when you open the safe. Let yourself feel it—you won't want to but you need to. Because this job isn't about saving everyone—if you go in with that as your expectation, your career in emergency medicine is going to be epically short. The job is to keep going . . . knowing you can't save everyone."

She stands straighter now, head lifted, breathing steady and eyes clear.

"Okay."

"You good?" I ask, just to be sure.

"I'm good."

I take the chart from the wall outside the exam room door. "Then let's go."

I stay at the hospital an hour past my shift to catch up on notes and charts. By the time I walk through my front door at 10:30 a.m., a heavy exhaustion has settled deep into my bones. It's more than just physical. I can barely muster a smile for Rosie when she greets me, her nails tapping the wood floor as she trots over to drop a mangy stuffed turtle at my feet.

But then I take a breath . . . and I'm infused with a deluge of delicious, sugary-scented goodness. The whole house smells fantastic, like a bakery—but in heaven.

I wander toward the kitchen like a damned soul in search of the light.

Violet stands at the stove dipping a wooden spoon into a large heated pot. She's wearing my gray T-shirt, tied at her stomach, and a pair of my black sweatpants that are huge on her—the waist knotted with a rubber band at her hip to keep them up. Her hair's in a messy chestnut pile on her head, and though her shape is lost in the mammoth clothes, she still manages to look sexy and adorable.

Standing next to her, Spencer sees me first.

"Dad! We're making homemade doughnuts!"

Brayden holds one in his hand at the counter, his cheeks puffed out with pastry like a chipmunk.

"They're soooo good."

Violet flashes me a smile before setting the spoon down and turning off the stove. "Give those a minute to cool and then you can dip them in the glaze," she tells Spence.

But as she approaches me, her eyes roaming my face, her smile sinks.

"Bad night?" she asks softly.

It was never Stacey's fault that she didn't work in an emergency department. That she couldn't understand what a bad night meant, no matter how hard she tried sometimes.

But Violet does. She knows exactly what this feels like, because she's felt it.

And there's a comfort in that. An embracing, easy respite from the persistent weight of guilt and melancholy.

"Yeah—I'll tell you about it later."

From the laundry room off the kitchen, the dryer alarm buzzes, signaling a load is done.

"There were wet clothes in the machine that were turning musty," Violet explains. "So I rewashed them."

"You didn't have to do that."

"It's no problem; I was here." She shrugs. "But I ran out this morning and picked up a new bottle of fabric softener. No offense—your fabric softener was kind of crappy."

"Told you," Brayden calls in a singsong voice as he slides on his socks into the laundry room. He comes out holding a freshly washed T-shirt, pressing it against his face and inhaling so deeply the fabric is momentarily snorted up his nostrils. When he speaks, it's in the voice of a stoner who just took a massive bong hit.

"Oh yeah . . . that's the good stuff."

I should probably start keeping a closer eye on him.

Before I can think any more about that, my firstborn pain in the ass graces us with his presence.

He strolls into the kitchen, not a care in the world.

And I try to stay calm, to hold on to my composure. . .

"Where the fuck have you been?"

. . . but I don't quite manage it.

He has the audacity to look surprised.

"I told you—Mia and I were fighting. I couldn't just leave in the middle of it."

"It's ten thirty in the goddamn morning, Aaron—I've been texting you for hours!"

"We drove to Sandy Hook to talk. We ended up falling asleep. My charger crapped out and my phone died. Why are you freaking out? Everything's fine—it's not a big deal."

It's the flippancy that really gets me going. The total disregard for anyone else's feelings except his own. You can teach your kids right from wrong, set an example of hard work and responsibility—but you can't make them give a shit.

"It *is* a big deal. You're seventeen, you have a curfew—I expect you to respect that."

"I'm going to be eighteen in six months. I'm practically an adult already!"

I rein in my response—because he's a kid and he's stupid and he's at an age where he just can't comprehend that he's not invincible.

"I lost a patient tonight. A kid just a few years older than you, in a car accident. I had to look his mother in the eyes and tell her her son was dead. That he was *never* coming home again.

And then I had to go through hours of you not picking up your phone! I was ready to send your uncle out looking for you!"

"Oh, please. You weren't worried about me." He jerks his chin toward his brothers. "You're just pissed because I wasn't here to watch the babies."

Spencer glares from across the room—his voice small and wounded.

"You suck, Aaron."

"Yeah, that's low, man." Brayden agrees. "We watched *Hereditary.*"

"We could've died!" Spencer insists.

But Aaron ignores them—tossing his resentment at me like an adolescent monkey flinging poo.

"You're no different than Mom. Neither one of you gives a shit about us. You only care about yourselves."

If you have kids, at some point in their lives you're going to want to look them in the face and tell them to go screw themselves.

They don't mention that in *What to Expect When You're Expecting.*

But I grind my teeth and clench my jaw.

"You're grounded. Two weeks—no going out, no car—give me your keys."

"Two weeks?! But it's the summer!"

"You want three? 'Cause I'll make it three, Aaron."

And now I sound like the asshole vice principal from *The Breakfast Club.* Perfect. Every dad's dream.

Aaron's furious gaze burns into me for a few seconds. Then he smacks his keys on the table.

"This is bullshit!"

And he stomps his way up to his room—slamming his door so hard the walls rattle.

And I stand in the kitchen and . . . deflate.

My shoulders cave in and my head throbs and my eyes ache.

Because Spencer is right—Aaron sucks.

And *I* suck. Everything sucks.

Such a goddamn mess.

Then I feel a hand on my arm—delicate but strong. Violet's palm slides up to my shoulder, massaging the knotted tendons, her caress so warm and soft and needed I want her to touch me forever.

"Bet you're glad you decided to help me out and stay over now."

My words drip with sarcasm.

But Violet's response isn't sarcastic. It's honest and bare and rock-solid supportive.

"Yes, I am."

I let myself fall into her gentle brown eyes. Take comfort in her warmth and understanding. I absorb her tenderness like a succubus—letting it soothe my sore soul—greedily taking all she so readily gives.

And everything seems to suck just a little bit less.

Because she's here . . . because she's her.

"I'm glad too," Spencer says. He takes a doughnut off the counter and gazes at it like he's just fallen in love for the very first time. "I'm never eating Dunkin' Donuts again."

The smile tugs at my lips and a chuckle rolls up my throat.

"Hey Spence—hook me up with one of those."

My son hands me a gooey, warm doughnut dripping with glaze. I sink my teeth in and moan, because—holy shit—it doesn't taste quite as good as one of Violet's blow jobs feel . . . but it's really close.

"Oh my God," I manage to mumble around another bite.

The three of them laugh at me—mocking my ecstasy.

And I almost forgot what this is like. The sweetness of sharing these moments—good or bad—with someone who's a partner, a lover, a friend.

But I remember now.

CHAPTER
Thirteen

Violet

A s summer shifts into August, Connor and I slip
further into each other's lives. Smoothly. Effortlessly.
We uncover even more about each other. For in-
stance, I learn that Connor has watched every episode of *The
Office*—three times—but it still makes him laugh. On one
Saturday afternoon when I'm driving us to the farmers market
because his truck is getting new tires, Connor discovers my occasional tendency to road rage.

Beep beep.

When a middle-aged woman in a shiny new Lexus commits
the unforgiveable sin of doing 40 mph in the left lane of the frigging Garden State Parkway.

Beeeeeeeeeeeeeeeeep.

"Move over! Get into the right lane!"

She eventually moves over. But as I'm passing her on the left,
she gives me the finger.

And my head practically explodes.

"Fuck me? No—fuck *you*! Learn how to drive!"

Connor just stares at me from the passenger seat. In shock. Bewilderment, perhaps.

"What?" I ask. "I would never talk that way if the boys were in the car."

"No, it's not that, it's just . . . are you sure you weren't born in Jersey? 'Cause it really sounds like you were."

I learn new things about the boys too—sometimes in not so great ways.

Like the night I pick up takeout for all of us from a Mexican place that's one of Connor's favorites. I get to his house while he's still hung up at his parents' place with his brothers, installing a new television in the living room. An hour after I get there, he comes through the door.

"Hey," I greet him. "Aaron's still at football practice, Brayden rode his bike to his friend's house when I got here, and Spencer's up in his room. Your food's over there—Spencer and I already ate—he was starving."

He brings his Styrofoam container to the table and I sit down next to him.

"What'd you two end up getting?" he asks.

"I got shrimp empanadas and Spencer got chicken empanadas. I accidentally put my plate in front of him at first."

Connor stops mid chew. "He didn't eat any, did he?"

"Only one bite. He realized it and—"

Connor bolts for the stairs, taking them two at a time.

I run up behind him and when he opens Spencer's bedroom door and stops short, I bump into his back.

"Hey Dathd."

It's sounds like Spencer . . . but something's wrong with his voice.

Very, very wrong.

"Oh, man," Connor groans.

Then he drops to his knees in front of his son, giving me an unobstructed view of Spencer's face.

I suck in a gasp—long and loud—covering my horrified mouth.

Because the little boy's lips are twice their size and his eyes look like he went a few rounds with Rocky Balboa in his Clubber Lang prime.

I shove in beside Connor, dropping to my knees.

"Are you having any trouble breathing, Spencer?"

Connor takes Spencer's pulse. "Usually his tongue and lips swell up but not his throat."

"Just because he hasn't developed anaphylaxis before doesn't mean he won't."

"I'm aware," Connor replies, his voice confoundingly steady.

Does he not see his kid's face?

"Nah, I cath breath othay. My thungs jus a lithel puthy."

Jesus. Connor entrusted me with his children and I broke one.

For the first time in my life, I understand the concept of self-flagellation. Because the depth of my guilt is so instant and bottomless, I want someone to punish me harshly, hurt me deeply—if only to relieve my crushing self-blame.

"My bag's in the closet by the front door, Vi. Can you grab it for me?" Connor asks, checking Spencer's arms and chest for hives or a rash, but his skin is clear.

"Yeah." And I'm sprinting for the steps.

When I round the corner back toward the bedroom with Connor's black physician's bag in my hands, I hear Spencer and Connor talking.

"Are you gontha gith me Benthadil?"

"I'm going to give you a shot of Benadryl this time, buddy." Connor says.

"A thot? Thots thuck."

"I know, but a shot will work faster and you're swelling up like the blueberry girl in *Willie Wonka*."

170

I hand Connor his bag and he takes Spencer's blood pressure—which is normal.

My voice is pleading and repentant as I crouch down on my knees.

"God, Spencer, I am sorry."

"Ith o-thay, Thi—you didnth know."

Connor opens the sterile packaging of a syringe and inserts it through the cap of the brown glass vial of diphenhydramine.

"Spence, why didn't you tell Violet you're allergic to shrimp when you ate the empanada?"

He shrugs, toddling his swollen little head.

"I didnth wanth Thi to theel badth. And I thoughth maythee I outhgrew ith."

Connor shakes his head. "It's not the kind of allergy you outgrow—we talked about this."

"Though it theems."

Suddenly Aaron's standing in the bedroom doorway, swallowing a gulp of water from a bottle and assessing the situation.

"Shrimp?" he asks his dad.

"Shrimp," his father confirms.

"Nice face, dweeble."

Spencer sticks his tongue out at his brother. At least I think he does—his engorged lips and inflated tongue make it difficult to tell.

After Connor gives Spencer the shot, I leave the bedroom so Spence can get into his pajamas. When Connor comes downstairs, I'm in the living room, in a tight ball of remorse on the couch, gnawing at my fingernails. Rosie lies beside me, her golden eyes brimming with human-like sympathy I don't deserve.

"How is he?" I ask, prepared to whisk Spencer away to the hospital in my own two arms if needed—faster than the Flash ever could.

He sits next to me, his firm thigh pressing against mine. "He's fine. The swelling's gone down and he's asleep."

My throat tightens anyway and my eyes ache with hot, unspent tears.

"I'm so sorry."

"Vi, he's *fine*. It's not your fault."

He says it in that final, definitive way like it's true—like he believes it.

"How can you be so calm about this?"

Connor shrugs.

"I have three kids. After the first one, you learn pretty fast that certain things are just not in your control. They fall down, they get sick, they have allergic reactions. The good news is, they also bounce, heal, and recover pretty quickly."

He puts his arm around me and I press my face into the soft cotton of his T-shirt, letting his warmth and scent surround me.

"Besides," Connor says, "I'm the one who didn't tell you about Spencer's allergy. If you're going to be upset with anyone, it should be me."

I wipe my eyes. "I want a complete medical history on each of them."

He chuckles.

"I'm serious. Blood types, broken bones, allergies, surgeries, serious illnesses—the full monty."

"You got it." Connor presses a kiss to my forehead.

Then he slides his arm off my shoulders and rests his hand on my knee. With his other hand he picks up his phone, pulls up his contacts, and I see *STACEY* across the screen before he brings it to his ear.

"Hey, it's me. I wanted to let you know Spencer might not be up to going out with you tomorrow."

He pauses and I hear the sound of her voice on the other end—too muffled to make out her words or tone.

I haven't given much thought to her in these last few months—the woman that Connor was married to for fourteen years—mostly because she's barely a presence in his life.

It reminds me of how it was for us when my dad would come and go. We'd gotten so used to living without him that nothing really changed for us whether he was around or not. It wasn't traumatic or upending, we just kept on keeping on.

"I realize that," Connor says evenly. "He ate some shrimp. No—he's okay—but he'll probably still be out of it tomorrow from the antihistamine."

Stacey is supposed to get the boys every other weekend, but Connor told me it's never been a rigid routine. In the last year her visitation has whittled down to only a Saturday or Sunday afternoon. Sometimes she cancels and when she doesn't, Connor feels that the boys are old enough to decide for themselves if they want to spend time with her or not. Recently, especially with Aaron and Brayden, it's been a not.

"It's a long story . . ." he says.

Connor's told me they met in college, got married after graduation, had Aaron when Connor was in medical school. She was a stay-at-home mom and wasn't a fan of his work hours, and when things ended it wasn't exactly amicable.

" . . . there was a mix-up with his food and he got shrimp empanadas by mistake."

Connor leaves out that Spencer got the empanadas from me. Someone he's seeing, someone he's in a relationship with, his girlfriend.

"Yeah, I know that. Fine. I'll have him call you in the morning when he wakes up."

The omission doesn't worry me, there are reasons—valid reasons—like that they're not on friendly terms and she doesn't seem to be someone Connor is eager to share his personal life with. Or maybe he just doesn't want the first mention of me to be in connection with the fact that I poisoned their child.

"Okay. Bye."

But still . . . I can't help but notice.

Two weeks after what is now branded in my mind as the Taco Saturday from Hell, Connor and I have plans to meet up with a group of people from work at a bar called The Piano Man.

On our way out the door, I start to tell Connor's youngest, "Remember, Spence, don't—"

He rolls his eyes. "Don't eat any shrimp. I *know*, Violet."

I may have reminded him once or . . . sixty times before.

But I can't help it if I'm more traumatized than either he or Connor. And I'll get over it . . . eventually . . . like when he's eighty.

The Piano Man is a bustling, old-school bar with gleaming mahogany trimmings and supersonic speakers connected to a jukebox. Every stool along the bar is filled, the round tables are packed, and the dance floor is hopping with hip-shaking, head-bopping people dancing to the best singable tunes.

And at the center of it all is our rowdy group of medical professionals. Because if anyone knows how to have a good time, it's people who work in the business of life and death every single day.

Two hours after we arrive, I'm on the dance floor, arms high and liberated, my feet stomping to Simon & Garfunkel's "Cecilia." I've lost count of the number of Hawaiian pineapple cosmos I've ingested, but what can I say . . . they're tasty. My limbs are loose, my vision is hazy around the edges, and my heart thumps with sweet, giddy happiness on every beat.

Connor's at the table, laughing at something Tanner just said. But his eyes are riveted on me—observing, like I'm something fascinating and rare. Like he could go his whole life never looking at any other woman and he'd be perfectly, absolutely content.

It makes me feel powerful. And emotional. Protected and wanted and rapturously sexy. He makes me feel everything.

The song changes to something slower that begins with a moving piano solo. The girls

I'm dancing with—Effie and Alice, the latter a mild-mannered anesthesiologist with a wild streak—head back to the table to wet their whistles.

But I stay right there.

Because Connor Daniels is on the move . . . and he's moving straight to me.

He wraps one arm around my lower back and folds his other hand into mine as the male singer's voice croons through the speakers. And I realize I know this song, I love this song—it's "Chances Are" by Bob Seger and Martina McBride.

"You look like you're having fun." His warm breath tickles my ear.

"Understatement."

I'm a little unsteady on my feet, but I don't have to worry . . . he's got me.

"Are you having fun?" I ask.

His grin is a little bit dirty, kind of suggestive—all ruggedly beautiful.

"Watching you? You have no idea."

I sink against him with a relaxed sigh. It's the sound you make when you're submerged in a warm, scented bubble bath and you don't have any worries or troubles because the heated water cradles you, surrounds you, and in that moment everything is just perfect. Connor is my happy place.

"This is a great song," he says above my head.

"I was just thinking that." But then another thought flits through my brain and out of my mouth. "This wasn't like your and Stacey's wedding song or anything, was it?"

"No," he scoffs.

Then he looks into my eyes.

"But I was kind of hoping it could be our song."

I feel myself smile—but *smile* doesn't really cover it. Because my lips stretch so broad and wide it feels like my mouth consumes half my face.

And my stomach and my heart are somehow smiling too.

"Really?"

"Yeah. It reminds me of us." Connor glances at the floor—almost shyly—and he's never shy. "When you weren't talking to me, I used to drive past your road on the way home from work."

My cosmo-soaked brain takes a moment to process the information.

"But my road isn't on your way home."

"I know . . . but it felt like it was. Like you were on my way home. I would park at the corner at the end of your street, just for a little while. Because I was hoping to get a glimpse of you. I wanted to be near you, in any way I could."

He shakes his head, glancing over my shoulder. "I can't believe I'm fucking telling you this. Pretty pathetic, huh?"

I stare at him meaningfully.

"I wrote a poem about your penis."

Connor found my box of poems the other day—to my ever-burning, napalm-level shame. It's my fault; I left the lid of the jewelry box open and he walked past and saw the top paper titled "Connor's Cock."

What man wouldn't take a second look at that?

He chuckles at me at the reminder.

"And it's not pathetic," I tell him. "I think it's romantic. The most romantic thing anyone has ever done. And it's a relief."

"A relief?"

"Yeah. For so long I had you up on this unreachably high pedestal. And then, at the wedding, you came down off of it and you were human. You were real. And I liked the real you even more. So it's a relief to know you liked me as much as I liked you. That we're on the same page."

He stares at our clasped hands, his voice hushed and soft.

"We are, Violet. We're on the exact same page."

CHAPTER
Fourteen

Connor

I DON'T TAKE VIOLET BACK TO HER HOUSE AFTER WE LEAVE The Piano Man. I'm not ready for our night to be over yet. Because I'm having too good of a time . . . and because Violet is just too damn cute when she's wasted. We get to my house a little after midnight.

Aaron and Brayden are playing the great unifier—Call of Duty—on the Xbox in the living room with what sounds like a dozen other kids online. Spencer is already in bed.

I grab two bottles of water from the fridge and tell the boys, "Violet and I are going to watch TV in my room for a little while."

"Yep," Aaron answers, but with his fingers working double-time on the remote, I'm not sure it's me he's answering.

"Watch your six!" Brayden says into the headset.

And my work here is done. I lead Violet up the staircase.

I'm the master and commander of my internal time clock, so I'm not worried about falling asleep. Doctors have a legendary ability to immediately crash into REM sleep or to stay awake and alert for hours on end, depending on the circumstances.

I close my bedroom door and lock it—in case Vi wants to

change into something more comfortable. And I honestly figure we'll hang out, talk, maybe watch a movie.

Violet's idea is so much better.

"Is it wrong that I want you to fuck me even though your kids are downstairs?"

My mouth goes dry and my voice rises an octave—from the stampede of blood descending toward my groin.

"Nope. Not wrong at all."

Her smile is naughty and her eyes are dark and shiny, and she's so frigging pretty she makes my chest throb.

Violet sinks down on her knees in front of me, keeping contact with my gaze. And there is nothing on earth that's hotter—nothing more arousing than a woman who is hungry for you and not ashamed to show it.

She opens my jeans, tugging them down my hips and pumping the already stiff shaft. Then she slides my cock between her lips. My head rolls back on my neck as her tongue swirls, and her head bobs and the sweet suction of her wet mouth is so divine it's like she's trying to suck out my soul.

My hands clench and a surge of rough urgency rises in me. I lift Violet up under her arms and we kiss hard. I slip my fingers under the straps of her lacy sundress, sliding it down her arms to the floor. I bend my knees, kissing across the swell of her breasts, unhooking her strapless bra and letting it fall. Then I spin us around and place her on the bed.

She looks stunning there, her long hair across my pillows, laid out just for me.

And I know at this moment I could do anything to her. Because she trusts me. Completely and unreservedly. It's there in her round, waiting eyes and splayed limbs. There's nothing I could want to do to her that she wouldn't let me.

It's heady and humbling and makes me wild to please her. Worship her with my mouth and my dick and hands.

To show her that I'll never let her down . . . I'll never let her go.

I slide my hands up her smooth legs and bury my head between her thighs. She gasps when I press my mouth against her smooth, bare skin—nuzzling and lapping at her hot flesh in deep, slow licks. Her clit is firm and swelled when I encase it with my lips, sucking until her back arches and her hands tug at my hair.

"Connor, please," she begs in a whisper. "Oh God, I need you."

I lift up to my knees, giving my dick a few swift strokes because she likes to watch me do that. I rub the head up and down against her, groaning at the warm wetness, and then I press inside her.

Violet curves her back when I slide home, lifting her hips, letting me sink in deeper. I roll my hips, rubbing her clit with my pelvis, dragging one of those high-pitched little whimpers from her throat that make me crazy.

I brace my elbows on either side of her head and mold our bodies together—giving her my weight. I can feel her heart pounding against my chest, in the same rhythm as mine. Our noses brush and our breaths mingle but we don't kiss. We look into each other's eyes, breathing the same air.

And it's so fucking intense.

I'm so deep inside her, her delicate muscles gripping me.

"Connor. . ."

My hips move faster—harder—in long slow jabs. I want to dip my head and feast on her breasts, suckle her until she moans. I want to kiss her mouth and give her my tongue. I want to let go and fuck her quick and rough until we're both coming, good and glorious, at the same time.

But I don't want to stop looking at her.

Soaking up every beautiful expression, watching those gorgeous brown eyes darken with need and adoration. Letting her see me, all of me, and all the things I feel for her.

Violet bites her lip, and her feet brace on the bed, lifting her hips—fucking herself up onto me.

"Connor. . ." she keens because she's close. I can feel the flutter around me, the rhythmic clasping as she starts to go over the edge.

"Not yet," I gasp, pumping smoothly.

"Please—" she grasps at my shoulders, my back.

"Not yet. If you come you're going to take me with you and I don't want it to end yet."

"It's so good," she pants.

"Not yet, not yet."

I'm groaning, because she's tighter now, squeezing down all around me.

"Please," she gasps.

Violet grabs for my hand and presses it over her mouth— sealing her lips and the sharp, soaked cry that seeps out behind my palm.

Then she's gone. Her eyes roll closed and her neck arches— her pussy contracts and her lips open on a silent scream as she loses herself in the cresting white heat of sensation.

And she pulls me right over with her, like I knew she would.

I press my face into her neck, inhaling the delicate flowery scent of her perfume—and pounding into her in blissful, wild thrusts. My mind goes blank and heat claws up my spine as pure, perfect ecstasy tears its way through me.

For several moments neither of us move. I love not using condoms with her—love being able to stay inside her just like this—where she's wet and hot and sticky with me.

I swallow hard and raise my head from Vi's shoulder.

"Are you okay?"

Her eyes remain closed and her voice is drowsy.

"I don't know. I think I might be dead. Or I died and came back. Either. Both."

And I laugh. Because every piece and part and moment with her is so insanely good.

Eventually, I roll over onto my back and Violet cuddles in against me—her leg draped over my hip, her arm across my stomach, using my chest as her pillow.

She mumbles a warning. "Don't fall asleep. You have to take me home."

I haven't had the chance to talk to the boys yet about Violet spending the night. I think they'll be fine with it, but since she's the first woman I've brought into their lives since the divorce, it feels like a conversation I should have with them.

"I won't." I give her a reassuring squeeze. "Just going to . . . rest my eyes for a minute."

"Connor! Connor, wake up—it's morning!"

What feels like five minutes later, Violet's panicked voice drags me awake.

Because in the history of the world, "eye resting" has never worked out the way it's supposed to—even for doctors.

I clear the sleep from my throat and run a hand through my hair.

"Yeah, I'm up."

The distinct sounds of life—the hum of the television, the closing of drawers, and the clatter of spoons against breakfast bowls—floats up to us from the kitchen.

"Oh my God, they're awake!" Violet's eyes dart to the sun-filled window like a vampire who's lost her coffin. "Should I shimmy down the gutter?"

"No," I chuckle. "It's too fucking early to shimmy down anything."

I dig deep into the recesses of my dad experience—past, present, and future—to come up with a plan.

And it's so simple it's genius.

"We're going to walk downstairs and act like everything is normal. If we don't make a big deal about you spending the night, they won't either."

Vi does not see the wisdom of my plan.

"You want me to do the walk of shame in front of your *children?*"

"They're boys, Violet. Men in training. Easily distracted, self-focused, not big on noticing details. Trust me—it's going to be fine."

We get dressed. Violet wears her sundress and sandals from last night, washes her face in my adjoining bathroom, and I find a new spare toothbrush in the vanity drawer for her to use.

And then we walk downstairs together—casually, nonchalantly—practically whistling.

All three of the boys are in the kitchen.

"Morning, guys," I greet them. Then I pull out a chair for Vi at the kitchen table.

She sits down carefully. "Hi, boys."

"Hey," Spencer replies, shoveling a spoonful of Froot Loops into his mouth.

Brayden nods, not even looking at us, keeping his unbroken focus on his phone.

But Aaron . . . well, I may have underestimated the power of the teenage snark.

"Didn't make it home last night, huh?" He immediately smirks.

And Violet looks like she wants to dissolve into the floor.

"You guys had a sleepover?" Spencer glances from Vi to me.

"Yeah." I shrug. "We dozed off watching TV."

He nods and goes back to his cereal.

Brayden doesn't care enough to comment at all.

That's my boy.

Aaron, I assume, files the information away to be used to his advantage at some later date.

"I'm going to make coffee." I grab the pot and hold it under the faucet. "Violet, do you want a cup?"

"Yes, please," she answers, looking slightly more normal and less mortified. "I should bring my French press over—it'll change your coffee life."

"Oooh, Franch," Spencer says dramatically. "You're fancy, Violet."

Then he and Brayden kiss their fingers and start saying every French word they know.

"Ooh-la-la."

"*Oui, oui.*"

"Bon appétit."

"Grey Poupon."

Violet laughs at them, then smiles up at me, relieved that we've survived relatively unscathed.

Since Violet and I both have the day off, we decide to ask the boys if they want to hit up Great Adventure—and we're met with yeses all around. Even Aaron agrees to come, which is extra special since he typically avoids "family time" like it's a death sentence.

We make a pit stop at Vi's house—the boys skip pebbles on the lake while she changes her clothes—and then we're on our way to the amusement park.

Violet sits in the passenger seat next to me with her window down, bathed in the late morning sunshine and looking pretty enough to eat. The warm breeze teases the tendrils that have escaped the thick bun on the top of her head. She's wearing hot-pink sunglasses, a black Led Zeppelin tank top, and cute cutoff white shorts that are going to have my eyes glued to her ass all the livelong day.

About an hour after getting to the park, I discover something I didn't know about Vi . . . something I'd never considered.

"Kingda Ka," Brayden announces, gesturing to the mammoth ride like a game show host unveiling the grand prize. "The fastest roller coaster in the country and the tallest in the *entire world*."

"The whole world, huh?" Violet gulps. "No Kingda kidding?"

"Nope. It's totally righteous."

Spencer extends his pinky and thumb on both hands in the surfer shaka sign and mimics Crush, the turtle from *Finding Nemo*—a film my kids have watched so many times it's permanently branded on their brains. And mine.

"Righteous, righteous!"

Aaron joins in the movie quoting fun, giving Brayden a high five. "Let's grab some shell, dude."

Violet's eyes grow bigger and more terrified the longer she stares up at the skyscraper-high roller coaster.

"You know, I think I'm gonna enjoy this one on the down low. Like, really low . . . over here," she gestures to a small grassy knoll. " . . . on the ground."

I lift my sunglasses to the top of my head.

"You don't want to go on?"

"Well, the thing is . . . I've never actually gone on a roller coaster before. Ever."

I've watched Violet jump on a moving gurney to administer chest compressions to a patient. I've seen her tie a tourniquet over a pulsing wound spouting arterial blood like a frigging geyser. I've seen her block the exit door to a domestic abuser after his wife told the cops how she really sustained her injuries.

This skittishness and fear is a totally new look for her—and it's pretty fucking adorable. It seems twisted and wrong to feel that way, but it's still turning me on something fierce. Making me imagine pulling her trembling little body against me and kissing her mouth long and deep until her anxiety is a faded memory. Kissing her . . . lots of places.

"Never?" Aaron asks. "Really?"

She shakes her head. "We didn't have the money to go to amusement parks when I was young, and when I was older there wasn't any time so, yeah, never."

"That's awesome," Brayden exclaims. "Kingda Ka can be your first—it's gonna blow your mind. And we'll all go on with you."

"I don't know about that, Bray." She looks to me. "Is it safe? It doesn't look safe."

I slide my hand up and down her back. "It's extremely safe. They inspect these things every day."

"You have to!" Spencer begs. "I went on last year and I barely made the height cutoff. It's so fun—pleeeease."

"Besides"—Aaron grins evilly—"you don't want us to think you're chicken, do you?"

Violet glances at each of them.

"You'd really think I'm a chicken if I don't go on?"

Children are like nature . . . cruel and predictable.

Aaron doesn't hesitate. "Yep."

Brayden concurs. "Totally and forever."

Spencer at least tries to soften the blow.

"Sorry—those are the rules."

Vi turns to me helplessly. "You have bad kids, Connor."

I wrap my arm around her waist, tugging her closer.

"Yeah, I know."

She takes a deep, cleansing breath. And shakes her head like she's going to regret this—like she already is.

"Okay, I have a rep to protect. I'm in. Let's go."

The boys cheer like she scored a touchdown. And I press a soft quick kiss to her tense forehead.

"You're going to love it."

And I think she almost believes me—until we're actually sitting on the roller coaster. Side by side, in the third row, because Aaron called dibs on the single front seat so Brayden and Spencer took the next best thing behind him.

"Connor," Vi whispers. "I don't want to freak out the boys, but I have to tell you something."

I lean toward her as much as the weighted industrial safety harness will let me. "What is it?"

"We're gonna die."

I laugh—I can't help it.

"No, we're—"

"Yes, we are!" And she's not whispering anymore. "I've never been on a roller coaster and now the breaks are going to fail and I'm going to die on one! It's gonna be just like the Alanis Morissette song!"

"Hey, man," the bearded guy in the row behind us grumbles, "you wanna chill her out? She's killing my buzz."

"Shut up," I shoot back. "She's fine."

I put my hand on top of Violet's clenched fists.

"Baby—look at me."

Her eyes remain firmly closed.

"I can't."

And I think she's praying.

But then we start rolling toward the launch point, and she snatches my hand up—her fingers strangling my circulation like killer vines.

"Hold my hand, Connor. Oh God, please hold my hand and don't let go."

"I am," I keep my voice calm, reassuring, rational. "I'm holding your hand right now."

But rationality has left the building.

"You're not doing it right!"

That's the last thing she gets out before we're shot forward like a ball out of a cannon—going so high and moving so fast, there's not even time to scream.

❧

"I wasn't *that* scared."

Violet leans back on her hands, her long legs stretched out in front of her, as she sits on a patch of grass with the boys, while I stand in line at the gift shop, watching and listening, a few feet away.

Spencer rolls back and forth on the ground—giggling uncontrollably like an insane gerbil.

"You so were!" Brayden laughs. "Look at your face—this is the best picture ever."

He's not wrong.

Because the hilarious five-by-ten shot of the five of us taken by the automatic camera as we crested the roller-coaster peak truly is a work of art.

It shows Aaron dangling his tongue out and flashing the peace sign, Brayden with both arms raised above his head, Spencer bright-eyed and smiling almost peacefully, and me gazing over at Violet . . . whose face is frozen in scrunched, open-mouthed, unadulterated terror.

I'm going to frame it and put it on the fireplace mantel.

Aaron takes the photo from Brayden and clenches his stomach as a new round of laughter rolls through him.

"It's so great."

Violet sticks her tongue out at them, taking their hazing like a champ.

"I was just acting really scared so you guys wouldn't feel bad if you were scared too."

"Really?" Brayden asks doubtfully.

"Maybe. It *could* be true."

Spencer scrambles to sit up.

"So does that mean you want to go on again? 'Cause I'll totally going on again."

Vi's response is immediate and sincere.

"Absolutely not. At least . . . not today."

I walk over to them and hold out my hand to Violet, helping her up and passing her the bag from the gift shop.

"You've earned it."

She bites her lip as she peeks inside. Then she tilts her head back and cracks up—pulling out the black T-shirt that says "I Conquered the Ka!" in big, bold letters across the front.

"I love it! Thank you."

Vi reaches up on her toes and touches her lips to mine.

It's a clean kiss, no tongue or lip smashing. But there's no awkwardness, even in front of the boys. It's not even a conscious thought—the kiss is more of a reflex—something that just comes naturally.

"I'm about to eat my hand," Aaron declares. "Can we get pizza?"

"Yes, pizza!" Spencer jumps to his feet.

I slip my hand into Violet's, folding our fingers together.

"Pizza sounds perfect."

Later that night, after we drop Violet at home and the boys have showered and are in their pajamas and Rosie's been fed and let out for the last time—the four of us sit in the living room watching a rerun of *The Office* before bed.

Spencer is squeezed in next to me on the recliner, Brayden's lying on one end of the couch, and Aaron's sitting up, on his phone, at the other.

"Today was a good day," Brayden says softly to no one in particular.

And I smile, because it really was. They don't know it yet, but I bet it's the kind of day they'll think of when they remember their childhood—a collection of simple, small, fun moments.

"Violet's your girlfriend, right, Dad?" Spencer asks.

"Yes, buddy, Violet is my girlfriend."

"I knew it. That's why you look so goofy whenever she's around."

"Goofy?" I give him a mock frown. "What do you mean, goofy?"

"Totally goofy," Brayden confirms. "Like how Aaron looked last year after he got his wisdom teeth pulled, but all the time."

"Yeah, you're right, he does look like that," Aaron chuckles.

"But it's okay." Spencer pats my leg, his little face honest and innocent. "I like it when you look like that."

When parents have a solid marriage and healthy relationship, it gives kids a sense of safety. Security. I used to worry that Stacey and I had robbed them of that. That the divorce would leave them lingering in a constant state of unease and shifting instability.

But looking at them now . . . I'm not worried about that anymore.

"So, I was thinking that Violet might stay over more often, like she did last night. It'll save on gas . . . and I like having her around and she really likes being here with us. What do you guys think about that?"

"Sure. I like Violet," Spencer declares.

"Me too," Brayden offers.

"Yeah, she's cool," Aaron agrees.

"Okay." I nod. "Great."

A sweet, warm contentment spreads through my chest that I haven't felt in a long time. It's that calm, satiated happiness that comes when life is just going good. Good for the boys, and for me and Violet . . . good for all of us. Together.

CHAPTER
Fifteen

Connor

AFTER OUR DAY AT GREAT ADVENTURE AND MY TALK with the boys, Violet starts staying over a couple nights a week. I clear out two dresser drawers; her shampoo and strawberry-scented body wash take up residence in the shower and her lavender toothbrush sits in the holder beside mine.

The boys handle the transition of having a woman around the house well—the only discernible change is that they're now putting on shorts in the morning instead of walking around in their underwear. Violet gets along great with them—and it's all just so . . . easy. Awesome and amazing.

The week before they're set to go back to school, on a Wednesday, Vi and I both have the day off and Garrett gives the football team a rest day, so he and Callie come over with the kids to swim in the pool and barbecue. Violet's in my bedroom changing into her suit, and when I walk in, she's standing in front of the floor-length mirror turning left to right, her decadent lips curved down in a pouty frown.

"What's wrong?"

She tugs her bathing suit down in the back, trying to cover the sweet sliver of ass cheek peeking out.

"I'm not sure about this bathing suit."

The suit is hot—a high-cut black bikini scattered with dainty white daisies that I plan to slowly peel off her later with my teeth.

"What do you mean? You look gorgeous."

Her skin is golden and warm as I splay my hands across her hips, pulling her back against me and rubbing against the semi I'm sporting, in case she had any doubt of just how gorgeous she looks.

Vi tilts her head toward the mirror, still concerned.

"That's what I'm worried about. Do you think it's inappropriate to wear around the boys?"

I will never not fucking love that. How she's always thinking of them, always putting their well-being before anything else. It just comes natural to her, and that makes me an even luckier bastard than I already know I am.

"It's not inappropriate, Vi—though I wouldn't mind seeing you in something that was."

My mind floods with tantalizing images of her languidly lying on a lounge chair wearing a brightly colored, barely-there, thong string-bikini. Or even better—at a topless beach.

"The boys know what a woman in a bathing suit looks like."

She fidgets with the triangular top, tucking her breasts in—and my palm tingles to be where her hand is, cupping and kneading that soft, pillowy flesh.

My dick goes from semi to full-fledged hard-on in no time flat. Because it's like my desire for Violet compounds daily, feeds off itself—every moment we're together only makes me want her more.

I crave her deeper today than I did last week, harder than yesterday, crazier than even this morning. It's a constant, insatiable need that dwells equally in my head, my cock, and my heart.

"I don't know," she sighs. "Maybe I should buy a few one-pieces."

I shrug. "If it makes you feel more comfortable, go for it. But don't do it for the boys' sakes. Trust me, you're my girlfriend—that means you no longer qualify as an actual woman to them. You're in the same category now as their aunts . . . and Angela and Callie wear bikinis too."

I wrap my arms around her waist, kiss her cheek and nibble at her jaw.

"Besides—if your goal is to ugly yourself down, don't delude yourself. You could walk around in a garbage bag and you'd still be smokin.'"

Her shoulders lose their tension and she aims her smile at our reflection. She turns in my arms and brings her lips close to mine as her hands coast down into the waistband of my swim trunks, squeezing my ass.

"You're pretty sexy yourself, Dr. Daniels. In case I didn't mention that yet today."

Then Violet kisses me—with tongue. And I love my life right now.

Having your entire family living within a ten-mile radius is kind of like eating Pringles potato chips—you can never have just one. So, while only Garrett and Callie and their kids come over in the morning, the entire family tree is here by the afternoon.

Ryan worked the night shift, so after a power nap, he, Angela, and my two teenage nieces, Frankie and Joey, show up.

Tim's already at my parents' house doing laundry, so the three of them arrive shortly after.

Food isn't an issue—with three healthy, perpetually starving boys in the house, I keep the freezer stocked with chicken, burgers, and hot dogs. Callie and Garrett baked cupcakes and cookies, Angela brought enough pasta salad and sliced watermelon to feed a small army, and since my mom likes to store up food like a doomsday prepper, she whipped up a ton of potato salad, macaroni salad, and canned peach crumble.

By 2 p.m. the sky is cerulean and cloudless, the sun is scorching. The Rolling Stones are blasting from the speakers scattered around the yard and everyone except my parents and baby Charlotte, who naps on a towel beside them under the shaded protection of the sun umbrella, is in the pool. Engaged in a heated game of water volleyball.

Because sports are woven into the fiber of my family's DNA—we're like working-class Kennedys—we're competitive and like to win.

And Violet Robinson fits right in.

She jumps up with a grace that still surprises me and spikes the ball over the net toward Ryan. He dives for it with a splash . . . and misses.

"Eat it!" Violet shouts like a baller.

"Niiice!" I hold my hand up and she slaps it high five.

"Did I mention I was the captain of the girls' volleyball team back in high school?"

"You didn't," I chuckle. "But I'm glad you were."

Ryan groans, "We've been hustled." He waves his team in. "Huddle up! Time for a new strategy."

My three-year-old nephew, Will, talks shit like a chip off the old block from where he's sitting atop Garrett's shoulders behind me.

"We're gonna beat you, Uncle Ryan!"

Ryan points at him like a WWF wrestler accepting a challenge.

"We'll see about that, little man. It ain't over till it's over."

Twenty minutes later, it's over . . . and we beat them. Afterward my championship team basks in the sweet glow of victory as we all sit around the patio table eating and drinking and talking.

"Dad, can we pleeeeease get a trampoline this year?" Spencer asks. "I'm ten now—that's double digits. I'm way more mature than when I was just nine."

As an emergency medicine doctor, there are certain items I've sworn never to own—in my mind it's a vow just slightly less sacred than the Hippocratic Oath. A garbage disposal, a motorcycle, and a trampoline are the top three—because they're disasters waiting to happen. Most people think falling off a trampoline is the biggest risk, but they're wrong. The bone snapping, ligament-tearing rebound and midair collisions are the real hazards.

"Not happening, Spence. Not now, not ever."

Plus—I have three *boys*. They're not exactly known for thinking through the consequences of their actions.

It was only last summer that I caught Brayden and two of his friends carrying my weights up from the basement, that they were going to tie to their ankles because they wanted to see how many pounds it would take to sink them to the bottom of the pool . . . and keep them there.

Yeah—that actually happened.

I don't even want to contemplate what they'd do with a trampoline and their bikes, their skateboards . . .

"But this one has an excellent safety rating!" Spencer whines, holding up his phone to display a trampoline marketed as "safe" that looks exactly the same as the rest of them.

In the chair beside me, Violet shakes her head gently.

"If you saw some of the gnarly trampoline injuries that come into the hospital, you wouldn't want one either, Spencer."

I'm not sure if she says it purposely, but few things will distract a ten-year-old faster than the detailed description of horrific injuries.

"Really? How gnarly?"

"Well, there was that time a guy came in with hyperextended knees in both legs—he needed surgery."

I nod. "That was a memorable one."

"What's *hyperextended* mean?" Spencer asks.

Violet demonstrates with her hands. "It means the knee bends backward."

He reaches down for his own knees. "Knees do that?"

"They're not supposed to."

"What else?"

As Violet recounts the tale of the mom and the multiple skull fractures, Brayden calls to me from the lounge chair by the pool.

"Hey, Dad!"

"What's up?" I call back.

"Mom texted me. She's going to Joyce's and wants to know if we want to go to dinner with her after."

Stacey was supposed to see the boys this past Saturday but she canceled the day before because she said she got called into work. It used to piss me off when she canceled on them—mostly because it bothered them. But it doesn't bother them anymore . . . and I can't figure out if that's good or bad.

"Tell her I'm a no," Aaron says from the diving board. "I'm gonna hang here a little longer and then a bunch of us are going to Smitty's house for an end of the summer party."

On the days she doesn't cancel, I leave it up to the boys if they want to go with her or not. At their age, I think it's important to give them that sense of control over their own time.

195

"It's your call, Bray," I tell him. "If you want to go to dinner with your mom, it's fine with me."

He scans the backyard, filled with his uncles and aunts, cousins and grandparents.

Then he shrugs. "I'd rather just stay here. If I go, I have to get changed."

Changing clothes is apparently a real burden for teenagers. Right up there with making sure the fitted sheet is actually on the mattress and not amassing a collection of empty water bottles under their beds.

"Mom texted me too, Dad," Spencer says. "I'm gonna tell her I want to stay here tonight. But I'll go with her this weekend."

I give him a smile. "Sounds good, Spence."

A few hours later I'm at the grill, cooking up another round of burgers and hot dogs for the crew. Through the hazy, fragrant smoke, my eyes find Violet across the yard—standing next to Callie and my mother, her hair in a long dark braid down her back, her face tilted up to the sun, laughing at something one of them said.

And for the thousandth time, I'm slammed right in the chest. Not just by how pretty she is but . . . by how fucking sublime it feels to have her here. The way she blends so beautifully into my life—with the people I love the most.

My parents are already enamored with her. It's there in the warm, affectionate tone of their voices and the gratitude in their eyes when they talk to her.

And I really get that.

Because I'm a father. And if one day one of my kids goes through a brutal end to a relationship, I'll worry about him.

I'll worry that he's lonely or hurting or unhappy. And someone like Violet is exactly whom I'd wish for him to find.

A woman who's loving and genuine—a woman who'll bring joy back into his life. Back into his heart.

I turn my gaze back to the grill, flipping the burgers and grinning like a goddamn idiot. Because today has been a great day. A perfect day.

Until it's not.

My phone pings on the counter next to me with an incoming text.

From Stacey.

I'm out front. I want to talk to you.

Awesome. The message every man wants to get from his ex-wife.

"Hey, Garrett." I jerk my head for him to come over. "Watch the grill. Stacey's out front, I have to go talk to her."

My family doesn't hate my ex-wife—that's not the kind of people they are—and she'll always be the mother of my kids. But it's safe to say she's not their favorite person on the planet either.

Garrett takes the spatula from my hand and lifts his beer at me.

"Enjoy. I'm sure that'll be all kinds of fun."

I slip my T-shirt over my head and walk through the house and out the front door.

Stacey's silver BMW is parked at the curb. She's standing next to the passenger-side door, her black shoulder-length hair styled in loose waves, wearing black shorts, sandals, and a sleeveless white blouse. Her manicured toenails and fingernails are painted the same deep red as her lips and the small designer bag that hangs from her wrist.

Objectively, I recognize that she's a good-looking woman—she always was. But there's no attraction or fondness for what I see—not even a stirring of nostalgia for the actual good moments we once shared.

What stands out most to me is the hard set of her mouth, her defensive stance, and the sharp narrowing of her eyes as I approach. Everything about her screams annoyed and bitter—and ready for a fight.

"What's up?" I ask.

"I was at my mother's and I asked the boys if they wanted to go to dinner and they all said no."

"Yeah, they told me."

Her voice is clipped and irritated. "I haven't seen Spencer in three weeks. Brayden and Aaron in over a month. I want them to come to dinner with me and it'd be nice if you'd help me out with that. For once."

"What do you expect me to do? Hog-tie them and toss them in your trunk? They don't want to go. And not to be a dick, but they were set to see you Saturday and you blew them off."

Her eyes flash. "I had to work, Connor! You of all people should understand that."

"What happened to Sunday? Were you working then too?"

Her handbag swings as she flails her arms. "Excuse me for needing a day to myself. That's a crime now, I guess."

I push a hand through my hair, tugging a little.

"I'm not saying it's a crime. But don't give me a hard time—or the kids a hard time—if they don't immediately re-arrange their plans because you've suddenly decided at the last minute that you feel like taking them out. That's bullshit."

Her relationship with the boys has been strained for a while—especially with Aaron. And I know it's not good, but I can't really blame them. When Stacey has them, she does what's convenient for her. She takes them to run errands or to the grocery store, or like a few months ago with Spencer to the nail salon and frigging Nordstrom.

"Well, I'm already here—can I come inside to see them?"

I gesture to the cars parked in front of the house.

"It's not a good time; my family's here. And . . . not that it's any of your business, but I'm seeing someone. She's here too. I don't want to make things awkward for her."

"Not any of my business? It's my business if she's around my children."

I'm actually surprised Spencer hasn't mentioned Violet to Stacy already. Out of the three boys—he's the talker.

I shake my head. "Not really."

Stacey's dated guys, guys who have met the boys. As long as I don't hear anything negative about them from the kids, it's not my business.

But she still folds her arms and shakes her head, tapping her foot like a ticking time bomb ready to pop.

"I want to see my kids, Connor."

"Well, I'm sorry—it's not a good day."

"I want to see my kids, Connor!" she screeches.

"Well, your kids don't want to see you! Maybe you should ask yourself why that is!"

She flinches. Pain flashes across her face before she has the chance to recover.

And I feel like an asshole.

Because I don't want to do this. I don't want to fight with her. I have no desire to hurt her. There's no satisfaction, or glee—there's only a sick, sad sensation twisting at my insides that this is what we are to each other now.

That every time we try to talk, to have some semblance of a civil, meaningful conversation, we end up screaming at each other over old wounds and ancient wrongs.

There's no water under the bridge . . . the bridge has been washed away.

I take a deep breath, making my voice go level.

"I shouldn't have said it like that, but your relationship with the boys is not in a good place right now. You have to see that. There's a therapist I know and I think—"

"I'm not going to therapy again," she spits out like it's absurd. "It doesn't work—it never worked for us."

"Not marriage therapy, Stacey, family therapy. For you and the boys."

And we're back to screaming.

"Jesus Christ, I said no!"

I fling my hands up. "Then I don't know what to tell you. If you want to work on your relationship with our kids, I'll support that. But I won't force them to see you if they don't want to."

"Of course you won't! God forbid you actually act like a parent and make them do anything."

"That's not true."

"God forbid you're not the fun-time dad—letting them do whatever the fuck they want, anytime they want."

"That's *not* true."

She jabs her finger at my chest.

"You were never there for us!"

"I'm here now! Every day, morning, and night, I'm *here*! Where the fuck are you?"

Stacey's voice drops to a lethal hiss.

"Oh, I did my time, believe me. You were just never around to notice."

I look away from her, pressing the tip of my tongue against the sharp point of my tooth to keep from saying things I can't take back. It's a joke anyway—this is how it's always going to be with her—as productive as banging my head against a wall.

After another breath, I meet her eyes and my tone is detached and indifferent and stone-cold final.

"Here's how this is going to go. The boys will see you when they want to see you. You're more than welcome to pick them up this weekend if you want. But they live here with me—that's how you wanted it. If you've got a problem with that now, get yourself a lawyer and take me to court. Otherwise, I'll tell them to call you before they go to bed tonight."

And I turn around and walk away.

"You're an asshole!" she screams after me.

I just raise my hand and wave without glancing back.

When I walk into the backyard, my jaw is tight and every muscle in my body is coiled with tension. The sun is starting to set and the kids are all gathered around the firepit roasting marshmallows. I feel my family's questioning stares following me, but I avoid eye contact. I snatch a bottle of beer from the cooler and sit down in a chair at the far end of the patio—twisting the cap off and taking a long drink.

But I still can't shake the frustration . . . the pointless, fruitless frustration. I just don't get why she has to be so goddamn miserable all the time. It's like she gets off on making me as pissed off as she is.

Two gentle hands land on my shoulders, just resting at first. Then kneading and squeezing—working at the knotted, tight muscle.

"Hey."

I tilt my head up into Violet's soft, concerned eyes.

"You okay?"

And I just look at her. Take her in. Take the time to absorb the calm sweetness that's always radiating from her. Letting it fill me and wrap around me like a fleecy blanket.

And I think about how lucky I am to have her in my life. How amazing she is with my kids, with my family—how awesome she is, period. She could have literally anyone . . . but she wants me. With her whole heart. And she shows me all the time, in big ways and small.

The frustration seeps out of me, my chest loosening and warming with her touch and scent and the nearness of her—leaving me soothed and happy again.

Violet makes me happy. When she's around, it's impossible to feel any other way.

And I've seen too much to ever take that for granted. To waste a moment of it.

I clasp her hand and tug her around to my lap, sitting her down and wrapping my arms around her. Her lips are supple and warm when I kiss her. We don't make out or anything—it's a brief, sweet peck—and then I just hold her.

Because that's enough. It's everything.

"I am now."

CHAPTER
Sixteen

Violet

THE TEMPERATURE AT NIGHT DIPS LOWER THAN USUAL for late September, but still warm enough that the heat isn't turned on yet. Connor likes to sleep with his window open—it's just one of a hundred wonderful intimate details I've learned about him in the last few months. The kind of sweet minutiae that truly makes two people a couple—the small facts that no one else is privy to.

Like how he knows I talk in my sleep. He discovered this a few weeks ago when I was mumbling in the dead of night and he decided to have a conversation with me. I didn't remember it in the morning, but apparently he asked me how sexy I thought he was . . . and I answered "purple, definitely purple."

The cat's already out of the bag about my poetry hobby—so, after that, there's really nothing I mind sharing with him. Connor Daniels has all of me now.

The crisp night air breezes in, coasting across my bare back. A delicious contrast to the heat of Connor's chest against mine. He's propped up against the headboard, and I'm straddling his hips, riding his cock in slow, deliberate strokes.

I love this position—not an inch of space separates us. And he's so deep inside me—his hardness, thick and unrelenting—making me feel impossibly full, making me come so easily.

My hips speed up, as I climb higher and closer with every hard drag of my pelvis against his. Connor's groan is hot and heavy in my ear and I know he's close too. His mouth slides across my chest, leaving a slick trail, before he takes my nipple in his mouth—sucking and flicking with his tongue and sending a spike of electric heat between my legs. I clench around him and moan his name.

And then I'm falling, flying, a swell of pleasure coursing through me so strong my head falls to his shoulder and I go slack against him—too caught up in the sensation to stay upright. His arms tighten around me, holding me, his fingers grasping at my shoulder blades, his hips snapping up roughly as his orgasm overtakes him.

We stay like that—joined and panting—for several moments. Connor's lips kiss my hair, my neck, and his hands slide up and down my back tenderly, soothing my exerted muscles. Eventually I slide off him, feeling that momentary emptiness when his cock leaves my body. And then my head is on the pillow and he's wrapped behind me. I let out a satisfied sigh and rub my legs together, because I enjoy the slick slipperiness of his come on my thighs.

We're quiet for a little while, but I can tell from Connor's breathing that he hasn't fallen asleep, even though I gave him quite a workout. His fingertip traces slowly up and down my arm and his voice is husky when he says, "Do you want kids?"

A bolt of excitement zings through me. Because spending time around the house with the boys these last weeks—giving them breakfast before school, helping them with their homework, just talking to them—has given me a hint of what motherhood could be like. I thought I had a taste of it raising my sisters and brother . . . but this is a whole other level.

Deeper. More.

I love being a part of their lives, a part of the memories they're making—it's an honor to have a hand in shaping them into the men they'll grow up to be. I love sharing the small, sweet moments with them as much as I love sharing them with their dad. It gives me a thrill to see little pieces of him in their expressions and mannerisms, to hear him in their words.

And Connor is an amazing father. I already knew he was, but seeing him in action up close has brought my ovaries to DEFCON level 1 on several occasions.

He's never more attractive to me—sexy and desirable—than when he's with his boys. The way he teaches them, guides them, has fun with them—always gentle and strong, and unconditionally devoted.

I can't conceive of a more beautiful future than one that includes me and Connor and children we'd have together. Seeing him and me blended into a precocious, incredible, new little human—making Spencer a big brother.

"Is that a proposition or an inquiry?" I ask.

"An inquiry."

I turn on my back because I want to see his face. I reach up and scrape my palm against the rough stubble on his jaw.

"You look so serious."

His eyes are intense and shining in the darkness.

"I'm feeling pretty serious about you these days. About us."

And God, I love him. With a deeply yearning worship that's a little terrifying.

Because if I lost him now—if I lost this—and Connor and his boys were no longer a part of my life . . . I don't know what I would do. It would be like one of my limbs were missing, one of my vital organs—I would never be the same.

"Yeah. Me too."

"I'm also twelve years older than you. A lot of our life experiences are similar, but some really . . . aren't. And I think it's important for us to talk about the ones that aren't. So there aren't any misunderstandings between us. Or disappointments."

I think about how to answer his question, the best way to word it. What I wanted for my life used to be simpler. Because I don't just have my feelings to consider. So much of what I want hinges on what he wants.

"I always assumed I'd have kids—it was always part of the plan. But it's not a deal breaker for me if—"

"Don't do that," he says sharply.

"Don't do what?"

"Don't equivocate because you think it's what I want to hear. I want to know what *you* want, Violet. What you hope for, what you dream about, not what you'll settle for." He brushes the damp strands of my hair back off my forehead cherishingly. "Hard, fast truth, Vi—do you want to have kids?"

I don't think this time—I just give him the answer.

"Yes. I do. One would be amazing; two would be even better."

He nods, unsurprised. But Connor's face is impassive, unreadable.

"Do you want to have more kids?" I ask softly.

He doesn't answer right away, and the heavy silence presses down around us.

"I don't know." Connor sits up, facing away from me, resting his elbows on his bended knees. "I've been thinking about it—trying to figure out how I feel. Kids are incredible . . . mine will always be the most amazing thing I've ever done."

He turns to me with dark, burning eyes.

"And I don't want to take that away from you. You deserve to have *everything* you've ever wanted."

I give him a small smile and he lets out a long breath.

"But kids aren't easy. And I've been operating under the assumption for a while now that having more wasn't going to be an option for me. I don't *not* want more. But . . . if we had a child together tomorrow, I'll be sixty when they're eighteen. That seems pretty frigging old to have a kid barely out of high school."

I'm not disappointed by his answer. It's a big decision and he's thinking about it, turning it around in his brilliant mind, examining all the angles. And the only reason he's doing that is because he's serious about a future with me, in the same way I want one with him.

And even if we don't know all the answers right this second, I believe in us.

And him.

I believe in a future where we're one of those annoying, disgustingly happy couples that go on fun vacations twice a year and do home redecorating projects together without even arguing. And we both have everything we want out of life.

We're too good together not to have that.

I walk my fingers up his spine and my voice goes flirty.

"You're going to be so fucking hot when you're sixty."

Connor chuckles, his shoulders jostling. He turns back toward me with a smirk and a flash of dimple.

"Oh yeah? You've got a thing for old guys, do you?"

"Well," I tease, gesturing between us, "I thought that was obvious."

"Ha ha ha ha!" Connor laughs mockingly. "Holy shit, you're hilarious."

And now I'm laughing too.

"If nursing didn't work out, stand-up comedy was gonna be my plan B."

"Oh yeah? Tickling was my plan B."

"Tickling is not an occupation."

"It is the way I do it."

"No! Connor, no!"

But he does.

Fast as a cobra, he snatches my ankle in an unbreakable grip and tickles the bottom of my overly sensitive foot—I can't even get professional pedicures—until I'm squealing and thrashing uncontrollably.

"Ahh!" I scream-laugh. "Stop!"

But he's relentless.

"Shh, shh—you can't scream, there are young boys in the house. They're going to come in here if they hear you and they'll see your perfect tits and it'll ruin normal breasts for them forever. You don't want that on your conscience. Shhh."

He moves to the other foot without mercy.

So I change tactics—activating my failsafe feminine wiles and capitalizing on his voracious sex drive.

I roll to my side and press all my naked parts against his, pelvis to pelvis, stomach to stomach, my "perfect" tits molded against his broad chest. I wrap my arm around his shoulders and tug him down, kissing him hard and hot, like my life—and my feet—depend on it.

And Connor . . . caves gloriously.

He groans low and rough—a sound that never fails to make me insanely wet. And then he's pulling me to him, biting and sucking at my lips, and lashing with his tongue. His stupendous cock grows thick and stiff against my thigh.

Then he's gliding on top of me, pressing me down into the bed with his weight.

And the possible-future-kids discussion is shelved . . . as we pursue our more immediate needs.

Connor

In the first week of October, I officially retire from D.U.H. Because "unattached" no longer applies to me. I'm extremely, happily attached.

It's tradition that when a member leaves the group, we all go out to dinner with the retiree and their new significant other to commemorate the occasion. And as any current or former athlete will tell you—you don't mess with tradition.

On a Friday night we all meet up at a Japanese hibachi restaurant—one of those places where they cook the food in front of you, do knife tricks, and launch pieces of shrimp at the mouths of each member of your party.

Violet looks gorgeous in a snug black sweater and boots, with blue jeans that are ripped at the knees. I got a cheap thrill in the truck on the drive over from slipping my hand into the torn hole and stroking the smooth skin of her leg with my fingertips.

In the atrium of the restaurant, we all stand in a crowd beside the indoor koi pond waiting to be seated. The D.U.H. crew are friendly and chatty with Violet, which doesn't surprise me in the least. She's easy to adore.

And they don't hold back on roasting me—also not a surprise.

"We tried to steer him away from walking around with his head up his ass when you two first got together," Delilah tells Violet.

"Thanks, Delilah," I interject. "Great visual."

"But he was determined to do it the hard way," Carl adds.

Violet glances at me sweetly, then says, "Yeah, Connor can be pretty thick sometimes . . . but I like him anyway."

Discreetly, I smack Violet's ass. Her eyes light up and heat suffuses her cheeks—and I make a mental note to explore spanking further when it's just the two of us.

The hostess calls our party and we each sit down around the large rectangular table, waiting for the chef to arrive.

Violet takes the menu from the hostess. "God, I'm starving," she says as she scans it eagerly. "I am Jack's growling stomach."

She laughs.

But I freeze. Just staring at her.

In medical school there are a shit-ton of facts you need to learn and memorize—dosages and the workings of body systems and how a multitude of external and internal factors can play cause and effect with everything else—directly and indirectly. But there are moments in medical training when all those extraneous pieces of information come together and crystalize in your mind. And it's not just something you know . . . it becomes your reality.

That's what this is like for me, sitting next to Violet.

The muffled chatter of conversations continue around me and the world keeps turning—but my brain is on pause—caught on a single phenomenal, indisputable, truth.

I'm in love with this woman.

Deeply, undeniably, rapturously in love.

She's perfect for me—precious to me. In every conceivable way.

"It's a line from *Fight Club*, Connor," Violet says, misunderstanding my silence.

I clear my throat, managing to get out, "Yeah, I know."

She smiles and my heart pounds with devotion.

"Oh good—you had me worried there for a minute."

The waitress sets Violet's cocktail in front of her—a tall pink fruity thing with an umbrella. And, Jesus Christ Almighty, even the way she sips her drink . . . the way her pretty lips pucker, is completely adorable to me.

I fucking *love* her. My happiness is inexorably linked to hers—to her existence in my life—her presence in my home, my bed, my heart. There's nothing I don't want to share with her.

I want Violet to be a part of my everything and my always.

And for a guy like me—who once upon a time believed I'd had that and ended up running face-first into a brick wall of mistaken—it's a huge realization.

Life altering. Future changing. Not just for me, but for my kids.

Still, the massiveness of it doesn't make it one bit less true.

And I'm almost sure Violet feels the same way about me. But "almost" only counts in horseshoes.

So I have to be sure. I have to tell her—go out on a limb and be the half of the couple who says it first.

And find out if Violet's up for everything and always with me too.

The sad but pervasive truth about life, that I think I know better than the average person—is that it's short and unpredictable. When you find happiness, you can't take it for granted.

You need to grab onto that shit with both hands and hold on tight. You can't waste time, you can't hesitate—if you do, chances are good you'll regret it.

And regrets suck ass in an especially brutal way.

I thought about telling Violet how I feel about her last night when we came back to my place from the hibachi restaurant. But Violet gets frisky when she's buzzed—and naughty. I'm not sure how much alcohol was in those umbrella drinks . . . but she started doing a striptease as soon as we walked through my bedroom door.

Not that I'm complaining. At *all*.

But I don't want Violet to think the first time I tell her I love her, that it's just the orgasm talking.

I want it to be perfect and right—I want her to know the words are coming straight from my soul. I'm also going to ask her to move in with me and the boys, full time—which is definitely a conversation she should be sober for.

It's a big step, but because it's her . . . it just feels easy.

"I'm walking across the parking lot right now," Violet tells me on the phone. She left for work from here this morning and was on shift until 8 p.m. "I'm going to head home and shower and then I'll be over in about an hour and a half for this late dinner you're cooking up for me."

Brayden and Spencer are sleeping at Ryan and Angela's, and Aaron's out with his friends and won't be home until midnight—so there won't be any interruptions.

"Sounds good, Vi."

"Do you need me to bring anything?"

"Just you, baby," I tell her. "All I need is you."

She releases a breathy, happy little sigh, and cool, cocky pride rushes through me at being the reason for it. When she speaks again, her voice is softer, sweeter.

"I'll see you soon, Connor."

"Okay. See you soon."

Forty-five minutes later, the lights in the dining room are dimmed and the table is set for two, with candles just waiting to be lit. One of the benefits of my re-upped bachelorhood is that I learned how to cook better. Not a wide variety of dishes, but the ones I know I'm Gordon-fucking-Ramsay-level awesome at.

So the homemade mashed potatoes are whipped and creamy, the foil-wrapped asparagus is dressed with butter and fresh-grated Parmesan cheese, and the steaks are perfectly seasoned and ready to be tossed on the grill.

It'll take me ten minutes to hop in the shower and change my clothes—and then everything will be set for the ultimate romantic night.

I don't lock the front door when I'm home—I don't think anyone in Lakeside does. So when I hear it open and footsteps walking into the house, it's unexpected but not unusual.

I'm at the counter drying my hands on a dishtowel when my brother Garrett walks into the kitchen. I'm about to ask him,

"*What's up?*" but the words get lodged in my throat when I see his face.

He's visibly pale and . . . shaken.

And it takes a lot to rattle Garrett.

"What's wrong?"

He swallows hard.

"Ryan called me. He told me to come get you and bring you to the hospital. There's been an accident."

CHAPTER
Seventeen

Connor

I ARGUED WITH AARON WHEN WE WENT SHOPPING FOR his first car.

I remember feeling excited that I could buy my kid a car, because it was more than my parents had been able to do for me and my brothers. I only had two rules: it had to be safe, and it had to be used. I don't believe a seventeen-year-old should own a brand-new car—they're bound to ding it up, get into fender benders—and there's a special sense of accomplishment when you purchase your first new car yourself as an adult that I wanted him to experience.

But still we argued—because I thought he should get a pickup truck, like mine. Trucks are practical, the bed space is always useful, they're big, high—safe. They can drive in any kind of weather, drive over almost anything, including another car.

But Aaron didn't want a truck. He wanted one of those low, loud, sporty street-racing cars like the ones in the *Fast & Furious* movies.

So we argued. And I gave in.

Because I wanted him to be happy. My work hours were so long for most of the boys' lives that when I had the chance to be with them, I didn't like to spend that time arguing.

Stacey was right. I was the fun parent, the lenient parent—the one who let things go when I should've put my foot down.

Because of that—because of me—I'm on the way to the hospital with Garrett while my son is being cut out of the small, fast car he wanted. Because an SUV swerved into his lane, hit him head-on, and pushed the entire engine block of his car onto his lap.

I've treated patients that were in head-on collisions. I know exactly what sharp metal and blunt force trauma can do to a human body... and it's always bad. Always.

Timmy's firehouse responded to the scene. He's there with Aaron right now as they extract him—keeping him talking. Tim called Ryan, who called Garrett, who came to get me. I wanted to go to the scene, but I couldn't take the chance of missing him and not being here when they bring him in.

Garrett pulls into the back parking lot of the hospital and I'm stepping out of the car before it's completely stopped. I tell him to meet me in the front waiting room. And when I walk through the sliding glass doors of my emergency department, the emotion that's swamping me—filling up my chest and drowning my lungs—isn't fear or grief. It's anger. Furious fucking anger. At myself.

Because Aaron's just a kid. And I should've known better.

"Connor."

Stella's behind the nurse's station as I head to the phone, looking for the paramedic notes because they call traumas in when they're en route.

"Is he out of the car?" my voice is ice-cold and detached.

Stella nods, her features soft with rare sympathy.

"They're five minutes out."

I locate the chart and scan his vitals. It's stupid that I'm shocked when I see how piss-poor they are, but I still am. And that makes me even angrier.

"Who's on trauma tonight?" I ask Stella.

"I am."

Makayla Davis is a trauma surgeon who's skilled and experienced—the best in the hospital. That fact brings no comfort, no relief.

"I can't imagine what you're feeling right now, Connor."

"No, you can't."

"We're going to do everything we—"

"Yeah, I know the pep talk. I need to see him when he comes in."

Makayla shakes her head—calm, steady, and in control.

"That's not a good idea."

"Makayla—"

"You're not the doctor right now, Connor."

"I know that!" I snap.

"Do you? Because I don't think you do."

I close my eyes and take a slow breath.

"I just need to be with him. If I'm with him, he'll be okay."

It's totally irrational; I know that. I sound unhinged . . . I sound like a patient. But I still can't help but believe it.

"Just let me in the room, Makayla. *Please.*"

She tears her gaze away, shaking her head like she knows it's a mistake—but she's going to do it anyway.

"If you second-guess my orders—"

"I won't."

"If you interfere—"

"I'm not going to."

"Aaron is *my* patient; he is my priority. If you get in the way of me treating him, I will have you hauled out in a hot minute—for both your sakes. Am I clear?"

"Crystal. I just"—my voice cracks—"I just need to tell him it's going to be all right."

Makayla nods and glances at the clock on the wall behind me.

"Let's go, then."

One of the hardest, fastest rules in medicine—not just golden, but platinum—is doctors don't treat their family members. There's lots of good reasons for it, the least of which is that emotions get in the way, even if you don't realize it. They slow your response time, cloud your memory, affect your decision making.

After Makayla gives the go-ahead, everything moves fast. The portable ultrasound and crash cart are wheeled into the exam room; gowns and gloves are donned. Everything moves in a blur around me.

And then the paramedics are pushing through the door, rolling the stretcher in, rattling off stats and injuries. He's just a form at first—packed in ice and a thin white blanket, a neck brace obscuring his face. Makayla counts it down and they lift him onto the table, the bright, hot light illuminating everything.

After they rule out a neck fracture, they remove the brace. And I see my son's face. His skin is waxy gray from the shock, there's dried blood caked around both nostrils, his lips are pale and cracked.

But I don't just see Aaron with my eyes . . . I see him in my mind too. So many versions of him all at once. I see him the night he was born, the night he made me a dad, when I held him for the very first time—his tiny lips and perfect fingers—his face scrunched and his lungs strong and his little limbs flailing with indignity.

I see him when he was three—his hair was blond—and he fell off the swing in the backyard. And he ran to me with his knee bleeding, crying these big, heartbreaking tears. And I scooped him up in my arms, and I hugged him and kissed his face and promised that I could make it better.

I see him when he learned to swim, when I taught him to throw a football, when he graduated eighth grade, the day he got his driver's license.

And I'm so proud. So grateful that I get to be the dad of this amazing, beautiful boy. A boy who needs me right now . . . more than he's ever needed me before.

I crouch down low beside his head, keeping out of the way as they evaluate him. I lean my face right next to his, so he can see me, hear me. The activity and voices going on around us fade away, and it's just me and Aaron here together.

"Dad?"

"Yeah, buddy, it's me. I'm right here."

I stroke my thumb back and forth across his forehead—because it's the only part of him I know I can touch without hurting him.

"I'm sorry about the car," he rasps.

My throat is hot, and my vision blurs and I have to blink to clear it.

"I don't care about the car, Aaron."

He struggles to drag in a breath—jagged and shallow. Somewhere in my brain a voice whispers, *possible pneumothorax*. A collapsed lung.

"I'm sorry I've been a dick—"

I shake my head.

"No, you haven't been. You're a good boy. A good son. I'm so lucky."

"Tell Brayden and Spencer I'm sorry I ragged on them so much."

I brush his hair back gently.

"I will. You can tell them yourself. As soon as you're feeling better."

Tears swell in his eyes and his voice hitches.

"Tell Mom I don't hate her, okay? Not even a little."

And it's like my heart tears open, bleeding out. Because I'm so fucking sorry. For every harsh word he had to hear, every second of confusion or heartache he felt.

It never should've been like that.

"She knows that, Aaron. But I'll tell her."

He closes his eyes for a moment.

But then he looks up at me, his face crumpling.

"I don't want to die."

"No—no, Aaron, that's not gonna happen." I rub at the tears trekking down my face. "I'm right here. I'm with you. I will never let that happen."

It's crazy sometimes . . . the lies we tell our kids . . . the lies we tell ourselves. Santa Claus and the Tooth Fairy and I'm going to keep you safe.

I think about Ms. Allen and the way her knees gave out, the sounds she made when she realized her little boy was gone. She would've done *anything* to bring him back. Ripped her own heart out, given up her lungs, she would've traded places with him in a second if it meant he would be okay again.

But sometimes . . . there's just nothing anyone can do. Nothing.

And I hate that I fucking know that. I wish I didn't. I wish I knew anything except that.

But Aaron doesn't know it and that's how it's going to stay.

I wipe his tears away gently, and my voice is calm and soothing, like when I used to read him a story before bedtime.

"You're going to be just fine, buddy. They're going to bring you upstairs and you're going to go to sleep and they're going to fix you right up. And when you wake up, nothing's going to hurt anymore . . . and I'm going to be right there. I'll be right there with you, holding your hand, I promise."

His features smooth out as he takes another breath.

"I love you, Dad."

I try so hard to keep my voice from breaking, but it does anyway.

"I love you too, Aaron. *So much.*"

He gives me a tiny nod and a small smile.

"I know."

I stroke his forehead with my thumb one last time, and then the rails of the exam table are snapped up with a metallic clang. And Makayla barks out orders.

"Okay let's go. OR 3 is ready for us."

They move as a group in rapid synchronized steps down the hall, some pushing the bed, others carrying equipment and saline bags. I jog behind them, keeping eye contact with Aaron for as long as I can. His eyes slide closed and stay that way as they wheel him into the elevator.

And I stand in the hallway watching the doors shut. Because there's no room for me and the OR is sterile, I can't go in with him.

My arms are numb at my sides and I'm just . . . useless. Blank.

Lost.

I don't know where to go or what to do. I never not know what to do. It's like I can't form a thought in my head. My knees go weak so I lean against the wall, bending over and gulping for air in tight, strangled gasps.

Above the rushing in my ears, I hear my name called from down the hall.

"Connor!"

I turn around and Violet slams into me. Her arms

wrapping around me, holding me up—solid and strong and here. And I needed her here so fucking much.

"Violet . . . Jesus, Violet."

I clasp at her like a drowning man, burying my face in her neck, breathing in her warmth and vitality.

"There was an accident," I tell her in a voice that's not even mine.

"I know. Callie called me."

"He's . . . hurt, Vi."

Her arms squeeze me tighter.

"He's hurt really bad."

"I'm here. I've got you."

We stay wrapped around each other for a few moments, until my heartbeat slows. I straighten up and rub at my wet eyes and try to pull my shit together.

"I don't know what to do." I press my hands against my skull, squeezing. "Fuck! What do I need to do?"

Violet's brown eyes are steady and clear—grounding me, guiding me, like a light in a pitch-black storm.

"You have to call his mother. You have to let Stacey know what's happening."

Right. Call Stacey. I can do that.

Having a direction, a task I can complete, helps. Helps to get my brain working again, helps to bring me back to me.

"Okay." I nod, reaching for my phone. "Okay."

Violet

I'm in full-on triage mode, my emotions on lockdown, moving on auto-pilot. My only focus is Connor and the boys—that they have what they need, that they're getting through this, that I'm here for them.

My own feelings about Aaron? The idea that's he's hurt, that we could lose him? No—I'll think about that later—when I can cry and fall apart.

Now is not that time.

We wait in the main waiting room outside the ED, because it's big with lots of chairs and accessible to everyone. Garrett stays, Connor's ex-mother-in-law Joyce arrives, Ryan and Angela bring the boys and wait with us too. Connor sits Brayden and Spencer in the two chairs between us, so we bookend them.

Connor's parents arrive next. Mr. Daniels, whose style is old-school and gruff, walks straight to his firstborn and pulls him into his arms for a hug.

"It's going to be all right, son." He pats Connor's back. "Don't you worry."

My armor cracks just a bit at his words, my throat clogging, but I manage to keep it together.

A few minutes later, Timmy walks through the doors still in his firefighter gear. His eyes are red rimmed as he sits beside Connor and quietly tells him what it was like at the scene. How they pulled up to the accident and Tim immediately recognized Aaron's white Honda Civic, but he didn't believe it . . . not until he saw his nephew pinned inside.

He tells Connor that Aaron was scared but he didn't feel any pain and that he begged his uncle to get him out. And Tim promised him he would, talked him through it, kept him calm, until they were able to extract him from the car.

Connor's expression is controlled and stoic. It's a mask he wears well . . . the same one he uses for patients so they're not burdened by what he's thinking or feeling.

"You did good, Tim." Connor puts his hand on his

little brother's shoulder. "I'm so grateful that you were there for him."

Timmy sniffs and blows out a big breath, the way guys do when they're trying not to cry.

"Yeah. I'm gonna . . . get some air."

He walks outside, and a moment later Garrett follows him, to make sure he's okay. Because even though they argue and mock each other . . . they're brothers.

As news of the accident gets around Lakeside, the waiting room fills up with more and more teenagers—Aaron's friends and members of the football team. They're somber, respectful, talking quietly amongst themselves or looking at their phones. Aaron's pretty girlfriend comes in wearing his varsity jacket, because kids still give those to each other when they're dating. She approaches Connor, her face awash with devastation, two of her friends flanking her for moral support.

"Hi, Dr. Daniels."

Connor gives her a gentle smile.

"Hi, Mia."

"Do you know how he's doing?"

"I talked to him when he came in; he was conscious, which is good. He's in surgery now and we'll know more when he gets out."

She points to an empty chair in the corner.

"I'll be over there."

Connor nods. "Okay."

Tim and Garrett come back in and Garrett tells his players that Aaron probably won't be out of the OR for hours— that they should head home and he'll update them.

"We want to stay, Coach D," one of the captains says. "If it's all right with you."

"Yeah, that's fine, Taylor."

"Do you guys need anything?" another captain, who's tall

with massively broad shoulders for a teenager, asks. "Coffee? We could make a White Castle run if anyone's hungry."

I smile softly . . . because these are good kids.

Garrett checks with all of us, but everyone declines—too worried to eat.

The waiting room is quiet for several minutes after that. But a little before 10 p.m., the air changes—when Stacey-formerly-Daniels walks in.

The tension between her and Connor isn't a secret to the people in this room. She's visibly agitated, frazzled—but still more beautiful than I'd pictured her. I don't know why that surprises me.

And the boys look like her. Up until now, I've only seen Connor in them, but the resemblance to their mother is there.

Her onyx eyes scan the room, finding Connor and glaring like he somehow caused Aaron's accident.

Her hands are clenched when she walks up to him.

"Where is he?"

"He's in surgery."

"I want to see him. Right now."

"You can't."

"Don't give me that shit again!" she raises her voice, pointing her finger. "You've been trying to turn them against me for months."

"I've been trying to turn them against you?" Connor stands, his mouth twisting. "You don't need my help with that—you've been doing a bang-up job of that all by yourself."

"Fuck you!"

He turns sharply on his heel, and walks out the doors with Stacey stomping after him.

Spencer watches them and his expression makes me remember lying in my bed, late at night, hiding under the blankets and covering my ears because my parents were screaming at each other in the living room—and it was awful.

"It's all right; they're just upset." I put an arm around his shoulders and the other around Brayden's. "They'll calm down after they talk."

"No. They're always like this," Brayden says.

And he doesn't say it in a petulant, my-parents-are-the-worst, teenager kind of way.

He's just sad.

"It's gonna be okay," I promise.

And I mean it. When this is over I'll talk to Connor—hell, I'll talk to Stacey—but I'll find a way to make the situation better for these boys, I swear.

Through the glass windows, I watch Connor and Stacey argue. I can't hear them, but I don't need to. I've seen this story play out between the parents of injured children dozens of times in the emergency department. The anger and blame, the cloying fear, the excruciating helplessness.

Stacey's back is to me, but I can tell the exact moment she asks Connor if Aaron is going to be okay. Because the frustration and resentment drains out of him, sinking his shoulders, making his mouth go slack with heavy words he doesn't want to say.

"*I don't know, Stacey. I really don't know.*"

They look dazed when they walk back in. Shell-shocked.

Stacey's arms are crossed over her middle like she's cold, or like she's barely holding herself together. Connor sits down beside Brayden, and Stacey comes over to the boys, her tone softening.

"Hey, guys. Are you doing okay?"

"Hey, Mom."

"Yeah, we're okay."

"Do you want to come sit with me and Grandma Joyce?"

Brayden doesn't look up from the floor. "I'm good here."

Spencer takes a moment before he answers.

"I think it might be bad luck to change seats while Aaron's in surgery. I'm gonna stay in this chair until he's out."

I can't help but smile at his sweetness, his endearing innocence. When I look up at Stacey, she's smiling tenderly at Spencer too.

But then her gaze shifts to me and the smile drops.

"I'm sorry, who are you?"

"Stacey, this is my girlfriend, Violet," Connor answers. "Violet, this is my ex-wife, Stacey."

Her gaze drags down over me from head to toe, slow and disapproving.

But I'm a goddamn nurse. I've had patients curse me out, throw things. One time a woman tried to stab me with a pen—and I still gave her the best treatment I'm capable of.

Nasty looks have no effect on me.

And the woman is distraught, her child on an operating table—I feel nothing for her but pity.

So I extend the olive branch. "Hi, Stacey. I'm sorry we're meeting under these circumstances."

She ignores me completely. There goes my faith in the Mediterranean diet.

Stacey shakes her head at Connor. "I can't believe you."

"Don't," he warns. "Not now."

She looks back to the boys and forces a smile.

"I'll be over there if either of you needs me."

And then she walks away.

Connor turns toward me, his eyes heavy-lidded with an apology I don't need. I reach for him, holding out my hand across the back of the boys' chairs. He takes it, folding our fingers together and clasping it tight.

And we wait.

Time moves differently in a hospital waiting room. Slower, more torturously, each second consumed with thoughts of what will be, what might be, what life will look like when you leave this room. Connor sits like a statue, hard and still, the cup of coffee I got for him sitting untouched next to him.

Brayden's phone starts to die so I borrow a charger from one of the nurses in the back and he moves to the floor, sitting beside the outlet. At some point, Spencer falls asleep against me, his little breaths puffing against the beige hoody I threw on when I got the call from Callie.

Just before 3 a.m., the surgeon, Makayla Davis, comes down. Connor and Stacey converge on her and I gently wake Spencer, shifting him over, moving to stand on Connor's other side as Makayla explains Aaron's condition.

"He got through the surgery without additional complications. He's critical but stable."

She goes on to describe some of Aaron's injuries—internal bleeding, broken ribs, a punctured lung, ruptured spleen, multiple fractures to his lower right leg that will require additional surgeries to repair. But there's good news too—no spinal cord damage, no apparent bleeding on the brain, and Aaron's vitals are strong . . . all positive signs.

"You and Stacey can come up to the ICU." Makayla glances at the crowd still gathered in the waiting room. "As for friends and family, we'll see how he does in the next twenty-four hours."

Connor nods, swallowing hard, because he knows if things are going to go bad, it's most likely to happen in that time period. Typically, only immediate family is permitted in the ICU, but sometimes they make exceptions if they think it could aid a patient's recovery.

He braces a hand on my arm. "You'll take the boys home? Stay with them?"

"Of course." I nod.

Garrett conveys the information to the students and Connor's family. Hugs are plentiful as everyone stands and starts to disperse. Spencer darts out of his chair and throws himself into Stacey's arms. She runs her fingers through his hair and kisses the top of his head. Connor embraces Brayden and tells him he loves him.

"Your mom and I are going to stay here with Aaron. Be good for Vi, okay?"

"We will," Bray assures him.

And then Connor turns to me, kissing me quickly, whispering a ragged, "Thank you."

My mouth is beside his ear, and I want to tell him that I love him. The words are right there on my lips . . . already his.

But I hold back. Because he's all over the place right now. His mind and his heart are scattered in a million different directions. And the first time I say those words to him, I want it to be a happy memory, a good thing—not associated with so much awfulness.

So I press a kiss to his jaw and let him go.

And I guide Brayden and Spencer to my car and take them home.

Rosie's worked up when we walk in the door—barking and spinning in circles—because dogs can sense when things are wrong. I open the back sliding door and let her out into the yard.

"Do we have to go to school tomorrow?" Spencer asks.

"No. We're going to take it easy tomorrow . . . today. We'll see how your brother's doing and we might go see him and your parents at the hospital." I look between him and Brayden. "Do you guys want to camp down here on the couch again?"

Trauma is sneaky. Sometimes you think you've got a handle on it, that you're doing fine. . . and then it crashes into you, knocking the breath out of your lungs and driving you to your knees. I don't want them to be alone right now—I want them close, in case they need me.

They nod and head upstairs to change into their pajamas.

My heart feels weighted and slow when I turn my attention to the kitchen, cleaning up the dinner Connor was making for me. A sad smile brushes my lips as I throw out the steaks that sat on the counter too long, put the unused dishes back in the cabinet and the dirty ones into the dishwasher.

Then I turn around and gasp, pressing a hand to my chest. Because Brayden is standing behind me.

"Is Aaron gonna die?"

His eyes are serious and somber—older than his thirteen years—older than he was this morning. And while I can see some of Stacey's features in him now, he still seems like a mini version of Connor to me.

"The doctors are doing everything they can to help him."

"That's what people say when they don't want to say someone's going to die." His lower lip quivers and his voice goes thin and pained.

"Just tell me the truth, Violet. I need to know. So I can be ready . . ."

The nurse in me says don't give him any assurances. No guarantees. Aaron could develop an infection, an unforeseen brain bleed, the surgeon could've missed something, a hundred things could go wrong.

But the woman in me—the woman who this sweet boy means everything to—demands that I shield him from those terrible possibilities. That I do everything I can to ease his fear and relieve his pain.

"Aaron's not going to die, Brayden. I think he's going to be just fine." I put my arm around his shoulders and kiss the top of his head. He leans into me, needing that comfort so much. "I think the first time you see him he'll be asleep because he's healing, but in a few days you'll visit him again and he'll be awake and talking just like normal. And in a few weeks he'll come home, and he'll let you sign the cast on his leg. And everything is going to be all right."

Brayden shudders out a sigh, nodding against me, wiping his eyes. "Okay."

I wish Connor was here. I have no idea if I just did the right thing or not.

As the boys lay out their pillows and blankets in the living room, I close my eyes and say a prayer. I didn't grow up particularly religious, but I believe in God. I believe in a God that loves us, accepts us, wants the best for us—the universe is too magnificent, the human body too perfectly intertwined not to have been planned by someone.

So I pray to God now. I beg and I plead . . . to not make a liar out of me.

CHAPTER
Eighteen

Connor

L AKESIDE MEMORIAL HAS FIFTY ICU BEDS, EACH IN private, small rooms to cut down on the spread of infection. Every patient's vitals are fed into a central monitoring station that is staffed by critical care doctors and nurses 24/7.

For the first ten hours of Aaron's stay in the ICU, Stacey and I sit beside his bed.

And we don't say a word to each other.

We stare at him. We watch the heart monitor, lost in our own thoughts. We talk with the doctor and nurses who regularly come into the room to check his status and administer his meds.

He's not intubated. He's breathing on his own but remains unconscious, which isn't unusual. Fifteen hours post-op he spikes a fever that triggers an arrhythmia—an irregular heartbeat. It's scary, but also not unusual after the trauma his body has experienced. They bring his temperature down with medication and monitor his heart, but due to the fever, additional visitors aren't allowed.

With her elbow braced against the arm of the chair and her head resting on her hand, Stacey sleeps for a few hours. I step just outside the room and call Violet to check in with her and the boys. She says she'll update my parents and brothers about not being allowed visitors and my chest aches with gratitude at having one less thing to worry about.

There's a gentle urging in Vi's sweet voice when she tells me to try and sleep, that I won't be good to anyone if I'm out on my feet.

I promise her I will . . . but it's not really true.

My brain's in hyperdrive; I couldn't close my eyes right now if I tried. I double-time it downstairs to the break room and pour two cups of bad coffee for me and Stacey. My coworkers inquire about Aaron, but they don't hold me up—they understand my need to get back upstairs.

Stacey's awake when I walk in the room, tying her hair back in a low bun and wiping under her eyes.

"Thank you," she says when I hand her the coffee, her voice thick with sleep that wasn't at all restful.

Forty hours after Aaron was admitted, it's still just the two of us in the room wearing the same clothes, watching our son take each breath, comforted by the beep of the monitor that lets us know his heart is beating regularly now.

And that's when Stacey speaks.

"Do you remember the night he was born?"

"Yep." I brace my elbows on my knees, leaning forward. "Blizzard of the decade."

"I thought for sure we were going to slide into an embankment, get stuck, and end up having him on the side of the road."

"So did I."

A smile pulls at my lips. "I remember wondering if I had anything sharp enough in the truck to cut the umbilical cord."

Stacey looks over at me, smiling a little.

"You never told me that."

I shrug. "Didn't seem worth mentioning after the fact."

"We should've known then that he was going to be the one to turn us gray," she says. "Give us all the wrinkles."

"Definitely." I nod.

And then we fall silent again.

But the memory of those shared moments hovers between us, linking us together, pulling us closer than we've been in years.

"I don't want to fight with you anymore, Stacey."

My words are gentle, but resolute. Because something has to give.

"It's bad for the boys . . . it's bad for us."

"I know." She nods tightly, gazing at our son.

"When they brought Aaron in after the accident, he wanted me to tell you that he doesn't hate you." My eyes burn, remembering his words. "Not even a little."

Stacey's chest hitches and her mouth pinches to contain a sob. She brings the tissue squeezed in her hand to her eyes.

"I know you think I'm a shitty dad, that I was a rotten husband—and I'm sorry for whatever I did to make you believe that. But we have to move on. To have things be . . . peaceful between us. We have to find a way to do that. I want to raise our boys to be good men and I want us to do it together. They need us to do it together."

Her voice is raw and scraping.

"I don't think you're a shitty dad, Connor. And you were never a bad husband."

After a quiet moment, she scrapes her teeth against her bottom lip, and her words come out soft, like a confession.

"Did you ever think . . . that we got married for all the wrong reasons? Like, we'd been together through college and then we graduated, and it was just expected that we take the next step?"

"Yeah, I have thought that," I say, my voice soft too. "But I don't regret it. We have the kids . . ."

"I don't regret it either." She looks over at me, her face gentle. Unguarded.

And it's like I'm looking back in time. Finally talking to the girl I knew . . . the person I used to love.

"Everything just went so fast," she says. "There was never any time . . . and one day I woke up and I was thirty-*eight*. And I . . . couldn't breathe. Because my life was rushing by and nothing about it was what I thought it was going to be. What I wanted it to be."

She inhales deeply, rubbing her palms on her jeans.

"It's hard to admit that when you have kids. Scary. So I blamed you for it. Because that made it easier to change it. To upend the boys' lives and blow our family apart."

I've wondered about this for so long. I knew we had issues—our marriage was never perfect—but her insistence on getting divorced took me by surprise.

"And then, this last year," she goes on, "it's like I went crazy on only having to worry about myself. I knew the boys were with you. That they were safe and happy, that you would take care of them. And I got to think about me. It had been *so long*, Connor, since I was able to only think about me. It's like I was drunk on it. The freedom of it. It felt like I was twenty-five again."

She glances my way.

"You probably can't understand that."

When we were married, Stacey took care of the details, the small things.

All of them.

The appointments, school paperwork, homework, schedules, playdates. The laundry and food shopping and housework. Even when we took vacations, she booked the hotel, reserved the flights, the rental car, packed the boys' suitcases.

I only had to pack mine. All the other stuff was just . . . taken care of.

Because I was working. Because my mind was on my patients—on becoming and being a doctor. And when I was home, I just wanted to spend time with the kids, with her. I needed that.

"I don't know if I would've understood it then, but I get it now," I tell her. "And I knew you were unhappy . . . in the end. But I was so tired of trying, and fighting. I just . . . stopped caring. It's fucked up."

"It wouldn't have mattered. You couldn't save us, like one of your patients. You couldn't fix us, Connor."

"I know. But it's still wrong. You were my wife, the mother of my kids . . . I should've cared." I look her in the eyes, my voice low and my words true. "I'm sorry."

She nods softly, sadly.

"I'm sorry too. For so much."

Stacey's gaze drifts back to Aaron. "And I've been sitting here thinking of all that time I'll never get back with them. With Aaron. And I've been praying—I've been praying, please, God, take me instead."

She shakes her head as tears flow from her eyes and down her cheeks, her voice louder and higher pitched.

"I just want one more hour with him, one more day. I want to hear his voice, Connor. Smell his hair. We can't . . . we can't lose him like this!"

I go down to my knees in front of her, pulling her into my arms and pressing her face to my shoulder as she unravels.

"I know, Stace. I know."

Her hands twist in my shirt.

"I wasted all that time and I'm so sorry!"

"Shhh, easy." I run my hand down the back of her hair, my voice calming. "You have to keep it together. I know it's hard, but this is the ICU; they will kick you out of here and I won't be able to do anything to stop it."

She nods against me, pulling in a shuddering breath.

"It's going to be different, Connor, I promise."

"I believe you."

"Everything's going to be different between us from now on."

I rock her gently while she cries.

"I know it will be. It's okay; we're going to be okay, Stacey. You and me and the boys—we're all going to be all right."

Violet

"It's going to be different, Connor, I promise."

Shit.

"Everything's going to be different between us from now on."

Shit, shit, shit.

"We're going to be okay, Stacey."

I'm going to be sick. My stomach coils and twists and it's all my own fault.

Garrett and Callie stopped by the house to see the boys, so I drove to the hospital to drop off coffee for Connor and Stacey. The good stuff, not the turpentine they've probably been drinking from the break room or the vending machine. I thought they could use it.

And then when I heard them speaking, I waited outside the door to Aaron's room.

Because I didn't want to interrupt.

I wasn't listening . . . I was waiting. But then the words were just *there*.

"You and me and the boys—we're all going to be all right."

And because curiosity didn't just kill the cat, it broke its fucking heart too—I peeked around the corner into the room. And I saw Connor holding Stacey in his arms, touching her hair.

I left after that—went down to the ED and talked with my coworkers, my friends. After twenty minutes, I walked back to the ICU. Stacey's eyes were puffy and Connor was somber, but they were sitting in their own chairs. I gave them the coffees and pretended like I'd just gotten there.

My stomach was still churning, but I didn't let it show.

Maybe he was just comforting her. Jesus—that would be understandable. It doesn't have to mean anything more than that.

But it *could.*

And now their words are in my head. On repeat. Burrowing like a worm. Sucking at my soul like some kind of evil alien parasite.

I'm not jealous . . . I don't work like that. I trust Connor completely. He's a good man, an honest man, he cares about me so much—I feel it every time I'm with him.

But I remember my parents. I remember one of the dozens of times my mom said it was "really over." And then Darren broke his arm skateboarding. And she called my dad because she needed someone, and he came home.

And it wasn't anything close to over anymore.

Emergencies clarify things. Show you what's important, strip away the trivial and petty, block out anything that doesn't matter. I've seen it, I know it, I've lived it. A sick child can tear a couple apart . . . or pull them right back together again.

That's how emotions work. How need and connections and histories work.

How family works sometimes.

And Connor's family is everything to him.

I can't think about this right now—and I can't ask Connor about it. His son is in the ICU, still critical. In the grand scheme of things, it's small and inconsequential.

Aaron is what matters.

So I put Connor and Stacey's words aside. And I do what needs to be done. Push on.

I don't let myself think about it. I don't get upset.

And I try my hardest to forget I ever heard it.

"He's awake."

Connor calls me the next day, his voice rough with exhaustion, but lighter than it's been in the three days since the accident.

"He's awake, Violet. He's weak and still running a temperature and he's out of it from the pain meds, but he knows what's going on."

This is good—it's everything. Cool, sweet relief shoots through my veins—for Connor and Aaron . . . for all of us.

Due to his fever, Aaron still can't have visitors, so I stay at the house with Brayden and Spencer. In the early evening I start to make them dinner. It's my mom's chicken cutlet recipe—a comfort food cure for all things. But just as I'm about to heat up the oil, my phone pings with an incoming text from Connor.

Stacey wants to come by to take the boys out to dinner. Is that okay?

I turn off the stove burner. And I remind myself that this is also a good thing—that whatever is going on between Stacey and Connor, whatever issues they had or have—she's always going to be the boys' mother.

I grew up with a parent who didn't want me or my brother and sisters, who had no interest in us. I never want Connor's boys to know what that feels like.

So I text him back.

Yep—sounds good.

Fifteen minutes later, there's a knock at the door.

Stacey is cool and stiff. "Hello."

"Hi." I give her a smile, because I have no reason not to. What Connor and I have is beautiful and solid and this woman is no threat to that. He's my boyfriend, and I'm in his house taking care of his kids because that's where he wants—needs—me to be. "Please, come in."

Rosie remembers Stacey—she trots into the foyer with her tail wagging furiously and her eyes wide.

"Hi Rosie-girl. I've missed you!" Stacey drops to her knees, letting the dog lick her face while she pets her behind her ears.

The boys' reaction to their mom is noticeably less enthusiastic. I told them she was coming. Spencer seemed excited at first, but then he changed his tune—following Brayden's lead. And now they drag their feet into the foyer, with matching expressions fit for a hostage video.

Stacey greets them with a big smile, but there's an almost desperate tightness to her features that says she's aware she's skating on thin ice. That she has things to make up for and this is step one.

"Hey, guys!" she says. "I thought we could go to that burger place you like—Diesel and Duke? Daniel, you can even get that double soda thing with the extra sugar?"

Connor's always said that Brayden's the easy one, but that doesn't seem to apply where his mother's concerned.

"My name is *Brayden*. You're the only one who calls me Daniel."

"I know. I love the name Daniel." Stacey reaches for him, but he steps back. Slowly, she lowers her hand. "I love it so much we named you it twice."

He crosses his arms. "I'm not hungry. Thanks for coming by, but I don't want to go to dinner."

Then he turns around and marches up the stairs.

Spencer seems torn—his soft brown eyes follow his brother, then turn back to his mom. Eventually, he sighs. "Sorry, Mom."

And he darts up the stairs too.

Stacey and I stand there for a moment, awkward and silent, and then I raise my finger.

"Give me one minute."

After I knock on his door and walk into Brayden's room, he immediately hits me with a "Don't make us go with her."

I hold up my hands.

"I'm not going to make you do anything—that's not really

my style." I sit down in his desk chair, swiveling. "I did want to tell you a story, though."

He gives me the distrustful eyes.

"What story?"

"About my dad. See, I had a dad who made a lot of mistakes over the years. Like your mom. That's why she's here—because she realizes she's made mistakes by not seeing you guys enough and she wants to make up for that. My dad was like that too . . . only he never realized it was a mistake. It's been . . . over ten years since I've seen him . . . and he still hasn't realized it. He probably never will."

Brayden frowns. "That sucks."

"Yeah, it does."

"But she wouldn't be here if Aaron didn't get hurt."

I nod slowly. "Sometimes it takes a bad thing happening to make us realize what's important. The people who are important to us."

"If your dad came here and wanted to see you after all that time," Brayden asks, "would you see him?"

And I give him the straight, unvarnished truth.

"I would. Because he's my dad, the only one I'm ever going to have." I look down at my hands. "Maybe that makes me a pushover. Maybe that makes me an idiot."

"You're not an idiot," Spencer gripes, like he's insulted on my behalf.

"Your mom's always going to be your mom. And she's here because she really does love you. You get that, right?"

"*You* love us," Spence insists in his sweet little voice, making my heart squeeze so hard.

I move from the desk chair to crouch down in front of them.

"I do. I love you. I love you, and I love Aaron and your dad. *So much*. But you know what I've learned in my thirty years?"

"What?"

I brush his hair out of his eyes.

"You can never, ever, have too many people around who love you."

Dinner is a go. The boys put on clean shirts and their shoes and head downstairs and out to their mom's car.

Halfway out the door, Stacey pauses and turns back to me. "Thank you, Violet. Really."

Her voice is smooth and melodious, and her eyes are shimmering dark and grateful. And for the first time, I can picture it—the beautiful couple she and Connor must've made for all those years.

And a sneaking, slithering voice in my head tells me how stupid I am—that I might be cutting my own throat. That it would've been so easy to do nothing and leave the wedge between Stacey and the boys right where it was. That the closer she gets to them, the closer she gets to Connor—and maybe, the further he gets from me.

But I could never do that. Not to them . . . not to him.

Still, I'm not a pushover and because I do love those boys, I tell her, "They're giving you a chance, Stacey. If you hurt them again, there probably won't be another. Don't mess it up."

She glances down at the floor, nodding.

"I won't."

CHAPTER
Nineteen

Violet

A WEEK LATER THINGS ARE BETTER . . . AND WORSE. Aaron continues to improve. His fever breaks and we're allowed to visit him briefly. The moment we walk into the ICU room, Spencer flings his arms wide and gently lays his head on his brother's stomach, in an awkward but heartfelt hug.

"I'm so happy you're not gonna die, Aaron!"

Brayden steps up beside the bed and holds Aaron's hand, his words thick with emotion. "Yeah, I'm really glad you're going to be okay."

Aaron's pale and his voice is weak, but he smiles. "Me too, guys. Me too."

During the visit, things are noticeably easier between Stacey and Connor. The tension and animosity that was so palpable the night of the accident have completely evaporated.

Before we go, I kiss Aaron's forehead and brush his hair back, telling him to rest up and that I know he'll be home soon.

Connor's been sleeping in the on-call room at the hospital,

showering in the locker room. I stay at the house with Brayden and Spencer and we see him, but only for quick snippets of time.

But it's okay. This is how relationships work. You're there for each other, support each other in whatever way is needed.

At least . . . that's what I thought.

Until a call from Connor at the hospital hits me right between the eyes.

"Vi, seriously it's fine. You've done so much already—my parents can stay with the boys for a few days. I want you to go home and relax."

"Brayden and Spencer are relaxing to me," I tell him, standing in his kitchen.

"And that means everything to me—really. But I'm not going to put this all on you—go back to your house for a while, recharge or go back to work if you want."

Work? He expects me to be able to focus on work knowing he's upstairs and Aaron is still in the ICU? Has he lost his mind?

"Maybe you can take them again in a couple days. I might be home by then, I'm not sure."

My stomach nosedives. So does my heart. A vertical drop, straight down from thirty-thousand feet—no safety net, no parachute.

"Connor—"

"I've got to go. Ortho's here to talk about Aaron's leg. I'll call you back when I can."

"Okay, I'll—"

But the line is already dead.

I didn't even get the chance to tell him I miss him. Or to give Aaron a hug for me. That I hope he's doing okay.

Brayden and Spencer hang out in Connor's room with me while I put a few of my things into a bag to take back to my house.

"I don't want to stay with Pop and Nana!" Spencer whines, lying dramatically across the bed—his head dangling off the edge—like he's being crucified.

"Pop snores and he doesn't share the TV remote—and he watches the news *all* the time!"

I turn upside down, so I'm right-side up in Spencer world.

"I know sweetie, but your dad wants your grandparents to stay with you. It'll only be a few days. Maybe you guys can come to my house and stay over there."

"Why can't we stay with you now? Everything's been fine," Brayden says.

I don't have any answer for him, because I don't understand it myself and Connor didn't have time to explain. So I come up with a good answer on my own.

"Maybe your dad wants you guys to stay with your grandparents because they need you, not the other way around? I mean, Aaron is doing better and that's fantastic—but maybe one of their grandkids being hurt has shaken them up? Maybe a little time with you guys will make them feel better?"

Brayden shrugs—like even if that makes sense, he wants no part of it.

Spencer considers this thoughtfully and nods . . . still upside down.

Connor's parents show up an hour later. I say goodbye to Rosie and hug both the boys at the front door. And then I go home.

Alone.

A sick, uneasy feeling follows me the rest of the day.

I can't write a poem about it. I don't even try.

Instead, I put a blank page of paper in my poetry box. I close the lid . . . and then I open it right back up again. I take out the blank page and tear it to pieces. Because that's how the thought of losing Connor, after everything we've shared, makes me feel.

Shredded.

Late that night I lie in my bed in the dark and talk to myself. And I finally give voice to my fears, to taste the terrible words—to hear them out loud.

"I think I could be losing him."

My throat narrows, making it hard to breathe.

"And the crazy thing is, if she's what he wants, if she'll make them happy—I would be okay with it. I love him *that* much. I want him to be happy, even if it's not with me." A sob tears through me and I cover my face with my hand, turning on my side and tucking my knees against my chest. "It just hurts."

Sometimes a good cry can make you feel purged. Refreshed. Stronger. But it doesn't work that way this time. When my eyes are swollen but dry, I feel even more fragile.

Like I could shatter at any moment. Like I'm already breaking.

I climb out of bed and go to the kitchen to pour myself a drink. I don't believe in drinking away your problems, hiding your heartache behind booze . . . but a vodka tonic never hurt anyone.

Scratch that—a double vodka tonic never hurt anyone.

I hold the cup under the ice maker in my refrigerator door, filling it up, watching the smooth oval-shaped pellets shine under the light.

When I was eight or nine, a woman down the street, Mrs. Dobfrey, used to keep an eye on me and my siblings after school while my mother was at work. She had a stainless-steel refrigerator—the latest model—that made oval ice too. Darren and I used to call it "the good ice."

I remember thinking that if one day I had a fridge that made the good ice like hers, I would have everything.

Life was a lot simpler then.

Connor

Two weeks after Aaron's accident, he's discharged from the ICU and admitted to the hospital floor. It's a big deal, a terrific milestone.

The next day, Garrett and Dean show up unannounced to his hospital room . . . and kick me out.

"Seriously, dude, go get a drink. Several," Dean advises, grinning in that easy, laidback way he's always had.

Because his daughter is still young—warm in her toddler bed at night and safe under his and Lainey's supervision during the day. He hasn't been subjected to the terror that comes with exposing your kid to the outside world. When they're little, you think the hardest part of parenting is the endless nights, teething and tantrums, always having them with you.

But it's not.

The hardest part is letting them go.

"And a shave," Garrett adds.

I rub my hand over the thick, coarse hair that's sprung up across my jaw because I haven't taken the time to scrape it off lately.

I thought it was looking kind of badass.

My teenager disabuses me of that notion.

"Yeah, you're starting to get that Tom Hanks in *Castaway* look after he was on the island for six months."

Garrett holds out his fist to my son.

"A-plus movie reference."

And for the first time in what seems like forever . . . I actually laugh. It sounds odd to my ears and unfamiliar in my throat, like the muscles are out of practice.

But it doesn't last long.

Panic slices through me when Garrett takes the chair on the left side of Aaron's bed, resting his feet on the corner of the mattress, and Dean parks himself in the right one—so there's no seat left for me.

"I-I can't just leave," I stutter.

I realize I sound like a shut-in—an agoraphobic—but I don't care. Stacey's been here practically around the clock too, leaving only to spend time with Brayden and Spencer, so she can reconnect with them. But I haven't left at all.

Because Aaron's mostly out of the woods, sure, but shit could still happen—really bad shit. He could develop another fever—an infection. He could try to get out of bed and crack his head open, or he could have an allergic reaction to one of his medications. He's not even on solid foods yet because he's scheduled for another surgery on his leg tomorrow afternoon.

Aaron looks me dead in the face, his voice kind but clear.

"Dad, I'm okay. Really."

Anxiety twists my stomach into a double knot.

"Yeah," Dean agrees. "And, hello—he's with two teachers who are also football coaches—first aid and CPR certified, thank you very much. Me and Garrett are practically first responders at this point."

"Also, I hate to point out the obvious . . ." Garrett gestures to the room around us. "We're literally in a hospital. Short of wrapping the kid in bubble wrap; it doesn't get any safer than this."

They're right. Rationally, I know this. But the rational part of my brain has been out of commission lately—I've been operating on base instinct and adrenaline.

"Where are the other two rug rats?" Dean asks. "I'm sure they'd like to see you."

"They're staying with Stacey tonight at her place in Hoboken."

"Good." Aaron nods. "Then why don't you go see Violet?"

Violet.

Christ, just thinking her name is like an oasis in a desert, a cool, beautiful glass of water on a scorching day. My chest loosens and my stomach unwinds, the knot replaced with simmering, exhilarating desire.

Because I've missed her so fucking much.

We've texted and talked in quick fragments. We've seen each other briefly, but really only in passing.

Not enough, not nearly enough.

My whole focus has been on Aaron—first on the paralyzing fear that he could crash at any moment, that we could still lose him—and then on his recovery, what he needed and making sure he got it.

But the thought of seeing Violet, talking to her, touching her, hearing her voice and her laugh . . . just being with her, fills every space inside me with a blessed, relieved joy that I almost forgot was possible.

"Seriously, Dad, go see your girlfriend," my wise child tells me. "You've probably been a crappy boyfriend lately; you might have to grovel."

I chuckle. "Nah, Vi's not like that."

Which makes it even more important that I not be selfish, that I treat her right. Because she's understanding and phenomenal—and she lets the small stuff go so easily.

"We're just going to hang here all night." Garrett pulls a bag of popcorn out of the gym bag he carried in with him. "And watch the Patriots get annihilated."

Dean grabs the remote from the tray and turns on the television on the wall behind me. "And mock Belichick's offense without Brady, because we're petty like that."

Aaron reaches for some popcorn, but my brother slaps his hand away.

"Ow!" My son retracts his hand, laughing. "I'm frigging injured."

Garrett points at him. "No popcorn allowed for you. You . . ." he reaches into the bag again—like a gender-swapped Mary

Poppins. " . . . get to enjoy this whole case of popcorn flavored Jell-O that Aunt Callie picked up from Whole Foods just for you."

Garrett looks at me. "And I already checked with Aaron's nurse on the way in—he's cleared to have it."

Aaron rolls his eyes.

"Great."

"No preservatives or artificial flavors," Dean says. "Yummy."

"I brought lemon flavored too, in case it tastes like ass," Garrett tells Aaron.

Then they all laugh.

And that's the moment when it clicks—when I know and feel that Aaron's going to be okay without me. I nod, surrendering.

"All right, all right . . . I'll head out."

I kiss the top of Aaron's head. "Love you, buddy."

He smiles. "Love you too, Dad."

My throat tightens and my eyes heat, because I'm just a fucking mess these days.

Still, I manage to walk out the door and down to my truck in the parking lot.

For the first time in weeks, there's nowhere I have to be—not at the hospital or talking to Stacey or Brayden and Spence, or in a conference with one of Aaron's doctors.

But *need*—need's a different animal. And there's only one person I need to see as soon as possible.

So I pull out of the parking lot and drive straight to Violet's house.

CHAPTER
Twenty

Connor

T WENTY MINUTES LATER, I PULL INTO VI'S DRIVEWAY behind her little blue Volkswagen.

I didn't call her on the way over, but the light in her living room glows a golden yellow behind the closed blinds. I kill the engine and gaze at her adorable house, the corners of my mouth inching upward, just because I'm here.

I walk up the path and knock on the door.

And then she's opening the door, standing at the threshold, her dark hair pinned up in a bun, her body encased in a white, fluffy robe.

And it's like my whole soul sighs with release, the tension draining out of me. I stand there for a moment . . . soaking in the sight of her, letting the sensation of coming home fill me up.

Violet tilts her head, watching me with liquid velvet eyes.

"You look tired."

My hand goes to the mountain-man beard.

"Is that a nice way of saying I look like shit?"

"Nope—that's not possible. You just look tired."

When I was at the hospital, I didn't feel the stress and worry and lack of sleep—I didn't let myself feel it at all. But now it's hitting me, full force.

"Do you want to come in?"

"God, yes. Please."

Violet steps back, opening the door wider as I step in.

"How's Aaron doing tonight?"

"Better. He looks good. I mean he's got screws in his ankle, and a metal cage around his leg and he's attached to a heart monitor, but overall . . . he's good."

Violet closes her eyes and exhales.

"I'm so glad."

"Garrett and Dean are with him. He's got surgery tomorrow afternoon so I'm going back in the morning, but . . . I wanted to see you tonight."

She gives me a smile, but there's something off about it. Something . . . sad. It doesn't light up her eyes.

Even when Violet was pissed at me all those months ago, there was a spark to her—bright and blinding. Now she seems . . . dimmed. Down. And I wonder if she's as exhausted as I am.

We walk into her living room and she moves to the kitchen.

"Do you want something to eat?"

"No."

"Do you want something to drink?" She opens the refrigerator door. "I have your beer."

I take her hand, turning her toward me.

"I'm fine, Violet. I just . . . I just want to be here with you. Talk to you."

Something flashes across her face that I don't understand. And she stares at the center of my chest.

"You came here to talk to me about something?"

"Well . . . yeah."

She folds her lips together tightly.

"I see."

I think about what Aaron said, how I haven't been a very

good boyfriend. It's true—I've been consumed with my son's situation, with myself. And I know Violet understands that . . . but I wonder if I've missed something.

Something going on with her.

I cup her cheek.

"Are you all right?"

"Yeah." She nods. "Sure."

"Is Darren okay? Your sisters?"

"Everybody's good."

And then she moves into my arms, hugging me, holding onto me—pressing her face into the hollow of my neck. It's like she forgot what I feel like . . . and she desperately needs to remember.

When she pulls back she says, "I was just going to take a shower."

A hot shower with her sounds like heaven right now.

"Do you mind if I join you?"

It shouldn't be a big deal—Violet and I have taken dozens of showers together—but for a moment she stiffens.

"Okay."

"Are you sure?" I ask . . . because she doesn't look sure. "I can stay—"

"It's fine, Connor. Really."

She picks up my hand and kisses my knuckles gently. Then she leads me to the bathroom and turns on the shower full blast, filling the room with steam. We're silent as we slip out of our clothes—she hangs her robe on the hook on the door, her smooth, beautiful back beckoning to me.

And it's not even sexual. I mean, I'm hard, obviously, but it's so much more than just that. Deeper. Needier.

I want to drown in the feel of her skin, surround myself in her scent and her sounds, sink into the sensation of her body pressed snug and vital against mine.

I don't even need to be inside her. Just being close to her is enough.

But there's a tension in Violet's shoulders, an anxiousness radiating from her that makes me hesitate. That tells me something is wrong. With her.

With us.

She releases her hair from its bun and steps into the shower first, the brown, wavy tendrils turning black beneath the stream. I follow her in, the scorching water hitting my shoulders and running down my back. She turns away from me, reaching for the shampoo and not meeting my eyes, like she's holding back—hiding.

My voice goes soft and coaxing.

"Hey, Vi?"

"Yes?"

"I know I'm missing something here. Something big. Can you tell me what I'm missing? Please?"

She licks the droplets of water from her upper lip, and her words come out slow, like they're being dragged out.

"I didn't want to bring this up now, I know you're dealing with a lot—"

"You can tell me anything. Anything at all, I promise."

And now she looks like she's about to cry, and whatever's twisting her up inside—I just want to make it better.

She takes a deep breath.

"Okay, I'm just going to ask and whatever your answer is . . . I need you to be honest with me, no matter what."

"Of course."

"Do you . . . do you have feelings for Stacey again?"

The shock of her question knocks me on my figurative ass.

"What?"

"I heard you and her talking in Aaron's hospital room. I heard her promise that things are going to be different between you from now on. And then you told me to go home and sent your parents to stay with the boys. Are you . . ."

Her dark eyes rise to mine—cracking my heart in two. Because she really believes that that's possible.

" . . . are you two reconciling?"

"No. God, no. I mean, she's finally got her head on straight about the kids and I'm happy about that. It's important that they have a good relationship with their mother. And she and I aren't going to be at each other's throats anymore; we talked it out and we both agreed. But that's it, Violet, I swear. I haven't had feelings for Stacey in a long time, and that hasn't changed. At all."

"Oh." She nods slowly, her face slack. "Okay."

Then she turns around, facing the wall. And a moment later, her shoulders quake, shuddering—as she sobs. She covers her mouth with her hand, shaking her head.

"Is that what you thought?" I ask.

"Yeah." She hiccups.

I think about what that must've been like for her. I imagine what I would feel if I thought she was slipping away. And it's like an invisible hand is crushing my insides, turning them to dust, leaving me achingly hollow.

"For how long?"

"A while." Violet's eyes are red and her lips swollen when she turns toward me. "I thought you might be here to break up with me tonight."

"Jesus Christ."

I pull her into my arms.

She comes easily, clasping herself against me, letting the tears flow.

And I think this could be about more than me and Stacey. She's been so strong for me, for my boys—pushing through, keeping everything together—bottling up all that emotion. Keeping it locked up tight inside.

Until now.

I stroke my hand down her wet hair, the words tearing out of me.

"I'm so sorry, Violet. I didn't want to take you for granted, I didn't want to put everything on you. The only reason I told you to come back here—"

"No." She shakes her head. "It's not really anything you did. I just . . . I know how these things work sometimes. I've seen it with patients, with my parents. I know in real life, tragedies can bring—"

"*You* are my real life. I love you, Violet. I'm so in love with you, I can't even see straight."

I frame her face with my hands, looking into her eyes.

"You make me so happy, Vi. Happier than I've ever been—than I ever thought I could be. And all I want to do for the rest of our lives is make you as happy as you make me."

She smiles through the tears. And it's her real smile—the one that lights up her whole face and my entire world.

"I love you too, Connor. I've loved you for so long and that's all I want to do, for the rest of our lives . . . is keep loving you."

I pull her back against me, murmuring sweet, worshipful words. And we stay in the shower holding onto each other, rocking slowly, until the water runs cold.

Afterward, we lie quietly in her bed, naked and wrapped around each other, as close as two people can be. Her head rests on my chest, and I slide my fingers through her long damp hair, her bent knee resting on my stomach. It starts to rain outside, the pattering of the drops against the roof enshrouding us in their rhythm—making Violet's room feel secret and warm.

"I want you to move in with me and the boys," I tell her.

She nods without a moment of hesitation.

"Okay."

"You can rent out your house or put it on the market, whatever you want."

"I'll sell it."

"Are you sure?"

I cradle her head in my hands and I roll her under me. Violet spreads her legs, letting me settle between her thighs. I trace the bridge of her nose with my finger, teasing, "You could hold onto it . . . it could be our love shack."

She laughs. And I will never not love that sound.

"I'm sure. It was always too small to be anything more than a starter home. And I'm ready to jump into this with you, with both feet."

I swallow hard, shaken by how much I feel for her.

"God, I love you."

Violet lifts her arms over her head, arching her back and lifting her hips, rubbing unabashedly and so fucking sweetly against me.

"Show me."

And I do.

CHAPTER
Twenty-One

Connor

THE FIRST WEEK OF NOVEMBER, AARON COMES HOME from the hospital. He'll be sleeping in the hospital bed we've set up for him in the living room, and he has lots of physical therapy ahead of him . . . but he's expected to make a full recovery.

The following week, I go back to work. Violet went back earlier, but now that she's living with us, we're able to coordinate our schedules so one of us is always home with him—at least until he's fully mobile again.

Knowing Vi's with him when I'm not—that she's calm and capable—lets me focus on my patients. It lets me be a doctor again. I don't know if I could've done that without her.

Stacey gets into a solid routine of seeing the boys every weekend—no more canceling, no more dragging them around on errands—when she's with them, she's with *them*.

And it's awesome to see on their faces, in the way they get excited about seeing their mom.

Sometimes Brayden and Spencer spend the weekend at her place, sometimes she hangs out here at the house because that's easier for Aaron right now. Last Saturday we all watched *Hereditary* in the living room in the afternoon because the boys wanted to see if it was just as scary during the day as it was at night.

All of us—the boys, Stacey, me, and Violet—who buried her face in my arm through most of the movie, because it's creepy as fuck.

It felt a little strange hanging out with my ex-wife and my girlfriend at the same time. But it was also good—really good. For the boys, for all of us.

Sometimes I think about what I've learned from the experiences of the last few months. If there's a lesson in it that I can pass on to my kids. And I've concluded that the moral of the story is simple but significant—the good ones usually are:

Sometimes life can be a straight-up asshole . . . but then it gets better.

And that better can end up being more perfect than you ever dreamed.

One Saturday afternoon, when Vi and I are both home, a bunch of Aaron's friends—the guys from the football team—come over. From the kitchen, I hear them talking in the other room.

"Only you, Daniels. You can't just break your leg—you gotta pulverize it. Overachieving motherfucker."

"It's a gift," Aaron replies dryly and I picture him shrugging and smiling in that smart-ass way he has.

Then they all laugh. I pick Aaron's laughter out of the din, and for a moment I stand there and close my eyes and just listen to my kid laughing.

"Best sound in the world, isn't it?" Violet says beside me.

Because that's how it is with us—we get each other—know each other inside and out.

"Yeah." I press a kiss to her forehead. "Though I can think of a few sounds that are definitely close seconds."

I slide my hand into the back of her jeans, palming her ass. And she squeaks out a sexy little surprised gasp.

I give her a wink. "There's one now."

After New Year's, the hospital bed gets tossed out of the house for good. And Aaron goes back to school on crutches for the spring of his senior year.

I've never seen a kid so happy to go back to school.

If all goes as planned, he'll hang up the crutches over the summer—just in time to pack up and ship him to the University of Maryland for his first year of college. He says he wants to major in sports medicine, to be a physical therapist or an athletic trainer.

My brother Garrett is thrilled by this development. And words don't exist to describe how proud I am.

In early April, a warm front sweeps into New Jersey, making the air feel more like June.

Vi and I have the afternoon off and the boys are in school, so I ask her if she wants to go for a jog on the trail behind her old house. I've always loved this town—it's why I was determined to raise the boys here—but these woods in particular have a special meaning to me now.

Because that's where Violet and I really started.

We jog beside each other in easy silence and then I stop for a water break—by the big boulder where she tied her shoe last year. I almost kissed her for the first time in this exact spot—and later, at her house, I did.

But I don't kiss her now . . . at least not yet, though that's on the menu.

Because she's just that awesome, Violet unknowingly puts my plan into motion when she says, "So your birthday's coming up."

"Yep." I nod. "The big 4-3."

"I don't suppose you want to give me a hint about what you'd like? You're kind of hard to shop for."

"Am I?"

"Yeah . . . I mean a motorcycle is obviously out of the question."

"Obviously." I chuckle.

She moves closer to me, running her hand up and down my chest.

"And I already spoil you with naughty lingerie on a regular basis."

I smirk, tucking a loose strand of her hair behind her ear.

"That you do—lucky me."

Vi grins up at me prettily, her long ponytail gleaming in the sun that finds us through the trees.

"So what do I get the man who has everything?"

I look into her beautiful eyes and my voice goes soft.

"A little girl would be really cool. Don't have one of those yet."

Violet's breath catches in her throat.

"Another boy would be awesome too," I continue. "They're always fun."

Violet's voice is airy when she speaks, her gaze tender.

"Connor . . . is that your way of telling me you want to have a baby with me?"

"It really, really is." I press a kiss to her lips and repeat her own words back to her. "One would be amazing, two would be even better."

"Oh my God!" Excitement flushes on her face and she lifts her arms to wrap them around my neck.

But I'm not nearly done yet.

I sink down to my knee—one bended knee—and reach into my pocket for the small velvet box I picked up from Zinke Jewelers last week.

"I was hoping we'd be married when the first one gets here . . . but that's up to you."

I open the box, revealing the round cut, two carat diamond set high in a platinum band.

It's simple and flawless—just like her.

Tears swell in Vi's eyes as she gazes at the ring. The sight of them makes my chest tighten and my throat narrow.

"I love you, Violet. Whatever life has in store for us, I want to share every day of it with you. Will you marry me?"

The brightest smile surges across her lips.

"Are you kidding me?? Yes!! Yes, I'll marry you!"

And she tackles me—like a linebacker in love—knocking me to my back and following me down.

The dirt from the trail rises up around us, floating on the air, and sparkling in the sunlight like golden pixie dust.

It's kind of pretty. Or maybe I'm just that deliriously fucking happy.

Because Violet is kissing me . . . and she said yes.

She wipes at the tears in her eyes and then I take her hand and slide the ring on her finger. Her chest shudders with emotion as she gazes down at her hand.

"I'm so happy, Connor. I never knew life could be *this* happy."

I kiss her again, holding her close, promising with everything that I am and everything I'll be, "It's only going to get better from here."

EPILOGUE
One

Violet

One year later

MRS. CONNOR DANIELS. MRS. DR. CONNOR
Daniels.
Violet Daniels.

God, I love my name.

We were married in June, on a sunny Saturday at the historical white chapel in Allaire State Park. We were able to put the wedding together in under two months, because neither Connor nor I wanted to wait.

Everyone was there—our friends and family—my LWW girls came in from New York and Darren got a weekend leave so he'd be there to walk me down the aisle. Aaron, Brayden, and Spencer looked dapper and adorable in their matching tuxedos and both my sisters were my maids of honor—wearing summery, strapless lavender gowns.

We held the reception in the glass enclosure of the Ridgewood Country Club. The food was amazing; the music was fun—Connor specifically requested that the DJ play MC

Hammer just for me. We cut the cake and fed each other teasingly. Chrissy caught my bouquet and Timmy snagged the garter. And Connor and I danced our first dance as husband and wife to our song, "Chances Are."

We spent an unforgettable, weeklong honeymoon at an overwater resort in Bora Bora.

And every single moment was more than I'd imagined—more than I ever dreamed it would be.

I still kind of can't believe it.

My pregnancy on the other hand . . . that I believe. My stomach is simply too massive not to.

And it's been extra-large from the very beginning. Three months after the wedding, at my eight-week ultrasound, we found out why.

I still remember the way Connor held my hand as my OB, Natasha Ferrini, ran the sonogram wand over my slick abdomen. How he squinted at the fluttering blobs on the screen.

Blobs with an *s*.

Plural.

"Is that . . . ," he'd started to ask.

"Two heartbeats?" Natasha answered. "Yes. Yes, it is. Sometimes the way the fetuses lay on top of each other makes it difficult to detect multiple heartbeats on the Doppler. But you've definitely got a two-for-one deal happening—you're having twins. Congratulations."

When Connor told me he was studly all those months ago, he wasn't messing around.

Now, four months later, I'm even bigger. Girthier. I realize this happens in pregnancy but it seems kind of ridiculous now.

The other day I had on light-green shorts and a royal-blue top and Spencer said I looked like a globe.

Out of the mouths of babes . . .

"I'm so huge."

Connor is propped against our headboard beside me in our bed, reading a medical journal on his iPad.

"You're not huge, you're pregnant."

"I'm *hugely* pregnant." I shift around, trying to find a position that doesn't cause battery acid to flow up my throat. "I'm ginormous."

I know he knows I'm at the large end of normal, even for twins—but he'll never admit it.

"You're probably retaining water."

"I'm retaining an ocean."

I turn on my side and reach around to massage my spine that feels like it's caving in.

Connor watches me, his brow scrunching.

"Maybe you should go on maternity leave now."

"I'm only six months along—I can't go on maternity leave at six months—the other nurses will never let me live it down."

Nurses are a hardcore, resilient breed.

"Six is enough," Connor argues. "Growing two new people is hard work."

He sets his iPad aside and moves down the bed on his knees, pushing away the covers and taking my foot in his strong hands—rubbing and massaging my aching arch and swollen ankle.

I moan long and low, because these days him going down on my feet feels almost as sublime as him going down on me.

"Think about it," he whispers like a seductive devil. "You can stay home, put your feet up anytime you want. You can snack and take naps in the middle of the day."

"You're a bad person," I moan. "So manipulative. But don't stop doing that."

A chuckle rumbles from his chest.

"I just want to take care of you, baby. That's why I'm here. Let me take care of you, Violet."

A thought occurs to me and I brace up on my elbows,

meeting my husband's dark eyes across the mammoth expanse of my body.

"Am I bigger than Stacey was with the boys at six months?"

I realize that Stacey never carried twins—but pregnancy is not exactly conducive to rational thinking.

Connor's fingers pause for just a moment.

"I'm not touching that question with a ten-foot fucking pole."

"Why not?"

"Because I'm not an idiot."

I inhale sharply, my lips forming a shocked O.

Connor stares at my lips—probably imagining sliding something between them—because he's a filthy, fabulous, dirty man.

"That's a yes! That means I am bigger than Stacey was! If I wasn't, you'd say so!"

And yes, wetness surges to my eyeballs. Stupid frigging hormones.

"No, I wouldn't," Connor says simply. "Because then you'd ask why I can picture what my ex-wife's body looked like over a decade ago."

He moves to the other foot.

And I pout.

"I look like Mount Vesuvius in human form. Like a sperm whale on the beach. A giant weeble-wobble . . ."

"All right, that's it." Connor sets my foot on the bed and leans over me, his eyes glinting and his gorgeous corded arms caging me in in a stern, sexy way that makes my heart race.

"I happen to think you look hot pregnant. You're having my kids—two of them—that's a huge turn-on. I would spend all day fucking you if I could."

I snort with disbelief.

"You doubt me? If my patients wouldn't find it off-putting, I would literally walk around with you on my dick from dawn till dusk."

Then I laugh.

But I admit, his words make me feel good. Desired. Wanted. Horny.

I don't mind that part of the hormones so much . . . and neither does Connor.

"You need a demonstration? Come here." Connor shifts back up the bed, pushing my pink cotton maternity nightie out of the way and gripping my bare hips, swinging me up and over onto his lap.

Because he's strong like that.

My knees dig into the bed on either side of his hips—his thick, prominent erection wedged perfectly between my legs. I rock my hips forward and back across his hardness, a bolt of sweet pleasure spiking through me.

"See?" he leans forward and nuzzles my neck, kissing a wet trail down my collarbone to my breasts. "Light as a feather, soft as silk."

I thread my fingers through his hair.

"I think the line you're looking for is stiff as a board."

He growls against my lips.

"I'll give you something that's stiff as a board."

I start to laugh, but it turns into a gasp when he thrusts his hips up. Sliding inside where I'm already slick and hot for him.

I cup his jaw with both hands, groaning as he fills me.

"I love your cock."

Connor smirks.

"It's got a major thing for you too."

And then he makes love to me—worships me, gentle and slow—drawing it out. Making me feel beautiful and lithe and always, wonderfully . . . his.

GETTING *Real*

Connor

Three months later

"I think you should take the morphine, Vi."

My wife spins around from her trek across the hospital room, her pretty face shocked, her hands cradling her stomach over the floral hospital gown that she somehow manages to make alluring.

Her round eyes bounce between me and Effie, Vi's friend and one of our labor and delivery nurses.

Because it's go time. The babies are coming.

Eventually.

"Are you both insane? I haven't taken a freaking Tylenol in nine months and now the two of you want to shoot me up with morphine like it's no big deal?"

It's been difficult to see Violet struggle these last few months. Everything's hard on her—walking and eating, sleeping and . . . breathing. Nature's a douche for putting it all on the woman. The toughest part for the guy—for me—is having to stand here and watch her suffer, see her in pain.

Anything that makes this easier for her I'm a hundred percent on board with.

"It's perfectly safe for the babies," I explain. "The only concern is if it's still in their system when they're born and it delays their ability to cry."

"Which it won't, honey," Effie adds. "You're only two centimeters dilated—these little ones are not making their debut until tomorrow."

Violet's water broke around 7 p.m., three hours ago, right after she got out of the shower. She's been having contractions ever since, but they're sporadic and irregular. We're two weeks to the day before her due date, but it's normal for twins to come a little early, so I'm not worried. Their lungs are fully developed, their measurements are right on target, and their heartbeats are steady and strong.

"You need to rest up for when it's time to start pushing," Effie tells her.

Before Violet can answer, another contraction hits. I move to her side, holding her arm as she bends at the waist, clutching her stomach and blowing out a succession of rapid *hees* and *hoos*.

When it passes, she looks up to me and Effie.

"Okay, you make a sound argument. Get me the drugs."

After Effie administers the shot to Vi's ass, she turns down the lights and moves to the door.

"Holler if you need anything."

I slip into bed beside Violet, careful of the monitor wires and IV line. Her features are relaxed and relieved as the medication takes effect. She breathes easily and gazes up at me with adorably shiny eyes.

"I feel so much better."

"I'm glad."

"I mean, I can still feel the contractions—I think I'm having one right now! But ask me if I care, Connor. Ask me!"

I stroke her hair back, running my finger along her cheek, because I love her so much.

"Do you care that you're having a contraction, Vi?"

"No! I can feel it, but it doesn't bother me at all! Isn't that great?"

"That's super great."

"Morphine is the best," she sighs, blinking slow.

"That it is."

I rest my hand on the hard, firm hill of her stomach.

After a quiet beat, Violet puts her hand over mine and asks, "What are you thinking about?"

"I'm thinking . . . how awesome it's going to be to have two little girls around the house."

Violet wanted to know the babies' sex, because like she said all those months ago—she's practical. And when you've got a double-decker on the way, it's easier to get everything ready when you know what you're having.

"I'm thinking," I continue softly, "how I can't wait to meet them. See what they'll be like, what they look like."

Vi strokes the side of my face.

"I hope they have your smile."

"I hope they have your eyes," I tell her. "But even if they come out with horns and tails they're still going to be amazing . . . because they're ours."

"Yeah," Violet's mouth opens in a slow, deep yawn—then she sighs. "Ours."

And I kiss her forehead.

"Go to sleep now, baby."

Her eyes drag closed as she snuggles in closer.

"You'll be here, right?"

"I'll be right here with you the whole time. No place on earth I'd rather be."

Fourteen hours later, the babies want to be here too. They've had enough of their tight living quarters—and they're ready to get out. Quickly.

Violet opted for an epidural, that they gave her when she was seven centimeters dilated, and she's progressed blessedly fast from there. We're perfectly in sync: I know exactly what she needs before she says it. I've held her hand and counted her through the contractions, fed her ice chips. We're a kick-ass team.

We always have been.

Vi collapses back on the pillows after the latest contraction passes, breathing hard.

"It's ridiculous that this is so hard!" She glances down to her lap. "I mean, they don't even have to go that far—it's like a couple inches at most."

I wipe her forehead with a cool damp cloth.

"You're doing so good, Violet. They're almost here."

"Okay, Violet," Natasha says from down between her legs. "Big push on this next contraction, okay? Here it comes."

Vi nods and lifts back up, grasping one of my hands in a death grip while I use the other to hold up her leg.

And then she's bearing down, her face focused and pinched, using all her strength to bring our children into the world.

"That's it, Violet," I coach her. "That's it."

And a moment later, a piercing cry tears through the room.

No matter how many times you hear that sound, it's never not incredible. Miraculous.

I look down to see the squirming, wet, beautiful bundle.

Our daughter.

"She's here, Violet!" I kiss her hair, laughing as my vision blurs. "She's here and she's perfect."

Natasha places her on Violet's stomach. We hold onto her together, my wife resting back against the pillow for just a moment, smiling down with exhausted eyes. Crying and laughing all at once.

And then another contraction builds. The nurses take the baby and I wipe the tears from Violet's face, helping her to sit up. Two more pushes later, our second daughter comes into the world.

And she's every bit as breathtaking as the first.

Later, after everyone has been assessed and cleaned up, Violet sits up in the bed, her arms propped on pillows, cradling both babies. I lie beside her, my arms around her, staring down at two identical sets of perfect little lips and noses, and ten tiny fingers each.

Violet raises her eyes to mine. "Look at what we did, Connor."

"Yeah," I say reverently. "Look at what we did."

It always takes you off-guard—the way your heart expands, the instantaneous, overwhelming love that swallows you whole.

"So what do you think?" I ask Violet.

Because we already have two names picked out, but we

wanted to wait until they were born to see which name was a better fit for which baby.

Violet lifts her right arm slightly.

"I think this is Peyton."

"Because she was born first?"

"Yeah." Vi nods, smiling wide and gorgeously. "She was like, look out—coming through."

She turns her attention to our daughter in her left arm.

"Whereas Hailey over here . . ."

"Was happy to hang back, enjoy the womb a little while longer," I finish for her.

"Exactly."

We gave them floral middle names in honor of Violet's mom.

She kisses each baby's nose and whispers, "Welcome to the world, Peyton Rose and Hailey Iris."

My heart pounds and my chest squeezes, because I'm so blown away by her . . . I always have been. By her strength and her beauty and the exquisite joy she brings into my life, just by being all that she is.

My voice is raw, humbled. "I love you, Violet."

I'll never not love her—I'll never stop being grateful for her.

She turns to me, smiling.

"I love you too, Connor. Just when I think I love you as much as I possibly can . . . you go and make me love you more."

I kiss her lips, long and slow. And then I run my fingertip across the powdery softness of our daughters' cheeks.

"Look at our sweet girls," I whisper.

They own me already . . . just like their mom.

And I wouldn't want it any other way.

EPILOGUE
Two

Connor

Six months later

O N A WARM, FALL, SATURDAY NIGHT, GARRETT AND
Callie have us over to their house for dinner.
My brother's still flying high about the Lakeside
Lions' blow-out victory the night before and Dean's happy to kick
back and relax after taking Lainey and their daughter on tour
with his band down the Jersey shore all summer.

Violet and I are pretty psyched too. With the boys' extra-
curriculars going full speed ahead and two new babies in the
house—we don't get out much.

"Peyyyyton," Spencer groans with patient exhaustion.

Because we're out on the back patio, overlooking the lake, and
my daughter has just dropped her plastic, multicolored toy keys
over the side of her Exersaucer for the millionth time. Spencer
takes his newfound big-brother responsibilities very seriously
. . . but everybody has their breaking point.

Still, Spencer dutifully retrieves the keys and puts them on
the tray in front of his baby sister.

And Peyton immediately tosses them over the side.

Again.

Then she lets out one of those, deep, loud, full-bellied baby giggles and everyone within earshot laughs out loud right along with her.

Because that sound is the Borg in audio form—resistance is futile.

Violet hit the bullseye when she named our daughters and guessed at their dispositions. They're both preciously gorgeous with dark hair and their mother's big, brown, heart-owning eyes. And Vi says they both have my smile—but their personalities couldn't be more different.

Peyton is demanding and mischievous, precocious and full of endless energy.

Hailey reminds me of Brayden when he was a baby—calm and thoughtful, low maintenance and content. Even now, she lies on a blanket on the grass a few feet away, gazing up at the sky and happily sucking on her big toe.

"How long can she do this?" Spencer asks, after yet another round of pick-up-the-keys-servant-brother.

"Forever," Violet tells him.

Then she laughs. "It's okay, Spence—you can go—I'll take over."

Violet is exactly the same kind of mother as she is a person—selfless and warm, strong and sensible, kind and gentle and amazingly loving.

"Thank you, Violet," Spence sighs, giving her a high five. "I owe you."

And he runs over to the firepit where Brayden, Aaron, and Lainey's son, Jason—who are both home for the weekend—are roasting hot dogs and talking about college and cars.

On the other end of the patio, Lainey watches Dean tossing a football with Garrett and Callie's son, Will. Beside her little

Charlotte and Ava sing an adorably jumbled lullaby and push a baby stroller gently back and forth together.

A stroller that contains Lucy—Dean's grandmother's black cat.

To hear Dean tell it, Lucy attempts to maim him on a regular basis—but Dean's daughter, Ava, can do no wrong—which explains the eyelet baby bonnet the formerly feral feline is currently comfortably sporting.

Garrett and Callie are at the grill—holding hands and occasionally kissing in between flipping steaks and sipping wine. And their never-not-happy golden retriever, Woody, lies at their feet.

I gaze out over the water and the surrounding trees that are just getting their autumn colors.

It's Violet's favorite time of day. The sun is going down, lighting up the whole lake with swirls of bright orange, pink and gold, and light shades of purple.

And it's a good night . . . a good life.

A *beautiful* life—for all of us—in a great little town, filled with the best kinds of people.

They say *home is where the heart is*, and that statement is totally true.

But sometimes, if you're lucky, it works both ways . . . and you find your heart right where your home's been all along.

If you want to stay in Lakeside longer,
don't miss the other books in the standalone
Getting Some series:

Getting Schooled
Getting Played

And continue reading for a sneak peek of ROYALLY
SCREWED,
the first book in the Royally series.

ROYALLY SCREWED

PROLOGUE

MY VERY FIRST MEMORY ISN'T ALL THAT DIFFERENT from anyone else's. I was three years old and it was my first day of preschool. For some reason, my mother ignored the fact that I was actually a boy and dressed me in God-awful overalls, a frilly cuffed shirt and patent-leather brogues. I planned to smear finger paint on the outfit the first chance I got.

But that's not what stands out most in my mind.

By then, spotting a camera lens pointed my way was as common as seeing a bird in the sky. I should've been used to it—and I think I was. But that day was different.

Because there were hundreds of cameras.

Lining every inch of the sidewalk and the streets, and clustered together at the entrance of my school like a sea of one-eyed monsters, waiting to pounce. I remember my mother's voice, soothing and constant as I clung to her hand, but I couldn't make out her words. They were drowned out by the roar of snapping shutters and the shouts of photographers calling my name.

"Nicholas! Nicholas, this way, smile now! Look up, lad! Nicholas, over here!"

It was the first inkling I'd had that I was—that *we* were—different. In the years after, I'd learn just how different my family is. Internationally renowned, instantly recognizable, our everyday activities headlines in the making.

Fame is a strange thing. A powerful thing. Usually it ebbs and flows like a tide. People get swept up in it, swamped by it, but eventually the notoriety recedes, and the former object of its affection is reduced to someone who *used to be* someone, but isn't anymore.

That will never happen to me. I was known before I was born and my name will be blazoned in history long after I'm dust in the ground. Infamy is temporary, celebrity is fleeting, but royalty…royalty is forever.

CHAPTER ONE

Nicholas

ONE WOULD THINK, AS ACCUSTOMED AS I AM TO BEING watched, that I wouldn't be effected by the sensation of someone staring at me while I sleep.

One would be wrong.

My eyes spring open, to see Fergus's scraggly, crinkled countenance just inches from my face. "Bloody hell!"

It's not a pleasant view.

His one good eye glares disapprovingly, while the other—the wandering one—that my brother and I always suspected wasn't lazy at all, but a freakish ability to see everything at once, gazes toward the opposite side of the room.

Every stereotype starts somewhere, with some vague but lingering grain of truth. I've long suspected the stereotype of the condescending, cantankerous servant began with Fergus.

God knows the wrinkled bastard is old enough.

He straightens up at my bedside, as much as his hunched, ancient spine will let him. "Took you long enough to wake up. You think I don't have better things to do? Was just about to kick you."

He's exaggerating. About having better things to do—not the plan to kick me.

I love my bed. It was an eighteenth birthday gift from the King of Genovia. It's a four-column, gleaming piece of art, hand-carved in the sixteenth century from one massive piece of Brazilian mahogany. My mattress is stuffed with the softest Hungarian goose feathers, my Egyptian cotton sheets have a thread count so high it's illegal in some parts of the world, and all I want to do is to roll over and bury myself under them like a child determined not to get up for school.

But Fergus's raspy warning grates like sandpaper on my eardrums.

"You're supposed to be in the green drawing room in twenty-five minutes."

And ducking under the covers is no longer an option. They won't save you from machete-wielding psychopaths...or a packed schedule.

Sometimes I think I'm schizophrenic. Dissociative. Possibly a split personality. It wouldn't be unheard of. All sorts of disorders show up in ancient family trees—hemophiliacs, insomniacs, lunatics...gingers. Guess I should feel lucky not to be any of those.

My problem is voices. Not *those* kinds of voices—more like reactions in my head. Answers to questions that don't match what actually ends up coming out of my mouth.

I almost never say what I really think. Sometimes I'm so full of shit my eyes could turn brown. And, it might be for the best.

Because I happen to think most people are fucking idiots.

"And we're back, chatting with His Royal Highness, Prince Nicholas."

Speaking of idiots...

The light-haired, thin-boned, bespeckled man sitting across from me conducting this captivating televised interview? His name is Teddy Littlecock. No, really, that's his actual name—and from what I hear, it's not an oxymoron. Can you appreciate what it must've been like for him in school with a name like that? It's almost enough to make me feel bad for him. But not quite.

Because Littlecock is a journalist—and I have a special kind of disgust for them. The media's mission has always been to bend the mighty over a barrel and ram their transgressions up their aristocratic arses. Which, in a way, is fine—most aristocrats are first-class pricks; everybody knows that. What bothers me is when it's not deserved. When it's not even true. If there's no dirty laundry around, the media will drag a freshly starched shirt through the shit and create their own. Here's an oxymoron for you: journalistic integrity.

Old Teddy isn't just any reporter—he's Palace Approved. Which means unlike his bribing, blackmailing, lying brethren, Littlecock gets direct access—like this interview—in exchange for asking the stupidest bloody questions ever. It's mind-numbing.

Choosing between dull and dishonest is like being asked whether you want to be shot or stabbed.

"What do you do in your spare time? What are your hobbies?"

See what I mean? It's like those *Playboy* centerfold interviews—"*I like bubble baths, pillow fights, and long, naked walks on the beach.*" No she doesn't. But the point of the questions isn't to inform, it's to reinforce the fantasies of the blokes jerking off to her.

It's the same way for me.

I grin, flashing a hint of dimple—women fall all over themselves for dimples.

"Well, most nights I like to read."

I like to fuck.

Which is probably the answer my fans would rather hear. The Palace, however, would lose their ever-loving minds if I said that.

Anyway, where was I? That's right—the fucking. I like it long, hard, and frequent. With my hands on a firm, round arse—pulling some lovely little piece back against me, hearing her sweet moans bouncing off the walls as she comes around my cock. These century-old rooms have fantastic acoustics.

While some men choose women because of their talent at keeping their legs open, I prefer the ones who are good at keeping their mouths shut. Discretion and an ironclad NDA keep most of the real stories out of the papers.

"I enjoy horseback riding, polo, an afternoon of clay pigeon shooting with the Queen."

I enjoy rock climbing, driving as fast as I can without crashing, flying, good scotch, B-movies, and a scathingly passive-aggressive verbal exchange with the Queen.

It's that last one that keeps the Old Bird on her toes—my wit is her fountain of youth. Plus it's good practice for us both. Wessco is an active constitutional monarchy so unlike our ceremonial neighbors, the Queen is an equal ruling branch of government, along with Parliament. That essentially makes the royal family politicians. Top of the food chain, sure, but politicians all the same. And politics is a quick, dirty, brawling business. Every brawler knows that if you're going to bring a knife to a fistfight, that knife had better be sharp.

I cross my arms over my chest, displaying the tan, bare forearms beneath the sleeves of my rolled-up pale-blue oxford. I'm told they have a rabid Twitter following—along with a few other parts of my body. I then tell the story of my first shoot. It's a fandom favorite—I could recite it in my sleep—and it almost feels like I am. Teddy chuckles at the ending—when my brat of a little brother loaded the launcher with a cow patty instead of a pigeon.

Then he sobers, adjusting his glasses, signaling that the sad portion of our program will now begin.

"It will be thirteen years this May since the tragic plane crash that took the lives of the Prince and Princess of Pembrook."

Called it.

I nod silently.

"Do you think of them often?"

The carved teak bracelet weighs heavily on my wrist. "I have many happy memories of my parents. But what's most important to me is that they live on through the causes they championed, the charities they supported, the endowments that carry their name. That's their legacy. By building up the foundations they advocated for, I'll ensure they'll always be remembered."

Words, words, words, talk, talk, talk. I'm good at that. Saying a lot without really answering a thing.

I think of them every single day.

It's not our way to be overly emotional—stiff upper lip, onward and upward, the King is dead—long live the King. But while to the world they were a pair of HRHs, to me and Henry they were just plain old Mum and Dad. They were good and fun and real. They hugged us often, and smacked us about when we deserved it—which was pretty often too. They were wise and kind and loved us fiercely—and that's a rarity in my social circle.

I wonder what they'd have to say about everything and how different things would be if they'd lived.

Teddy's talking again. I'm not listening, but I don't have to— the last few words are all I need to hear. "…Lady Esmerelda last weekend?"

I've known Ezzy since our school days at Briar House. She's a good egg—loud and rowdy. "Lady Esmerelda and I are old friends."

"*Just* friends?"

She's also a committed lesbian. A fact her family wants to keep out of the press. I'm her favorite beard. Our mutually beneficial dates are organized through the Palace secretary.

I smile charmingly. "I make it a rule not to kiss and tell."

Teddy leans forward, catching a whiff of story. *The* story.

"So there is the possibility that something deeper could be developing between you? The country took so much joy in watching your parents' courtship. The people are on tenterhooks waiting for you, 'His Royal Hotness' as they call you on social media, to find your own ladylove and settle down."

I shrug. "Anything's possible."

Except for that. I won't be settling down anytime soon. He can bet his Littlecock on it.

As soon as the hot beam of front lighting is extinguished and the red recording signal on the camera blips off, I stand up from my chair, removing the microphone clipped to my collar.

Teddy stands as well. "Thank you for your time, Your Grace."

He bows slightly at the neck—the proper protocol.

I nod. "Always a pleasure, Littlecock."

That's not what she said. Ever.

Bridget, my personal secretary—a stout, middle-aged, well-ordered woman, appears at my side with a bottle of water.

"Thank you." I twist the cap. "Who's next?"

The Dark Suits thought it was a good time for a PR boost— which means days of interviews, tours, and photo shoots. My own personal fourth, fifth, and sixth circles of hell.

"He's the last for today."

"Hallelujah."

She falls in step beside me as I walk down the long, carpeted hallway that will eventually lead to Guthrie House—my private apartments at the Palace of Wessco.

"Lord Ellington is arriving shortly, and arrangements for dinner at Bon Repas are confirmed."

Being friends with me is harder than you'd think. I mean, I'm a great friend; my life, on the other hand, is a pain in the arse. I can't just drop by a pub last minute or hit up a new club on a random Friday night. These things have to preplanned, organized. Spontaneity is the only luxury I don't get to enjoy.

"Good."

With that, Bridget heads toward the palace offices and I enter my private quarters. Three floors, a full modernized kitchen, a morning room, a library, two guest rooms, servants' quarters, two master suites with balconies that open up to the most breathtaking views on the grounds. All fully restored and updated—the colors, tapestries, stonework, and moldings maintaining their historic integrity. Guthrie House is the official residence of the Prince or Princess of Pembrook—the heir apparent—whomever that may be. It was my father's before it was mine, my grandmother's before her coronation.

Royals are big on hand-me-downs.

I head up to the master bedroom, unbuttoning my shirt, looking forward to the hot, pounding feel of eight showerheads turned up to full blast. My shower is fucking fantastic.

But I don't make it that far.

Fergus meets me at the top of the stairs.

"She wants to see you," he croaks.

And *she* needs no further introduction.

I rub a hand down my face, scratching the dark five o'clock shadow on my chin. "When?"

"When do you think?" Fergus scoffs. "Yesterday, o' course."

Of course.

Back in the old days, the throne was the symbol of a monarch's power. In illustrations it was depicted with the rising sun behind it, the clouds and stars beneath it—the seat for a descendent of God himself. If the throne was the emblem of power, the throne room was the place where that sovereignty was wielded. Where decrees were issued, punishments were pronounced, and the command of "bring me his head" echoed off the cold stone walls.

That was then.

Now, the royal office is where the work gets done—the throne room is used for public tours. And yesterday's throne is today's executive desk. I'm sitting across from it right now. It's shining, solid mahogany and ridiculously huge.

If my grandmother were a man, I'd suspect she was compensating for something.

Christopher, the Queen's personal secretary, offers me tea but I decline with a wave of my hand. He's young, about twenty-three, as tall as I am, and attractive, I guess—in an action-film star kind of way. He's not a terrible secretary, but he's not the sharpest tack in the box, either. I think the Queen keeps him around for kicks—because she likes looking at him, the dirty old girl. In my head, I call him Igor, because if my grandmother told him to eat nothing but flies for the rest of his life, he'd ask, "With the wings on or off?"

Finally, the adjoining door to the blue drawing room opens and Her Majesty Queen Lenora stands in the doorway.

There's a species of monkey indigenous to the Colombian rain forest that's one of the most adorable-looking animals you'll ever see—its cuteness puts fuzzy hamsters and small dogs on Pinterest to shame. Except for its hidden razor-sharp teeth and its appetite for human eyeballs. Those lured in by the beast's precious appearance are doomed to lose theirs.

My grandmother is a lot like those vicious little monkeys.

She looks like a granny—like anyone's granny. Short and petite, with soft poofy hair, small pretty hands, shiny pearls, thin lips that can laugh at a dirty joke, and a face lined with wisdom. But it's the eyes that give her away.

Gunmetal gray eyes.

The kind that back in the day would have sent opposing armies fleeing. Because they're the eyes of a conqueror… undefeatable.

"Nicholas."

I rise and bow. "Grandmother."

She breezes past Christopher without a look. "Leave us."

I sit after she does, resting my ankle on the opposite knee, my arm casually slung along the back of the chair.

"I saw your interview," she tells me. "You should smile more. You used to seem like such a happy boy."

"I'll try to remember to pretend to be happier."

She opens the center drawer of her desk, withdrawing a keyboard, then taps away on it with more skill than you'd expect from someone her age. "Have you seen the evening's headlines?"

"I haven't."

She turns the screen toward me. Then she clicks rapidly on one news website after another.

PRINCE PARTIES AT THE PLAYBOY MANSION
HENRY THE HEARTBREAKER
RANDY ROYAL
WILD, WEALTHY—AND WET

The last one is paired with the unmistakable picture of my brother diving into a swimming pool—naked as the day he was born.

I lean forward, squinting. "Henry will be horrified. The lighting is terrible in this one—you can barely make out his tattoo."

My grandmother's lips tighten. "You find this amusing?"

Mostly I find it annoying. Henry is immature, unmotivated—a slacker. He floats through life like a feather in the wind, coasting in whatever direction the breeze takes him.

I shrug. "He's twenty-four, he was just discharged from service…"

Mandatory military service. Every citizen of Wessco—male, female, or prince—is required to give two years.

"He was discharged *months ago*." She cuts me off. "And he's been around the world with eighty whores ever since."

"Have you tried calling his mobile?"

"Of course I have." She clucks. "He answers, makes that ridiculous static noise, and tells me he can't hear me. Then he says he loves me and hangs up."

My lips pull into a grin. The brat's entertaining—I'll give him that.

The Queen's eyes darken like an approaching storm. "He's in the States—Las Vegas—with plans to go to Manhattan soon. I want you to go there and bring him home, Nicholas. I don't care if you have to bash him over the head and shove him into a burlap sack, the boy needs to be brought to heel."

I've visited almost every major city in the world—and out of all of them, I hate New York the most.

"My schedule—"

"Has been rearranged. While there, you'll attend several functions in my stead. I'm needed here."

"I assume you'll be working on the House of Commons? Persuading the arseholes to finally do their job?"

"I'm glad you brought that up." My grandmother crosses her arms. "Do you know what happens to a monarchy without a stable line of heirs, my boy?"

My eyes narrow. "I studied history at university—of course I do."

"Enlighten me."

I lift my shoulders. "Without a clear succession of uncontested heirs, there could be a power grab. Discord. Possibly civil war between different houses that see an opportunity to take over."

The hairs on the back of my neck prickle. And my palms start to sweat. It's that feeling you get when you're almost to the top of that first hill on a roller coaster. *Tick, tick, tick…*

"Where are you going with this? We have heirs. If Henry and I are taken out by some catastrophe, there's always cousin Marcus."

"Cousin Marcus is an imbecile. He married an imbecile. His children are double-damned imbeciles. They will never rule this country." She straightens her pearls and lifts her nose. "There are murmurings in Parliament about changing us to a ceremonial sovereignty."

"There are always murmurings."

"Not like this," she says sharply. "This is different. They're holding up the trade legislation, unemployment is climbing, wages are down." She taps the screen. "These headlines aren't helping. People are worried about putting food on their tables, while their prince cavorts from one luxury hotel to another. We need to give the press something positive to report. We need to give the people something to celebrate. And we need to show Parliament we are firmly in control so they'd best play nicely or we'll run roughshod over them."

I'm nodding. Agreeing. Like a stupid moth flapping happily toward the flame.

"What about a day of pride? We could open the ballrooms to the public, have a parade?" I suggest. "People love that sort of thing."

She taps her chin. "I was thinking something…bigger. Something that will catch the world's attention. The event of the century." Her eyes glitter with anticipation—like an executioner right before he swings the ax.

And then the ax comes down.

"The *wedding* of the century."

To keep reading, purchase at your favorite online retailer.

Also by
EMMA CHASE

Dirty Charmer

GETTING SOME SERIES
Getting Schooled
Getting Played

THE ROYALLY SERIES
Royally Screwed
Royally Matched
Royally Endowed
Royally Raised
Royally Yours

Royally Series Collection

THE LEGAL BRIEFS SERIES
Overruled
Sustained
Appealed
Sidebarred

THE TANGLED SERIES
Tangled
Twisted
Tamed
Tied
Holy Frigging Matrimony
It's a Wonderful Tangled Christmas Carol

ABOUT
the Author

New York Times and *USA Today* bestselling author, Emma Chase, writes contemporary romance filled with heat, heart and laugh-out-loud humor. Her stories are known for their clever banter, sexy, swoon-worthy moments, and hilariously authentic male POV's.

Emma lives in New Jersey with her amazing husband, two awesome children, and two adorable but badly behaved dogs. She has a long-standing love/hate relationship with caffeine.

Follow Emma online:

Twitter: twitter.com/EmmaChse
Facebook: www.facebook.com/AuthorEmmaChase
Instagram: www.instagram.com/authoremmachase
Website: authoremmachase.com

Subscribe to Emma's mailing list for the latest book news, exclusive teasers, freebies & giveaways! authoremmachase.com/newsletter

Printed in Great Britain
by Amazon

81056240R00173